Valley of Souls

AJ Cooper

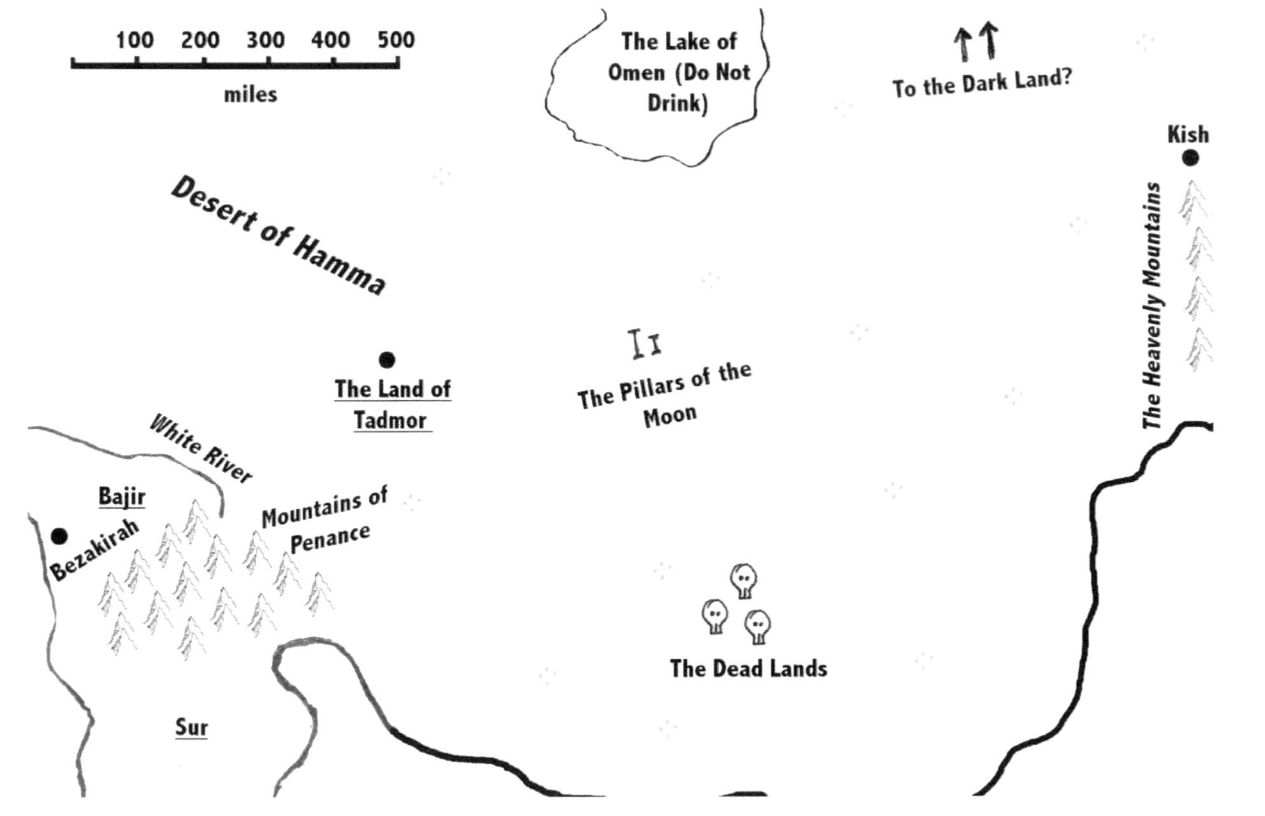

100 200 300 400 500
miles
Desert of Hamma
The Lake of Omen (Do Not Drink)
To the Dark Land?
Kish
The Heavenly Mountains
The Land of Tadmor
The Pillars of the Moon
White River
Bajir
Bezakirah
Mountains of Penance
The Dead Lands
Sur

Part One: The Woman at the Well

In the village of Adwar, the well had stood for centuries, giving water to a parched and desolate land.

The well was deep, so deep that no one could see the bottom of it, even in midday, and those who drew water had to stand there for minutes before the bucket reached its destination. Those who fell in were assured of death, by blunt force or by drowning. In Adwar, the well was revered and feared as much as the one god Mazda himself.

Faraad, a merchant passing through the valley, stopped by the well in the afternoon to draw water for his horses.

A woman stood there, garbed in a black hooded cloak. She was alone, remaining still, amid the burning midday sun. The shadow she cast was long, stretching many yards.

"Greetings, good lady," he said.

She remained silent as Faraad yanked the rope and allowed the bucket to descend.

Nervously, Faraad tried to keep up the conversation. "Where are you from, good lady? From Adwar? From here? Or Bezakirah? Kish?"

Still, she said nothing. There was something wrong with this woman, Faraad knew—something he couldn't explain.

A chill was creeping across Faraad's skin but he remained still, intent on dredging up the water. His horses were barely functional, and he needed to get away from this accursed valley before sundown… and away from this accursed woman.

It seemed an hour had passed before the bucket hit the ground. A loud clinking sound echoed. It had hit dry rock.

The well had run dry? The well of Adwar, which had provided water for ages? How was it possible? How could it be?

When Faraad looked up at the woman in the well, she had lowered her hood.

Her skin was gray, her eyes red and bright as coals. From the sleeves of her robe clawed hands emerged.

Faraad staggered back.

In the distance, a sandstorm was blowing. The desert had come to claim the valley and all its denizens.

This woman was its herald.

Chapter One: Precious Yara

When Yara was young, she had learned several things. In Tadmor, even in the capital city, Mahara, a girl was never to laugh, sing, or dance. To eat good food was a sin; to live richly would ensure your soul's damnation.

Yara looked out her balcony onto the streets of Mahara, the capital city of the Land of Tadmor. Her father had control over these streets, over its marketplaces and its wealth. In her life, she felt she'd never been afforded any of it. All money in the coffers went to Father and Mother, not her.

At least, on her thirteenth birthday, they'd stopped making her cover herself head to toe. Now she walked naked-faced like the heathens, wearing only a headscarf. She loved every second of it, even now, four years later. The devout of Mahara considered her a harlot and an idolater, but she didn't care.

The sun was setting over the distant hills. *After sundown*, her mother said, *you may never leave the house*. Tonight, she had an inkling that she would. She had turned seventeen yesterday, the age of womanhood. Her parents should have no power over her, not anymore.

~

When Yara was a girl, dinner had been mostly bread and water. On holidays celebrating the prophets, they might have had a little meat. Even that was considered sinful. Her family had been considered blasphemers by several of the city's clerics. One had given a fiery sermon before the people, condemning the heathens who ruled over them—and that was, of course, before her father had him executed and set his head on a pike for all to see.

The clerics did not dare speak out now, as a feast was prepared for them, of clams and crab-legs, of fresh-baked bread and boiled ostrich eggs, and of rose water sweetened with sugar.

Yara's mother sat at the head of the table. She was glaring. "Yara, you look like a pauper."

It was true, she did not look her best. But she didn't ever understand why her mother cared, not when it was just them. Who cared what her servants thought? Who cared, if no royal official or man of importance wasn't visiting?

"Who cares what I look like?" she said out loud.

Mother stood up from her seat. "Go change into nice clothes, you tomboy, or I'll make you do it!"

Yara wanted to stick her tongue out at Mother, say some of the curse words she'd learned from her friends, but she thought better of it. Mother was old, but she was fierce. She was as formidable an enemy as any Yara had met on the streets.

In her white silk gown, which Mother had purchased from merchants of Cathay, Yara stirred uncomfortably, wanting badly to don her tattered smallclothes once more.

She ate an entire ostrich egg as Father prattled on about problems he was having with the king, about unrest in the wider world, about things Yara had no time for and no reason to care about.

"Eat your beans," Mother said, looking at her.

She pushed a bowl of steamed lentils to Yara, knowing full well how much she hated lentils, how they felt grinding through her teeth and her mouth.

Yara knew Mother would watch her until she'd eaten every last bit, until the bowl was empty and porcelain sparkled in the candlelight.

And so she ate, and ate, and as Mother talked, and grew distracted, she lowered the bowl until her dog came skipping up from the other room and began to devour the remainder.

Sure enough, by the time Mother and Father had finished their chat, the bowl was licked clean, sitting on the table.

"You devoured that, Yara," Mother said.

Yara had an inkling that Mother was suspicious.

But she dismissed Yara soon afterward.

~

In her room, Yara peered out the balcony onto the streets below.

They were lit by torches, and few people walked around outside. The clerics were known to drag any so-called "night walkers" out into the city square and flog them with a scourge. But Yara wasn't afraid of them. Her father was the wazir. If they laid a hand on her head, they would face full justice.

In faraway kingdoms, the clerics ruled. But here in Tadmor, Father and Mother kept an iron grasp over things. No threat of hell would stop Father from protecting "precious Yara."

The silence of the night was shattered: a male voice shouted, "Yara! Yara!"

She recognized the voice instantly. It was a boy she had met in the marketplace just weeks ago.

She tiptoed up to the edge of the balcony.

Yes, it was him… it was Hiraz.

She had met him when Mother left Yara unsupervised and she'd slipped out of the house. She and Hiraz had eaten date honey and candied lemons. He had promised to seek her out. She had rebuffed him.

Would she rebuff him now?

"Yara!" Hiraz continued. The street torches illumined his slender form.

She didn't know what to say. She wasn't one to back down from an invitation.

"Come down! You and me… let's have some fun! My friends

are in the marketplace…"

Yara was seventeen but she knew better than to trust a boy like Hiraz.

Still, when he threw up the length of rope, she caught it.

If Mother and Father found out she was gone, she'd be locked inside for life.

She had fashioned a doll for just such an occasion. She laid it in her bed and covered it with her blanket and pillow. If Father and Mother checked on her, they wouldn't know any better.

She blew out the candle beside her bed. She hurried out to the balcony and, fastening the rope tight, shimmied down to the streets below.

"You are fearless," Father had told Yara.

"You are reckless," Mother had insisted.

In the end it didn't matter what they thought. She followed Hiraz down the darkened streets without skipping a beat. In such a situation, a dagger would help Yara, but her parents—though open-minded—would never allow a woman to carry a weapon. There were limits to their willingness to offend the clerics.

The city square of Mahara was silent and empty. The buildings surrounding it were dark and unlit, and the only noise that carried over the complete stillness was that of the desert—many miles away, but wracked by storms and wind and blowing sand. In Tadmor, an island amid the desert, it still made its presence known.

Like Hiraz said, a group of young men and women were gathered by the edge of the square. They were eating sweets together:

candied lemons and date pastries, sugar puffs and king raisins.

And yet, standing there among them, though they smiled and greeted her warmly, Yara felt out of place.

Something wasn't right.

The night deepened. One by one Yara learned their names. Yohar. Samia. Yibaz.

Yet they kept themselves distant from Yara. They did not speak much about themselves.

Eventually, all the sweets were eaten.

The night was dark and deep, and against the distant moan of the desert storms, it dawned on Yara that what they were doing was wholly illegal.

Everyone was to be inside by sundown; the Thul, leader of the clerics, demanded it. Father agreed to the law.

"I think I'll be heading home," Yara said. She had not enjoyed this venture nearly as much as she'd thought she would.

Fearful of the clerics, she darted away.

It wasn't until she'd gotten halfway home that she realized she was being followed.

Hiraz was there. He had changed. He was different.

His expression was no longer warm. It was a scowl.

And now, in the blink of an eye, Yara was in danger.

Hiraz had expected, had demanded, something more.

Something Yara was not willing to give to Hiraz, or anyone.

And so Yara took off at a sprint, running like hell for home.

But Hiraz was gaining on her.

When his hands reached her shoulders, she knew it was over.

Hiraz tackled her to the ground. He forced a kiss on her.

Yara wept and wailed, knowing no one would save her, not Father, not Mother, not the one god Mazda himself.

Chapter Two: Tomb Raiders

Amid the howl of winds and the sting of desert sands, Ahram sighed in relief as the lost city of Zeved-Du emerged into view.

For a city, not much was left.

The only standing structure was a ziggurat, an ancient stepped pyramid which served as a tomb for kings and a temple for priests.

That is how the ancients lived.

The Naamer, the ancient people who lived here before the desert claimed them, had incredible wealth. The kings of the Naamer were buried in these structures, together with their royal treasure hoard.

If Ahram and his team were right, Zeved-Du was untouched, unrobbed and unspoiled. They had found it on an ancient map, and here it was.

Ahram, honesty, couldn't believe it. More often than not, these cities had shifted beneath the ever-changing dunes, or the maps were wrong altogether.

"We found it!" Ahram cried. "Zeved-Du…" He unloaded his pack and got out the map. He had copied it from a stone tablet. He had navigated the desert, using the stars, and here it was.

He could hardly believe his luck.

There were too many tomb raiders about. Soon all ziggurats would be found, all kings' treasures would be plundered, and Ahram would have nothing to do.

Traveling the desert was dangerous, and it was growing more dangerous each year.

Strange things were happening. Something was not right about these howling winds, about these shifting sands. Ahram had lived thirty-two years, and something had changed. It had not always been this way. The storms had not always been this constant, this violent.

Ahram drew his scimitar. Often vipers and spitting cobras could be found in these sheltered areas, away from the sandstorm.

He untied his sandals, preferring his bare feet in the event of unexpected pitfalls and traps.

He unwound the cloth of his headwrap. He needed to be as mobile and clear eyed as possible.

Behind him, his team of a dozen fellow tomb raiders were making similar preparations.

Except one.

Akil was staring ahead blankly. His eyes were bulging. He had frozen up.

"What's wrong?" Ahram asked before immediately seeing the source.

They were not alone.

Someone was near the edge of the ziggurat, stooped over a corpse.

Had he murdered this tomb raider or adventurer?

Ahram had no idea.

But they were prepared.

Every member of Ahram's team had a weapon, a scimitar or a saber. They were ready for this. They could prevail.

Ahram took the lead, charging ahead, and the silhouetted figure slinked away, darting into the shadows, leaving the corpse alone.

The moon illuminated the corpse in its ghostly light.

The smell of the acanthuses and the desert wildflowers could not mask the overbearing stench.

The corpse's stomach had been ripped apart. A hollow red hole was all that was left.

"Where are his intestines?" cried Akil from behind.

"He's been eaten…" muttered Warez. "Look at the bitemarks."

Indeed, this corpse had been disemboweled, its stomach and innards consumed like no animal Ahram knew of.

He looked to the ziggurat, stony, silent.

"A wildcat must have gotten to it," Ahram said.

His statement was met with silence. They didn't believe it. Neither did he.

"Perhaps we should go back," Warez said.

Ahram's team was getting skittish. He had thought better of them. "And do what?"

The camels were waiting. They could leave at a moment's notice. But Ahram wasn't having it.

"All because we found a body? How many skeletons have we seen in these ziggurats? We are tomb raiders!" Ahram's words weren't calming his team. He could see by their faces. But he wasn't going to let their cowardice get in the way of a good treasure.

There was still a problem, of course. Who was that man, already here? And where had he gone?

~

The ziggurats, built by the Naamer in ancient times, had an identical structure and an identical blueprint throughout the thousand miles where they could be found. Each one faced toward the setting sun, and the entrance was in the back. When they were abandoned amid the encroaching desert, the entry was piled with stones to prevent robbery.

But the tomb raiders had found a way.

The door, as expected, had mostly rotted away, leaving the stones piled up, preventing entry to the inner chamber.

The Naamer made it difficult for the tomb raiders.

But before the hour was gone, the stones would be removed, and treasures of gold, silver, ruby and emerald would be found: images of ancient gods, now banned from society—gods with three heads or in the shapes of cows and reptiles. They would be melted down into gold ingots so that the wazirs and sultans of this world could fuel and feed their armies and expand their empires.

They began hauling the stones out of the entryway, one by one, amid the sound of the howling windstorm. Like shrieking ghosts the storms continued without cease. They would never end. They consumed all.

The night deepened. Soon they had all broken out into a sweat, and their light clothes became unbearably hot. Bit by bit, they were piling the stones out of the way of the entryway. They were almost done.

Out of the corner of his eye, Ahram saw a shadow.

It was a lanky silhouette, strangely formed, with a head a bit too big for his body. Who was this strange man?

He was watching them from just beyond the ziggurat, crouched over like an animal. His arms were long and spindly. Something was not right.

Ahram stood up, taking a break from his work and wiped some sweat off his brow.

For the first time, he grew worried.

There were more shadows behind the creature, as many three, their dark shapes reflecting in the moonlight.

Ahram drew his scimitar.

His team stopped their work.

Akil screamed. Warez unsheathed his dagger.

Ahram turned and saw more shapes, another four of them, on the other side. They were surrounded.

Ahram took a step toward the creatures and shouted. They scattered, retreating into the sands.

"This place is haunted," Akil said. "We're disturbing the spirits of the Naamer... what we do is a desecration. A blasphemy."

Ahram didn't appreciate the moralizing. These were not

ghosts. Ghosts, mara, lilitu… those were things of fantasy, of wives' tales and fiction. The creatures before them were real. And now they had retreated into the desert sands.

"We should go," Akil said. "We shouldn't desecrate this ziggurat any further."

"I agree," said Warez and some other teammates murmured assent.

Ahram wasn't having it. "Keep removing the stones," he said, "I'll keep watch."

As they hauled the stones out of the entrance chamber, Ahram looked out into the desert and took stock of what he'd seen. The creatures nearby, who had retreated into the sands, were certainly not human.

And though he had no way to prove it, he suspected they, and not a wildcat, had feasted on that corpse.

He could be wrong. But the more he stood watch in the night, listening to the howls of distant storms, the more he wondered.

Sohail was holding the torches while Akil and Warez worked. Ahram beckoned the torch from his hand.

He would take a look, while the rest of his team labored.

Around the ziggurat, structures—the remains of ancient houses, and pieces of pavestone streets—tripped up Ahram as he walked. Zeved-Du had once been a town. The Naamer homeland, a thousand miles in length, had once been spared from the desert's sand and heat; the Naamer had grown crops, and irrigated their farms. It had not always been so desolate and so unforgiving.

But the desert encroached for centuries, until it consumed all in its wake.

The city continued for longer than Ahram was willing to walk. The creatures had slinked away somewhere here. The dunes surrounding the ruins were a good distance away.

The creatures were gone. Had they hidden in one of these structures?

In the distance, above the moan of desert storms, the skittering of feet echoed. He followed the sound instantly, running toward it.

A skeleton was there, fresh and picked clean of all its sinew. Nearby was a shredded tunic. The bone of the skeleton was bright white. This was a recent find, a victim these hunters had seized upon.

Were they tomb raiders? It was hard to know.

But the map to Zeved-Du they'd found could have been copied.

The ziggurat remained unpenetrated, its stones left in a pile on the entryway. If they were tomb raiders, they had not gotten far.

These creatures had gotten to them.

A wail lit up the night, echoing through the ruins.

Ahram's team was in danger.

Ahram bolted back toward the ziggurat, suspecting he was not fast enough, that he shouldn't have left at all.

A bloodbath greeted him at the ziggurat's entry door.

Ahram's team had been dragged away, seized by the gangly creatures.

Just a short distance away were the bodies: Akil, still twitching, disemboweled and yet gasping for air: the bony-faced, purple-headed creature sucking out his entrails with its white wormlike tongue; Warez, torn to shreds, being gobbled up by two feuding creatures at the same time; together with everyone who had come here, everyone except Ahram. He had led them here to Zeved-Du; their deaths were as much his responsibility as these creatures, these subterranean creatures who fed on corpses in the dead of night.

One came bounding toward him, arms low to the ground, black claws glinting in the moonlight.

Ahram swept his saber out of its sheath, nicking the creature's bony knuckles.

Pebbles skittered across the ziggurat's steps. He looked up, and saw near the top more creatures emerging. By Ahram's count, there were thirty of these monsters. He was outnumbered. He could not possibly defeat them all.

In cities across the land, in desert temples, the clerics had spoken of people like Ahram—how robbers were condemned to damnation, how those who robbed tombs would suffer in the hellfire prepared for them.

Now, at the cusp of death, he wondered if he had made a mistake. He had riches beyond anyone he knew. Now he could lose it all because he robbed the wrong tomb; he could perish, all because he followed the map to Zeved-Du.

Had fate placed that map in his hands? Was he, and Akil, and Sohail, destined to die this night?

There was a loud flash of lightning and thunder.

The earth shook, and seemed to groan. Bricks from the ziggurat jolted from their place; a crack opened up in the earth.

The creatures screamed, and began to flee.

Abandoning their food, they fled toward the desert sands, but another brilliant flash of light echoed through Zeved-Du and they fell to their knees, shielding their eyes from a coming doom.

Billows of dust entered the air as the ground as disturbed. From beyond the desert came a gleaming figure in a white robe, dazzling in his brilliance. In his sunburnt hands was a green book; he was raising it up as a weapon, even as he caused the creatures to cower in paralysis. Who was this man? Who was this creature? Was it a messenger of Mazda, sent from heaven?

In terror, Ahram bolted to where the camels were tied up. He was no safer than these creatures.

The creatures cowered, immobile, their lanky forms casting

long shadows against the moon and the flashes of light. Ahram ran by them, up to the desert's edge.

The camels had broken their binds in terror. Who knew where they had gone off to?

Ahram was trapped here, without food, without water. There was nowhere for him to run.

Instead he turned back as the heavenly figure approached. Lightning was flashing, consuming the creatures and setting them alight.

Ahram ran for the desert but tripped. Soon he too was cowering, just like the tomb creatures.

His heart was beating out of control. He'd grown slick with sweat. The desert air would soon become ice cold, and his only chance of surviving was gone with the camels.

The repulsive creatures had driven them mad with fear. They'd terrified the camels so badly they'd burst free from their binds.

And now Ahram had nowhere to go as the heavenly figure drew near.

Like a beacon of light he was walking up to Ahram.

As he walked ahead, some of the brilliance began to fade.

An old man in sandals was revealed as the light died down, an old man clearly sunburnt by the desert. The book he carried was green and enameled, and surely heavy. He spoke in a gentle voice which nonetheless echoed above the whispering sands: "You are lucky to be alive."

By the time Ahram looked up at his face, the brilliance had entirely faded. He was an old man with a long gray beard that needed trimming and care.

"You have not met a ghoul before," the man said. "They can only be defeated with fire. Fire is what they fear most…"

Perhaps the torch Ahram had carried caused the "ghouls" to leave him alone. But he had a feeling even that lone torch wouldn't protect him for long.

He owed his life to the old man, standing over him.

"Who are you?" Ahram said.

He had stopped shaking. The fear was gone, replaced with peace and deep relief.

"Zathustra," he answered. "I've come to warn the Land of Tadmor of the danger she is in."

Tadmor, the Bride of the Desert, the halfway point between Bezakirah and Cathay: her value was beyond any human price, and she stood as an island amid the brutality of the sand and wind. She lay some hundred miles from here, if Ahram navigated by the stars. A ten day journey in the best of circumstances, its plentiful water and food were far from Ahram's mind.

He had been to that blessed land more than once. In his youth, when Ahram was growing up in Bezakirah, Tadmor was a legend for its wealth and its plentiful farmland. The clerics cursed it as a land of vice and sin, but Ahram had nursed a desire to visit from his earliest days.

"You're going to the Land of Tadmor," Ahram said. "And where are you coming from?"

"You will find out soon enough," Zathustra answered, "if you join me on my venture. I could use a hired sword. I will pay you in gold when we get there."

Ahram didn't have much of a choice.

He looked to his friends, the tomb raiders, their bodies splayed on the ground. He would bury them tonight. Then, he would go with Zathustra to Tadmor.

~

In the desert, the sun rises; and the mind-numbing cold of the night begins to dissipate.

Soon, as Ahram expected, the warmth became oppressive. The sun was searing in its intensity as Ahram and Zathustra left on their camel train.

Zeved-Du was soon gone, replaced with the rolling dunes of the desert.

Zathustra donned a cowl to hide from the oppressive sun. Ahram tied up the cotton strips of his headwrap. It wasn't enough. It was never enough. When the sun beat down on the glaring sand, its heat could never leave you. There was no way to get rid of it, only to soldier on.

Zathustra's camels were laden with waterskins. But he had brought other things on his journey as well: reading material, not only books but codices, scrolls and parchments. Zathustra was a man of learning, and wherever he had come from, he had thought it necessary to bring all this.

Where had Zathustra found it in his heart to travel all this way for the sake of saving Tadmor? Wherever he came from was far away and foreign. His sandals were strangely tied, and the white silken robes he wore were embroidered with gold thread, in patterns Ahram had never seen before. Why had Zathustra taken it upon himself to travel all this way?

Tadmor was indeed a majestic place, a place worthy of its title "The Bride of the Desert," but was it worth this difficult journey?

Ahram had a feeling there was much for him to learn. Whatever had brought Zathustra out here, the reasons had to be dire, with consequences to Tadmor and to the world.

The day grew hot, and the sun burned like fire. Even the camels seemed reluctant dipping their toes into the scalding sand. Ahram had gone through five waterskins, and he feared they'd run out soon. Zathustra, however, encouraged him to drink as much as he'd like.

"We are stopping at the Well of the Oath tonight," he explained.

In normal circumstances, the camels would be weighed down with silk from Cathay; now books were the heaviest of the cargoes. In passing, despite the glaring sun, he caught some of the titles, seeing they were books of history on the Naamer together with treatises on sorcery and herb-lore. Ahram had already seen proof he was traveling with a sorcerer; it was those strikes of fire and lightning that had put an end to the ghouls.

In Tadmor, and across the land, the clerics demanded all sorcerers be put to death.

Ahram was never afraid of risk, especially at the hope of such a great reward. Ahram would do anything for gold, anything at all. Tomb robbery wasn't any more esteemed than sorcery.

Up and down dunes, throughout the scalding desert, it seemed the day would never end, that the fires of the wicked sun would consume them and burn the whole world to ash. Like a sea, the endless crests of sand continued. Ahram worried that Zathustra didn't know where he was headed. But he had a good feeling that they would reach their destination. Perhaps they'd never reach Tadmor, but at least for now, Ahram was in good hands.

The sun was low in the sky, and the horizon began to grow pink in its dusky colors. The dunes faded away into a dry rocky bed, overgrown with tamarisk trees. Another caravan was gathered there: merchants, huddled around a well.

Lizards darted away like shadows as Zathustra led the camel train downwards into the coolness of the sanctuary.

Wells were scattered throughout this rocky valley and the green tamarisk trees provided shelter from the sun. From the burning hellscape of the desert, Ahram felt they had entered a paradise. He had never been here before. But he was glad he had accompanied

Zathustra. Finding the way home would have been impossible alone; and it seemed Zathustra knew every corner of the desert, and how to get there.

Zathustra tied his camel to a tamarisk, and the others circled around her.

One by one they refilled the waterskins from the clear, cold waters of the well.

Zathustra had brought waybread with him.

It crumbled to the touch; it was dry, tasteless, but it nourished Ahram's empty stomach.

They set up beds around one of the wells.

As the night grew dark, they spoke in hushed tones.

"This place is called the Well of the Oath," Zathustra said. "Do you know why?"

Ahram shook his head. He guessed there was some religious significance, some great Prophet of Mazda who swore an oath here. That was the best explanation.

But before Zathustra could speak, the howl of the winds picked up in the distance. As the darkness of the sky became complete, the storms were starting.

"Why," Ahram muttered, "does it always storm at night?"

Chapter Three: Runaway

As the Wazir of Tadmor—according to the law—Javan answered to one person and one person alone, the king.

That was how it was supposed to be. In life, things often worked out differently.

A daughter was supposed to respect her father, and obey his command; Yara had proven the opposite could happen.

A wife was supposed to obey her husband. No such luck with Marit.

And he did have to answer to others beside the king, like the cleric who stood before him now.

Though Javan was seated on his throne, indicating his high status, the bearded cleric in his black turban wore a disrespectful scowl on his face. Whatever his complaints were this time, Javan was sure he'd heard them before.

He knew what the Thul thought of him and his family—that they were heathens, that they were impious, that they disregarded the law of god.

In all honesty, Javan did not much care what these clerics thought of him. Yet they held sway over the masses. They could rouse the crowds against him. Javan despised the clerics, but he'd be foolish not to fear their power.

"What do you want?" he repeated, this time with an edge to his voice.

"There are revelers in the streets during the holy days," the cleric replied. "You have soldiers. What are you doing with them?"

"That's not my concern," Javan answered.

"Then will you allow the Thul to raise his own army?"

"Absolutely not."

The anger in the cleric's eyes was unmistakable. He clenched his two fists together. He could not harm his lord Javan, but if he could, he would.

Yelling curses, the cleric turned and stormed out of the throne room.

The clerics were growing irate. That was all fine. Javan was, too.

"Lord Javan." His court page, Abgar, drew near. "There is another who wants to speak with you. He is from Adwar… his name is Faraad."

"Adwar." He spoke the word like a joke. The village on the perimeter of Tadmor was hardly known to anyone. It certainly wasn't worthy of a royal audience. "Tell him I am busy."

Abgar looked uncertain, but he knew better than to question his lord Javan.

~

He had not seen Yara all day.

In his private chambers, he found Marit sitting on their bed, twiddling her thumbs. There were tears in her eyes.

"She's run away," she muttered.

Chapter Four: A New Identity

On the outskirts of the city of Mahara, Yara took a razor to her hair. She judged her look in the mirror.

Did she look like a boy?

It still didn't look convincing to her, but the merchants in a caravan might not question her, if she offered free help.

She had purchased men's breeches in the marketplace, saying she meant them for her husband. The tunic she'd bought was somewhat ill fitting, but she had cut the sleeves to fit her size, and added some padding to hide her breasts.

In short, Yara was as convincing as she could possibly be.

She would leave the city of her birth to escape what happened to her.

Perhaps somewhere, in some far flung kingdom, she'd regain her sense of self, her ability to think, to reason and to feel.

She wept. There were people passing down the road, staring at her.

"Are you all right, sir?" said a woman.

Her deception was working. She wiped her eyes, taking comfort in the fact that one of her goals had not yet escaped her.

She stood up and went about her way.

The village of Magdala, on the desert's edge, was a landing spot for caravans. In Magdala, Yara would have her best ever chance to escape Tadmor once and for all, to forget the violence which had been wrought on her, to become a new person altogether.

What would her new name be? She settled on Yaro.

~

Magdala's white, flat-roofed buildings lay on the very edge of the dunes. In the center of town, scraping the sky, was a giant stone tower. Its immense bricks were stained brown from years of sand and wind.

Father told Yara that this tower was once Tadmor's greatest bulwark of defense, that—long ago—the people would retreat into the stone fortification in times of attack.

Now it was just a relic of the prior age, a symbol of Tadmor's rich history.

Several caravans were gathered in the village square. The scent of spices and dried goods was thick here. On the square's edge was a train of camels. They were heavy laden with bushels of dried raisins and dates.

Back in Mahara, a cleric had once shouted at Yara that raisins "are the fruit of the Devil.

"They came from grapes, and grapes are made into Devil's water!"

Yara had laughed in his face.

Devil's water—that is, wine—was banned altogether, though certain enterprising criminals were known to sneak it into the border.

Yara had done many things the clerics detested, but one thing she dared not do was have her fill of Devil's water. To be merely caught with a cup of Devil's water was a crime worthy of flogging; to drink it meant death. Perhaps Father would allow her to get away with it, but Yara was too wise to risk it.

When the soldiers guarding the caravan looked away, Yara grabbed a handful of raisins and stuffed them in her mouth.

They were sweet and chewy, a mouth full of heaven. She had not eaten all day. Now, in the blazing heat, she finally found her dinner.

These caravans brought in goods from the wider world: silk and porcelain from Cathay, iron swords and axes from Dwemer, whalebones and pipeweed from trading posts across the east. Caravaners had one goal: to profit. They knew the farther they traveled, the higher a price they'd find for their goods. Silk could be found nowhere other than Cathay; the further from the Dragon Emperor's realm they ventured, the higher the price would be.

On the other edge of the square, a camel train was empty. They had sold their goods, perhaps in Mahara. Now they were disembarking.

A dusky man stood at the front of the camel train. He was dressed in white, wearing a cotton headwrap. A scimitar was buckled to his side.

He regarded Yara with his dark eyes as she approached.

He laid a finger on the hilt of his scimitar. "What do you want, boy?" he said.

Clearly he thought Yara was some sort of thief. "May I join your caravan? I will work for just food and water."

"Food and water," he replied. "I saw that you like food. You reached in and grabbed some raisins for yourself, and at no cost to you at all…"

Yara flushed with embarrassment. She almost told him, "I was hungry." Instead she remained silent.

The man smiled. "Can you wield a sword? Or a dagger?"

"Of course," Yara lied.

"We leave tomorrow morning," he said. "We are going to Cathay, by way of Kish. Our first stop is the Pillars of the Moon in seven days. Can you make it that far without complaint?"

"Of course," Yara guessed.

She spent the night with the caravaners. The man, whose name she learned was Rafiz, handed her a dagger of her own, crafted of iron, with serrated edges. There were thirty on the caravan, plus Yara.

She realized she had never ventured more than a mile into the desert. Now, Yara would see the world.

She wept that night, privately, like she had wept every night since the incident. She missed Father and Mother. She missed the warmth and love of her home.

But she had no options. The world had changed. She had seen its ugliness. She had seen its pain.

Chapter Five: The Sons of Darkness

In the Well of Oath, covered in blankets, Ahram remained awake, listening to the howling wind of the desert night.

The air had grown icy; his breath turned to fog as he lay there. The scalding heat of the desert was a bitter memory. Now it was replaced with something different, and not altogether better.

When he shut his eyes, and heard the howling winds, he could almost hear voices, a chorus of them, ghostly in their tone and timbre.

He was likely just imagining it, but those sounds in the desert were unsettling him even more as he grew older. In his youth, when he traveled from town to town, from well to well, he thought little of these storms.

Now he dreaded their sound.

The Well of the Oath had held its own against the encroaching sand. But this sanctuary could not bear out against the desert forever.

How many towns, how many villages had the desert claimed?

The Well of the Oath, where—according to Zathustra—a holy man fought against the forces of darkness, was little protection against those howling winds, against that ghostly chorus.

They had days before they reached the relative sanctity and security of Tadmor. Ahram couldn't wait to end this venture altogether.

Zathustra, after all, had offered him ten pounds of gold, as much as Ahram was likely to have seen in Zeved-Du.

The ghouls had claimed his hopes for the treasure, as well as the lives of his friends.

That night he dreamed of those ghouls, standing over the body of Zathustra as they chittered in the dark. They stared at Ahram, as if waiting for something, before he looked at his hands, and saw he had become one of them.

Zathustra led the way the next day, up and down the scalding dunes. Their waterskins were filled to the brim with cold water. They would last a week in the desert and face no problem of thirst.

The memory of the nightmare lingered on, in the brightness of day.

Ahram had thought often of the ghouls, especially at night, when he heard the winds pick up and the storms howl. He could not forget their chittering teeth, their purple skin stretched tight across abnormally-shaped bones. They had the look of humans, but they were deformed, gangly. Had they once been people? Would, one day, Akil or Sohail rise again in the form of a ghoul?

"Zathustra!" Ahram shouted, one camel behind his partner. "What took you to Zeved-Du? How did you know where we were?"

It was enough to raise suspicions.

"The Lost City is a stopping point for me," Zathustra said. "Few know it, but the wells are deep there. It has held out against the desert for centuries, even in ruins.

"I did not expect the Sons of Darkness to be there…"

"The Sons of Darkness?"

"The ghouls were once only found in the deep desert. But they've spread north, south, west… everywhere. There is a change underway… one which bodes ill for Tadmor, for the world…"

"You speak of Tamor," Ahram mumbled as they began their ascent up a dune. "Where are you from, Zathustra, and why do you care about the Bride of the Desert?"

"You will know, in time… if you stick around long enough."

~

Over the scalding dunes, the camels took them, mile after mile without complaint, lurching their tall bodies from one side to another.

In the burning heat, oases appeared, which he knew where mirages. But the hotter the sun grew, the more intense the heat, the more he reached for his waterskin, and the more he was unsatisfied.

By Zathustra's estimate, they had three days before the next stop. It couldn't come soon enough.

~

That night, they pitched their tent.

The innumerable stars shone like beacons across the vast, open sky. The moon was gone; it had completed its cycle.

As Ahram rustled with the tent pegs, Zathustra was looking around pensively, scanning the dunes and the environs.

He was afraid of something, clearly. He was worried.

Over these days of travel, Ahram had begun to suspect Zathustra wasn't telling him everything he knew.

Ten pounds of gold was a huge payment for one man to accompany him.

They were being followed.

As he worked to erect the tent, Ahram finally decided to ask him. "Zathustra," he said, "what are you looking for?"

Zathustra straightened up and tightened his robes against the quickly-cooling wind. "Jackals are known to roam these parts."

"I'm not stupid," Ahram said.

"This I know." Zathustra didn't sound convinced.

"You aren't worried about jackals. You slew all those ghouls with your sorcery."

"Ghouls may be here, among us…"

"And yet you killed them. There's something greater that you fear…"

Zathustra was strong willed. He wouldn't tell Ahram what he knew.

Instead he continued watching the desert, surveying the outlines of the dunes amid the night sky.

Ahram continued his work, with no help from Zathustra. "I'm

an old man," he'd complain. "You're being too hard on me." Ahram couldn't believe Zathustra, a sorcerer, would have the gall to refuse work, so easily and so gladly. For the price of ten pounds of gold, he was Zathustra's slave. Was it worth it? Ahram would soon find out.

The camels formed a circle around the tent, and Ahram had them lay down.

"I will keep the first watch," Ahram said.

"I insist," Zathustra said, standing as straight as a rod. "In fact, I don't feel much like sleeping tonight."

"*I* insist," Ahram snapped. He'd had enough of this old oaf. "You've complained about aches and pains all day. You should get some rest, so I won't get an earful tomorrow."

Zathustra snapped toward him with a glare. In the blacks of his eyes, Ahram saw a shimmer like lightning. He had never seen Zathustra so angry.

But to Ahram's surprise, Zathustra calmed down quickly. "Very well," he said. "The first watch goes to you."

He passed by Ahram with an arrogant glance, and entered the tent.

Not long after, as Ahram sat, huddled, against the cold, the winds began to pick up.

Out of boredom, Ahram began to count the stars.

He lost count at three-hundred.

In ancient days, astrologers predicted the future by signs in the sky and constellations. Now the clerics overruled them, sentencing all "star-seers" to death.

He wondered what the stars would say about him now.

Lahiv, one of the camels, stood up and awakened her sisters.

Ahram scrambled to ease her down.

Her ears were twitching.

She was afraid. But of what?

Ahram stood up and put a hand on the hilt of his scimitar. He could see nothing in the dark outlines of the dunes. The winds, blowing against the sands, sounded like howling voices.

He eased Lahiv down, brushing her trembling neck. "Shhh," he whispered to her. Perhaps she wouldn't react this way if her master was keeping watch.

When Lahiv had calmed herself, Ahram looked again into the dark shapes of the dunes. He couldn't make much of them, what was on top or around them. The stars were brilliant, but the night shrouded the landscape in secrecy.

Off in the distance, on a dune, there was a stirring of the sand, a shadow.

A lump formed in Ahram's throat, but this was his watch. It was his duty to protect.

The camels had awoken and grown restless. They wanted to break free from their ties. Lahiv, ever a leader, remained seated and kept them relatively calm. She was the leader of the pack, whom Zathustra rode and gave the greatest affection. Ahram hopped over her and took the first tentative steps toward the sight of the disturbance, down the sloping sand.

Perhaps he had overreacted.

But as he stopped, halfway down the slope, half fearful and half worried he was losing his mind, he reminded himself this was his duty. Zathustra was sleeping. Those ten pounds of gold were Ahram's payment as a hired sword. He was there to protect, not to hang on and travel as a fellow passenger.

When he reached the summit of the dune in question, he could see nothing save sand, illuminated in the starlight. The shadow he saw was gone.

Perhaps it had never existed.

The winds were picking up, and the sand was hitting his bare legs like darts.

He hurried back toward the tent, knowing a storm was upon them.

He entered the tent convinced that the shadow was real, that whatever Zathustra was running from lay close-by.

~

In the darkness of the tent, the winds blew, and the sand was shifting ever-so-slightly underneath him.

Zathustra was snoring, as if making a mockery of Ahram's concerns and worries.

The wind, driving along the sand, had begun making the ghostly sounds of voices. The infernal chorus was no longer far away, in the distance, but right here, upon them, and around Ahram's tent.

He wouldn't give Zathustra the satisfaction of waking him up. He could just imagine the smug look, the condescending words.

He realized, in all this time, in all his adult life, he had never ventured out, deep into the storms. Instead, he had huddled in his bed, assuming the winds were nothing more than just that, winds.

Again he headed back outside. He grabbed a torch from Lahiv's saddlepack, a flint, and some tinder. He struck the oil-soaked torch until it burst into flames.

Lahiv, still sitting down, looked at him with a questioning glance.

Sweet thing.

Ahram stepped over Lahiv and, a torch in his right hand and a scimitar in his left, he ventured out toward where he'd never been before.

He descended the dune into the quickly cooling night. A lump had formed in his throat, but he'd made up his mind. He would scour the desert for the shadow, for the demon, for whatever lurked in each desert night.

~

At the summit of the next dune, the torch's light failed to reach the tent. He was alone, far from Zathustra and his pack animals. A cold sweat had formed on Ahram's forearms. The storm seemed permanently close, but always out of reach. Like a ghost it was hidden from sight, wailing in its infernal chorus.

He traversed up and down three separate dunes, circling the tent from a distance. At the summit of the third dune he heard something different, rising slightly above the noise of the storm: chittering.

Something stank.

There were ghouls nearby. They had followed them from Zeved-Du.

Or perhaps there were some bodies close-by, some lost wanderer who had succumbed to the desert heat. These creatures of darkness feasted on rotting flesh. They did not prefer the living, Zathustra had told him.

He followed the sound and the smell. To his surprise they scattered; he caught sight of their shadows fleeing from view.

Emboldened, Ahram pressed the charge, sprinting after them as they ran away.

Their features were long and lanky; their arms almost touched the ground as they scurried this way and that. As they ran they jabbered and chittered their teeth. The scent of death and decay followed them wherever they ran. The powerful miasma would be enough to knock many foes off balance, but Ahram continued his pursuit, refusing to relent.

He had run along time; he was panting and sweating when at last they stopped. They turned to face him, white teeth glistening in the starlight.

Their tongues were white and segmented, like worms. Their black and beady eyes gazed at him.

They were not alone.

A shadow stood behind them, twice as tall as any of the ghouls.

They had run to her in shelter. Or perhaps they had drawn Ahram here, as a trap.

The shadow before him was long and wispy, its eyes bright and blazing red. Amid the blackness of her body, there were bits of color: traces of white corpselike hands. There was the sound of buzzing like a million insects were swarming within her.

He backed away.

At the first trace of fear, a ghoul charged him, swiping at him with its rancid claw. He slashed hard with the scimitar, severing its arm. It wailed and screeched as black blood came pouring out from the injury.

The rest of the ghouls scrambled into the desert, cowards all, as Ahram landed the killing blow, severing the ghoul's head.

The shadow remained before him, lurking like a vapor. The buzzing rang in Ahram's ears.

She was half physical, half insubstantial. Wisplike, she was on the edge of existence. Two horns sprouted from her head.

The shadows began to coalesce. She began to shrink. More of her began to substantiate, gaining form and substance. Beyond the wisps of shadow, a beautiful white face appeared, luscious breasts, feminine hands and arms. Her eyes were bright blue, like the waters of an oasis; their beacon-like red color was gone. She was as beautiful as an houri, as radiant as a jinn.

Lust replaced Ahram's curiosity. He had not been with a woman in weeks.

He drew near, knowing it was unwise, unable to help himself.

When he held her hands, a sensation of crawling crept over him, but by that time her grip was iron hard, and she wouldn't let him go. She drew him near. Her lips were red. Her brilliant eyes seemed to stare into his soul.

As he moved in to kiss her, he saw that her teeth were fangs; her tongue white and dead; and bugs were inside her.

Lust was replaced with panic; in a moment he was inches from death.

But lightning struck and thunder rolled.

She relinquished her grip and fled.

Zathustra was hobbling up the hill, lifting his book. "Flee!" he was shouting. "Flee, daughter of darkness."

Now that she was gone, he turned to Ahram with a stormy glare.

"You idiot!" he was shouting. "You fool!" A string of curses followed. He slapped Ahram with his book, so hard he fell down.

Ahram scrambled to his feet and Zathustra struck again, bruising him.

"We must leave," he cursed. "We must leave now. The darkness is consuming the desert. The Lamia are near…"

Chapter Six: The Desert Encroaches

"The desert is consuming all," the man name Faraad stuttered to Javan. "The woman… the woman… the Woman at the Well."

Javan examined this man, standing before him in the throne room. Javan gathered he was a caravaner. But he'd been stricken mad. Perhaps he had drunk something foul, or contracted dysentery or some kind of wasting disease. Javan's officials had found him in possession of great cargoes: a bag of cold coins, a fine camel, topaz and sapphire and beryl. His clothing was resplendent: a bright blue silk tunic and green breeches.

Whatever happened to Faraad in the village of Adwar, whatever he had seen, or eaten, or drank, had caused him to lose his mind.

If he were a Tammuri, he'd be placed in the ward of some rich family; no one was allowed to suffer and die in a land of such wealth.

But Faraad was not a Tammuri. He was a foreigner. He did not belong here. He did not deserve Javan's mercy, only his sorrow.

"Send him away," said Javan.

The guards grabbed Faraad and dragged him screaming to the door.

Javan was not without his troubles: a daughter, lost; a wife beside herself, unable to function. Yet Tadmor had to go on, and therefore so did Javan.

Faraad struggled against the guards but couldn't overcome them. Soon he was gone from Javan's sight.

Javan raised his scepter, indicating he would tolerate no more visitors today, but as the guards moved to shut the door, a cleric came barging in, dressed in black, together with a gaggle of servants.

Javan seethed at the sight. He'd seen enough of these clerics. Over decades, over centuries, they had been given too much power in Tadmor.

The brazenness with which the cleric stormed in would have

outraged a wazir in ancient days. And yet he did not fear Javan, because he did not have to.

For centuries, they had preached in their kabakh*s*: black temples, shaped like squares, which had spread in every corner of the city of Mahara. They had grown wealthy through tithes, through extortion, and the sum of money Javan was forced to pay into their coffers. They held great power over the minds of the citizens, and because of that, they were to be feared.

But this was no ordinary cleric. This was Rahul, the second-highest ranking cleric in Tadmor. He was the enforcer of the will of the Thul, leader of the faithful, a ruthless deputy for "His Holiness." He would not seek an audience with Javan unless this was important.

Unlike Javan's other visitors, Rahul did not fall prostrate, nor did he so much as bow. Thinking himself an equal to the wazir, who controlled the armies of Tadmor, he did not bother to show any respect. He met Javan's gaze with an icy glare.

"Javan," Rahul said—not "Your Majesty"—"the Supreme Leader of the Faithful wishes to speak to you."

Javan muttered curses through his gritted teeth. "What about?" he said. "You've received your money apportioned from the Treasury… I haven't harassed your clerics or street preachers on their sermons. And I will never, ever, allow you to arm yourselves. There is nothing to talk about."

"It's about the desert." Rahul wore a black turban like the other clerics. He was younger than the others. There wasn't a trace of gray in his beard, nor any wrinkles on his face. He was handsome, in fact, though wives were forbidden to the clerics. There were reports of clerics and young women meeting together, in secret; but marriage was illegal according to their religion. All was forgiven for the clerics, when it came to their god Mazda; but death and torture was a fitting instrument of punishment for the common people.

Once, in his youth, Javan had paid heed to the religion of Mazda, hearing the so-called wisdom of the street preachers. But he had grown jaded. He had seen their evil: the severe punishments the clerics dealt for crimes that they themselves had committed.

Now his respect for the clerics, and for Mazda himself, was linked only to his fear of them.

"The desert," Javan repeated, rather floored by the strange statement. "He wants to speak of the desert.

"Speak to me, desert. Speak to me, mountain and sky." He quoted the pagan poet Uru and watched the anger build of Rahul's face.

He watched the furrowed brow, the upturned lip with a smile.

"It's not a joke," Rahul said.

Javan knew better than to think the clerics ever joked or made a jest about anything. "Well, I laughed."

Rahul was glaring at him, outright, now. "The Supreme Leader of the Faithful demands you come join him in the Grand Kabakh. He must speak with you instantly."

He had done so before. He had brought himself to travel there. No longer would he do so. He wouldn't degrade himself by traveling there. "If the Thul wishes to speak to me," Javan said, "let the Thul come here."

Rahul rushed him.

"Take him away!" Javan screamed, and the guards around him instantly seized Rahul and all his servants, wrestling them until they were firmly into their grip.

"You will regret this!" Rahul screeched. "You will regret this!"

As he was dragged away, Javan knew he was probably right.

~

That night, riots broke out. From the palace balcony, Javan saw the unruly mobs, bearing torches, marching through the streets.

He had seen such mobs before, the blindly pious, shouting of Javan's "pagan ways" and his "infidelity." Like all mobs they were composed of the common people, whipped up by the clerics and believing their every word. If they followed their edicts, if they paid their money to the kabakh, one day, perhaps, Mazda might grant them mercy and entry into paradise. That is what they thought.

Who knew if this mob, like the rest, would dissipate, or if something far more dangerous would arise?

Javan wouldn't count on Mazda's mercy, or the Thul's. He would rely on his wit, his strength, and his armies to ride out the storm.

Chapter Seven: The Pillars of the Moon

"To Cathay, by way of Kish."

That, as Rafiz explained it, was where they were headed.

Yara would follow them there, to escape her past, to escape her family and the troubles of the world.

When she finally reached that far-off destination, totally remote from Tadmor and all Yara knew, she didn't know what would happen next. The Cathayans spoke a strange tongue she did not know. She could not communicate with them.

So what would Yara do in that far off land?

For now, she would put one foot ahead of the other. She would treat each day as its own battle.

Now she lurched along, riding a camel, following the caravan as it wound through the scalding desert.

The danger of her situation did not escape her. She was traveling with thirty men. So far, none had seen past her disguise, her thick-cut tunic, her short hair, her torn and dirty breeches. But how long before something happened, before they knew that the "Yaro" traveling with them was not a little boy but instead a young woman?

She would do her best to keep up the ruse, to fool them all and ensure they never knew. It was a wonder that she pulled it off, but she had become an expert of sorts in cosmetics and appearances.

The night before, she'd inquired of Rafiz where Kish was and how far away it lay.

"Far enough," he had answered, "that you will wish you'd never embarked on this journey."

Yara's friends back home had told her that silk grew in the Cathayan seas, and floated like flotsam and jetsam for ships to gather. But these traders said that worms spun the silk, like spiders, and that Cathayan maids wove it into the most precious fabric in the world.

Yara didn't want to think the rich robes her mother wore came from an insect's spinneret. But many precious things were made from filth.

If all went well, if bandits did not strike the caravan dead, if a storm did not overtake them, if the sun did not scorch them beyond recognition, then they'd return with reams of silk, purchased from the markets of Cathay, and sold back home for ten times the price.

It surprised Yara how much she enjoyed the caravaner's life. She wore a dagger without fear. She cussed and spoke whatever words came to mind.

Gone was the fear of the clerics. Gone were the loose-fitting oppressive robes, whose heaviness and black color sapped her strength in the sun. Gone was the demand that she'd never be armed, that she wouldn't wield a dagger, that she couldn't protect herself.

She couldn't protect herself back then.

She thought of that evil night as she lurched back and forth on the camel. Tears formed in her eyes. She wiped the moisture away. She had to be strong. She couldn't show weakness, not with these rough caravaners. She couldn't let a bit of her hurt show. She had to face the day firmly. She couldn't give in to the dread, to the sadness, to the negativity that still lingered inside her.

That night, they made their first stop.

"The Valley of Dates!" Rafiz shouted.

The well-watered oasis was covered in weeds and algae, surrounded by a forest-like thicket of date palms.

Near the edge of the oasis, a town of sorts was set up: mudbrick buildings overgrown with vines and vegetation. The scent of cooking meat filled the air.

Farmers had dug irrigation canals and raised goats and cows in this lush island in the middle of the desert. The tall date palms protected from the heat. Frogs were chirping as the sun began to sink beneath the horizon. The heat of the day began to wane.

Treasure this moment, Yara told herself, *because tomorrow you'll be saddle-sore, traveling the desert.*

Under the vibrant sky, beneath the vast sea of stars, Rafiz tied the camels down and, together with his men, fashioned a fire.

Another caravan had joined them; they were headed west, from Cathay, to Bezakirah.

Their leader looked shaken.

As the night wore on, and the caravaners mingled, he began to speak: "There are bandits on the road," he said. "They killed a dozen men passing through, near the Pillars of the Moon… and they were women."

Female bandits. Yara had never heard of such a thing.

But in the coming days, when she passed the Pillars of the Moon, she would keep an eye out for them.

~

Up and down steep dunes, beside scorched salt pans and fields of twisted rocks, through the burning desert and the relentless sun, Yara continued her journey for five days. She learned why caravaners were so well paid, and why few chose to take up this profession.

And yet she relished not having something handed to her. Whatever she was paid, she had earned. It wasn't just given to her as the daughter of the wazir.

The night before they passed the Pillars of the Moon, heading due east toward Kish, a storm erupted.

The howling winds were like a chorus of voices, echoing through the deeps. Yara, taking refuge behind the tent, couldn't fall asleep. Amid the ghostly howls, she thought she could hear the screaming voices of women, of loud wailing, of shrieks.

Even her fellow caravaners seemed perturbed. Rafiz was tossing and turning. Ali had his eyes open. No one, as far as she could tell, was asleep.

Stepping over their bodies, she opened the tent flap and,

holding her sleeve to her mouth, stepped outside amid the biting, blowing sand.

There were shadows moving in the dunes ahead, hundreds, marching in a column. Tomorrow they would be gone.

Chapter Eight: The End of History

Javan had ruled the nation long enough to know these riots were something new.

Normally, when the clerics whipped the faithful into a frenzy, they would peter out after a few days.

But now, they continued, and as the riots endured, the destruction and devastation spread. Entire neighborhoods had been burned to rubble. The mobs had taken torches to the houses of anyone who did not join them.

Javan rose from his throne, knowing it was time to act. He had to stop this. He had to do something which he'd never dared.

He summoned his emirs, his commanders, his sergeants-at-arms.

"We are going to make peace," Javan told them. "We are going to put sense into the mob. And we are going to drive the clerics from Mahara, once and for all."

Chapter Nine: The King of the Dark

At a rushed pace, Ahram and Zathustra continued through all hours of the night. Zathustra was running from something—from what, Ahram was not entirely sure. He cried out nonsensically, sputtering about the Lamia. The fact that such a powerful sorcerer was afraid made it clear Ahram should flee as well, that he should run as quickly as possible to find shelter in the safe valley of Tadmor.

Eventually, Zathustra stopped out of exhaustion. The sun was beginning to rise over the dunes.

"How far to Tadmor?" Ahram asked.

"Days," Zathustra said. "Five days at best. We can't outrun them. They are coming. They come at night…"

The exhaustion was clearly wearing on Ahram's client.

Ahram had a job, to protect Zathustra, to keep him alive. It was hard to know if the stress of the journey was eating on him, or if his panic was justified.

Soon after the sun rose, the darkness would dissipate, and faster than Ahram knew, the heat would blaze down upon them, sapping their strength and energy even further.

"Who is coming?" Ahram asked. "What do you mean? The Lamia? The ghouls?"

"The Lamia," Zathustra repeated. "The ghouls. The King of the Dark."

~

They used the tent to protect from the sunlight, though the stifling heat within intensified and grew as the day wore on.

Zathustra slept soundly, snoring loudly, but Ahram—try as he might—couldn't get any rest. He stepped outside the tent and surveyed the dunes, watching the endless sea of sand which shifted for centuries, and would shift for centuries more.

He questioned why he had agreed to this, why he hadn't stopped in some fertile oasis town and left the horrific memories of Zeved-Du behind him. Was ten pounds of gold worth it? The ghouls only came out at night, but they were surely close-by.

Before dusk, Zathustra arose. He began to dismantle the tent, but Ahram took him by the hand and pulled him aside.

"You have to tell me what you're running from," Ahram said. "Otherwise, I'll leave you here to die."

It was an empty threat; Ahram knew his presence was little more than companionship for the powerful sorcerer Zathustra.

But his hard features and steely gaze softened. "Very well," he muttered. "I will tell you everything."

With a hand on Ahram's shoulder, Zathustra began to speak in hushed tones of "The King of the Dark."

"He is the greatest of the ghouls," Ahram muttered. "Immune to mortal weapons."

The skies were still dark when Zathustra spoke. "In times before human reckoning he arose… the King of the Dark, raised by the Lord of Darkness himself."

Shemesh, the Lord of Darkness, was an idea predating Mazda, a relic of the ancient religions of the past. He was still spoken of, and feared, but the clerics laughably dismissed him. It seemed that Zathustra still believed.

"The King of the Dark was the first of the ghouls. He fashioned the monsters from the spirits of those slain: from the dead who feasted on man's flesh in their prior life."

It seemed like madness.

In his youth in Bezakirah, he had listened to the fiery sermons of the street-side preachers, condemning the pagans and the adulterers, pronouncing that Mazda would torture them for eternity after death. He had heard tales of the jinn, calling up lightning and spiriting people away in vast whirlwinds. Ahram had heard much, but he believed little. Would this be any different?

He had to take Zathustra seriously. He had come to respect this old man.

"His powers were restricted by the gods for millennia, but in these past years, the chains have been loosened…"

"The gods," Ahram repeated. "Are you a pagan?"

Zathustra answered with a blank look.

"They will not accept you in Tadmor," Ahram continued.

Zathustra smiled. He thought it was funny.

"And you've never told me where you came from, Zathustra."

"I come from far away," he answered. "Beyond the desert. Beyond Kish. Beyond the Tower and its environs. I come from a mountain, and a temple built on its slopes. Does that satisfy your enquiries?"

"It will have to." Ahram smiled.

Zathustra's happy demeanor faded. In an instant, he had grown weak again. "The King approaches. Soon enough he will lay siege to Tadmor and all its wealth. The desert follows him; it is at its beck and call."

~

That night, and for the ensuing four nights, they heard drums.

Chapter Ten: The Lily of the Valley

Days after the caravaners' journey began, the Pillars of the Moon appeared, and Yara found herself disappointed.

The Pillars did not dazzle in the slightest. Decades of wind and sand had turned the marble a shade of brown. The leaf details on their capitals were almost completely worn away. The only thing notable was their immense size, and the thought that one day, long ago, the ancients had fashioned them with their hands.

Yet these pillars were as good guideposts for the caravaners as the stars.

Long before the sun set, Rafiz ordered the camels to stop, and they decided to set up camp for the night.

The caravaners, thirty in total, quickly went to work setting up tents, fastening them with hammers and tent pegs. Yara wandered away from them, into the surrounding fields.

Sagebrush had replaced dunes. Their blue color was a welcome reprieve from the monotony that had greeted Yara all this time. The ground was flat and dry, cracked and parched in the sun's direct glare. Yet there was game here, Rafiz had said: gazelles and wild birds were known to haunt this region, "from here until we reach Kish." The whirling sands and the endless climbs were gone, for now. The Pillars of the Moon were the stopping point; from here, the caravan would turn east until they reached Kish, until they embarked on the mountain path toward Cathay and returned, at a breakneck pace to Tadmor, and eventually the great cities and towns of the coast. That is how caravaners made their fortune: by traveling to the impossibly far land of Cathay, filling their packsaddles with silk, and reselling it for exorbitant prices.

Yes, Yara had grown to respect these caravaners and their lifestyle. But over these past few days, she had grown more uneasy. The looks Rafiz and his men gave her were beginning to make her uncomfortable. She had let her guard down at times: she had forgotten to lower her voice every once in a while. And she wasn't sure the padding on her tunic was convincing.

Did they know "Yaro" was actually a girl? She had begun to fear they were catching on. They were not as stupid as they looked. And "Yaro" was a part she played well, but she'd begun to have nagging doubts. Did Rafiz believe her? Was Masdjar looking at her lustfully? The way they talked about women, and the eagerness with which they talked about the "whorehouses of Kish" made Yara realize what danger she was in.

That night in Mahara scarred her to this day. She doubted she'd ever recover. She doubted she'd ever look the same way at life again.

To have it happen once more was beyond imagining.

She decided to wander further into the wilderness. Perhaps she'd never return to the caravan. Starvation and thirst was one thing; to have that trauma return to her was another.

~

As they'd approached the Pillars of the Moon, Masdjar and Yahul had spoken of the rumors they'd heard: of a tribe of female bandits who were known to waylay caravans.

Yara hadn't believed it at first. But then she thought of herself, posing convincingly as "Yaro" and wondered if there was a grain of truth to the legend.

Lizards skittered across the ground like fleeting shadows, running from Yara and departing their sunning spots. Yara had grown hungry. The stale waybread failed to satisfy her. She hoped to Mazda that Rafiz would find a gazelle and roast it for dinner… anything but stale, flaky waybread, even one of those lizards.

She wondered what they'd taste like, dropped into a pot still squirming. With enough sauce and salt, would they make a good substitute for the feasts she'd enjoyed back home?

Home. Her soul ached for Tadmor.

Though a dark shadow had fallen over it, though the clerics had gained in power and commanded vast mobs of the faithful, though its ancient wealth had begun to taper, still Yara wanted nothing more than home.

But she could not return. She was different. Her childhood had been ripped from her. She would never go back.

But here, in the blazing sun, as dusk approached but the heat lay thick on the land, she thought of the juicy pomegranates in her father's garden; of the fruits hanging of the trees, of figs, of lemons and melons. She was far from her luxuries as the wazir's daughter; she lived like a pauper, like one of her father's subjects. She was no longer pampered.

In a way it was a good thing for her, to see how the date farmers lived, to see how grimy the shepherds got, each day; but she did miss her home.

And she missed Father and Mother more than she would have thought. She missed Father and Mother most of all.

Now, with her life shrouded in uncertainty, they were a beacon—a distant memory now, of better times. They were a candle in the dark.

Rafiz was hollering at her. She could just barely make out his voice above the wind.

With some reluctance, she turned. She could not survive out here, by herself. She had to risk it. She had to stay with the caravan. Perhaps, when they reached Cathay, she'd join the silk weaving maidens who spun the world's most precious cloth. She wouldn't have to return to Tadmor at all.

But would the Cathayans accept a foreigner into their midst? She supposed she would find out.

~

Rafiz's men built a fire from sagebrush and gumtrees. It was roaring, bright and warm, not long after Yara returned to camp. "Any luck with the gazelles?" Yara asked. Her stomach was an empty chasm, crying out for anything but waybread.

Rafiz laughed. "You're a strange one, Yaro," he said.

Was there more meaning to his words than he let on?

Yara was being paranoid.

"I'm sick of waybread," she explained.

Rafiz laughed, and nodded. "We aren't prepared for gazelle hunting, little Yaro."

She still did not trust Rafiz. When she looked into his eyes, she saw a crafty man who hid his thoughts and disguised his intentions.

That night, in the tent, Yara couldn't sleep. She had a terrible feeling about this night.

She had not felt this much dread since the night she was assaulted.

In the dark, Rafiz's form rose above her.

"Yaro," he said, "may I call you Yara?"

As Yara unsheathed her dagger, chaos overtook the camp. Horns blew and the caravaners scrambled to their feet. In the confusion, Yara dashed out of the tent, to see women in blue, naked-faced and wearing nothing but headbands, storming the site. In their hands were thick sabers which gleamed in the moonlight. The blades were curved and shone like polished silver.

A slaughter began; Yara turned and ran into the desert.

A bandit was right behind her.

Chapter Eleven: The Storming of Mahara

Javan stood before his soldiers, marshalled together in Mahara's City Square. All around him were pillars of fire and columns of smoke. The wicked clerics had set fire to the city, stirring up their zealous mob into a violent frenzy. They had spoken ill of their wazir for generations; but now they had ratcheted up the rhetoric. They had called Javan "the son of the devil" and "the blasphemer prince." No wazir had drawn the blood of a cleric in history.

When the clerics first came to Tadmor, their power had not been sudden. Like leprosy or red itch their faith had spread, until the old gods were forgotten and a kabakh was built in each village, city and town.

Now was the time to end this pox, this rash, this leprosy on the body of mankind. It was time to break the power of the clerics, and to drive them from Tadmor. Javan would be the dagger that stuck them in the heart.

~

After midnight, the attack began; hundreds of Javan's men, on horse, on camel, on chariot, drove the endless mobs before them. Before dusk hit, the clerics began to retreat. When the sun dawned, they were gone from Tadmor.

Chapter Twelve: The King Approaches

After endless days in the burning sun and many long nights punctuated by drums, Tadmor appeared: a green horizon bursting with the promise of pomegranates and plentiful water.

Ahram stared at the blessed land, so close yet so far. He was parched. The waterskins had run out this morning. His tongue was dry. The thought of water made him want to dismount and sprint the rest of the way into Tadmor's embrace; but in this state, it would kill him.

Zathustra was mumbling, as he had begun to do: mindless jabbering about the King of the Dark and the Lamia.

Ahram would leave him to die if he had to. He didn't care about the gold anymore. Just water, and the sweet taste of pomegranate.

As the sun sank beneath the horizon in its gold and pink colors, it became clear just how far that green horizon was.

"We must stop here!" Zathustra shouted, "and prepare for the night."

"Tonight, I will be in Tadmor," Ahram said. "With or without you."

"You are a fool, Ahram. Don't let your thirst get you killed."

Ahram wanted to strike Zathustra. He didn't understand. He didn't know how Ahram felt, how his tongue was as dry as the sand that swirled beneath his camel's feet. He didn't understand Aharam's desperation.

The drums began not long after the sun set. They were louder than they had ever been before, echoing across the dunes. As Ahram and Zathustra waited, there was the sound of chanting; and in the distance, green signal flares lighting up the night, casting ghostly shadows against the nearby mountains.

"I'm not waiting," Ahram said. Panic was welling up inside him. But still, in the heat of the moment, the thing he thought about the most was his tongue.

Zathustra turned. He handed Ahram a waterskin. "The last bit. I was saving it for myself. I won't need it, not anymore. Run, Ahram. I will hold off the King of the Dark as long as I can. I will die."

For the first time, Ahram hesitated. "You come with me."

"Leave the camels behind you," Zathustra said. "They'll panic. Run. Run as fast as you can. Tell the wazir to take all his subjects, everyone who lives in Tadmor, and leave. Everyone must take shelter in the coasts. Flee to the west! Flee to the west!"

Part Two: To the West

Down a desert road from Bezakirah, along the rocky coast, the city of Huddin hugged the shore. The smell of seasalt and fish filled the air, as rumor of conflict spread throughout its streets.

"War in Tadmor!" said a merchant passing through. "The wazir has gone mad, and taken on the faithful…"

"Tadmor?" a woman answered him. "The Bride of the Desert?"

And so the rumor spread, and reached the Wazir of Huddin's ear.

"A rebellion against the faithful!" his advisors cried, and the clerics joined their call. "We must rescue them!"

But the Wazir of Huddin was undecided, and entered his private chambers for solitude.

Chapter Thirteen: The Temple of the Moon

The bandits had bound their hands and feet in rope.

Yara watched, trembling, as the beautiful women circled around, examining them.

They were naked faced and wore their long black hair in braided ponytails. Their blue midriffs revealed their muscular bodies. To wear such garb in Tadmor would earn many lashes in the town square. Here, the law of the desert ruled. There would be no punishment. They could wear whatever they wanted. They could do whatever they wanted.

Too bad they had chosen to kill Yara along with the caravaners.

Rafiz they could kill; the rest, she would weep for.

Their circling stopped.

One of the young women stood in front of Yara, her black hair crowned with a silver-and-emerald tiara. She wore baggy blue pants of silk and a midriff woven with gold thread. Her eyes, unlike others, were a crystal blue. Her lip was pierced with a ring. She had colored her eyes with dark shadow. This was the bandit whom the others called "The Lily of the Valley."

"You come here, caravaners, passing through our sanctuary," she said. "You cross the Pillars, hoping to become rich men."

The Lily of the Valley stepped up to Yara and kicked her onto her back. A cloud of dust billowed into the air and Yara choked on its fumes.

"Do you know that the Temple has been rebuilt?" the Lily continued.

Yara struggled to get back up on her knees. The ropes were tied so tight they were chafing against her skin.

"Do you know that the old world is returning?" the Lily said.

"Did you know that the Goddess's worship has been restored? That her servants are growing in number each day?"

"I spit on your pagan gods!" Masdjar cried. He was the most religious of the group, but for his own sake Yara wished he'd bitten his tongue.

The Lily leapt many feet to where Masdjar knelt, blindfolded, and sliced off his head with a saber.

Rafiz screamed. Yara retched. The other caravaners renewed their struggle to flee, but the ties that bound them were too tight; and the bandits surrounded them.

Yara did her best to remain calm, knowing this might be the end of her life, the end of all things.

"You! Leader! Rafiz!" the Lily snapped. "Tell me. Say 'I reject the new faith. I pronounce my allegiance to the Goddess.'"

"I reject the new faith! I pronounce my allegiance to the Goddess…"

She cut him down.

Rafiz, a worm, a coward to the end, had no principles except self-preservation.

Yara wouldn't give these bandits the satisfaction of hearing her renounce Mazda, even though she never cared much for clerics or the One God. She would face her death in stony silence. She would curse them before the saber struck. She would pray for their destruction.

"You have not come here to venture to Cathay," the Lily said. "You're going north. North, to the Place of Shadow. To the Altar of Sacrifice. Who are you bringing for the blood offering?"

At her words, the struggle returned anew. Nazir broke free from his binds. Yalon tossed and turned mightily, but fell over. In an instant, the bandits had cut them down, even as a cold calmness overtook Yara. She remained still like a statue.

The bandits made their rounds, cutting down the caravaners.

At last they came to Yara. She was shaking and weeping.

The Lily of the Valley approached, brushing her cheek with her finger. She wiped away some of the salty tears.

"I kill all the men who pass north from the Pillars. But you... you are not a man."

She made an incision with her scimitar, and the padding that hid Yara's breasts fell from her tunic.

"You almost had me tricked," the Lily of the Valley stated. "But not quite. I have a better eye than these oafish caravaners."

But Rafiz had found out, Yara told herself. *I wonder if he'd known all along.* The terrible night in Mahara's city square had almost repeated itself. Yara wasn't sure whether she was shaking from that, or from the Lily of the Valley and her depraved "sisters."

"Aila..." The Lily nodded to one of her underlings behind Yara.

Yara's binds on her hands were severed. She fell flat onto her face.

Next, the ties that bound her legs fell free. Yara leapt to her feet and grabbed her dagger, hidden inside her boots.

The bandit women backed away.

The Lily of the Valley laughed. "We are freeing you," she said. "Don't test our kindness."

"I don't want your kindness," Yara answered. "You're savage killers."

"Quaint," the Lily purred, "that you defend these men, who no doubt intended to sacrifice you on an altar."

Mad blabbering from a bandit, Yara knew. She didn't care. "Leave me alone. Kill me, or run away!"

"You'll be dead before the sun sets. Come with us. Or don't. Traveling isn't safe anymore by yourself." The Lily was adamant.

Yara glared at the bandit women. "I don't need your advice."

She watched as they filtered away, forming a line.

She was left alone in the night, with only the wind, grating against the Pillars of the Moon, to comfort her.

Rafiz had stuffed precious goods into the camels' saddlebags. In the moonlight, Yara began to pilfer through them. She found in one saddlebag a cachet of silver and gold coins, mixed with diamond rings and emeralds. She'd seen such splendor in her own home in Mahara. She passed it by.

Among more coins and jewels, there were whalebone figurines with black eyes and primitive faces; jet-black stones which Yara could not identify; and in the saddlebag of Rafiz's camel, what she recognized as a sacrificial knife.

It was impractical for combat, crafted of silver, with red rubies inset in patterns along the blade. She had seen such a blade, when clerics offered cows on an altar during a religious feast.

So the bandits were right. She had lost track of them. They had disappeared, leaving her alone in the night.

Directly ahead, the North Star was shining brightly. They had indeed turned down a different path than Yara expected. Instead of turning east toward the mountain stronghold of Kish, they had changed direction, toward a place Yara didn't know.

They had tried to sacrifice her. To whom? To what? The ancients sacrificed human beings, but not even the clerics stooped to that level.

Yara wondered if she should have stayed in Tadmor.

No, she reminded herself. She couldn't look her parents in the eye after what had happened. She couldn't be a burden on them. All this journeying, all this action, had taken her mind off the sorrow.

Now she was far from Tadmor, far from home, in the middle of the desert. There was no easy way back, anyway. It was impossible to return by herself.

She would remain by these Pillars, these ancient guiding posts for caravaners, and she would find a way out, or she would die. She turned once more to those immense structures, built thousands of years ago. In the darkness they were mere silhouettes. Their marble was worn and faded. Their beauty was gone, but the structures remained intact for countless centuries. Was there any better place for Yara to face her end?

She recalled, not long ago, the mirage she had seen: of an army marching across the desert in pitch blackness.

She did not have to worry about such hallucinations. But there were dangers in the desert: cobras whose poison could kill an elephant; ravenous wild dogs, hyenas and jackals. She couldn't let her guard down. There were several full waterskins tied to the camels, and wells not far from the Pillars themselves.

And yet Yara bristled as she stood there. Peering into the darkness, she did not feel safe. The moon's pale light did not allow her gaze to travel very far. Despite the silence of the night, broken only by the wind, she was not alone—she could sense it.

She led the camels into a circle around her, and spread her bedroll out onto the dry soil of the desert. A night bird had begun to sing, perhaps a stridge or a hunting owl.

Mazda would strike her dead tonight, according to the word of the clerics. By now, having dressed in the attire of a man, she'd be labeled an apostate and sentenced to die; and her father would be loathe to protect her. He'd have to face off the mobs like he'd done throughout his life. And they'd blame her for what happened in Mahara's city square. At the thought of that night, she grew vulnerable again. Tears formed in her eyes as the desert night turned colder, and the winds began to pick up.

Not long after Yara shut her eyes, the sound of dirt scraping jerked her out of the bedroll and onto her feet.

She could just vaguely make out the silhouette, reflected in the light of the moon. If humanoid, it was strangely shaped, with long, lanky arms that almost touched the ground and an oversized head. The camels had awakened and were beginning to grunt.

A fetid stench was wafting towards them, a smell of death and rot.

Yara shoved past the camels to face off this creature. A true caravaner protected his camels; they were his lifeline in the treacherous desert.

The creature's face was oblong, and a few needle-like fangs jutted upward from its hulking jaw. Its eyes were black and beady. As she drew near, the scent of death and rot grew stronger, and she grew faint, almost falling down. She tried to breathe from her mouth, but even then the scent managed to get to her. She wanted to vomit. She held firm.

Brandishing her dagger, she took a tentative step forward, and the creature backed away, shielding its head with its large, ape-like hands.

This creature was fearful of her. It could not sense the building terror in Yara's face. It was opportunistic, as craven as it was cruel.

She charged it, swinging her dagger. It leapt toward her and in one frenzied moment tackled her to the ground.

It scratched her with its claws, and opening its mouth, took a deep bite out of her with its needlelike fangs.

In a moment, it was all over as shadowy figures overtook the creature.

But the pain remained, deep and throbbing, consuming every bit of her, filling her with matchless agony.

She barely realized that she was being picked up and carried across the desert on the Lily's shoulder.

Careening in and out of consciousness, Yara at some point came to, seeing—through the throbbing pain—that she'd arrived in some sort of pillared temple.

She was placed on a mattress beside a pool. Above she could see the gleaming stars. There were statues all around, and wandering the perimeter of the pool she saw a tiger, orange- and black-striped, pawing the waters and splashing.

There were fish swimming around in the pool, and despite this one of the bandits was bathing, swimming around in the nude.

The pain caught up to Yara and she screamed.

The Lily was crouched over her. "Hush," she whispered. "You are going to be fine, my sweet."

Gently the Lily touched Yara's wounded arm. There was blood everywhere, and her flesh was torn open in a gash. Already signs of infection were beginning to spread.

"The Sons of Darkness have the worst bite of any creature," the Lily said. "No one can survive the aftermath. Not without medicine. And we have it. Tell us, young woman... What is your name?"

"Yara," she answered. Tears of pain had caused her eyes to become blurry.

"Yara," the Lily said. "That is an old name. It means 'Love.'"

Yara knew that as well as anyone; it had a specific meaning in Old Tammuri. "And yours. Surely, it is not the Lily of the Valley."

"That is what people call me," she answered with a laugh. "But I know you well enough, Yara. You may call me Saboo."

That name was an archaic one, though Yara didn't recognize it from anywhere in her lessons of Old Tammuri.

Yara watched as the Lily was handed a metal pot filled with a dark liquid.

With a rag, she dabbed Yara's wounds. She screamed in pain as a burning sensation overtook her arm. The liquid had a fruity smell. "What is that?" she said.

"Wine," the Lily said. "The strongest we could make. It's not for drinking."

Wine. Yara had never seen it close-up. To the cleric it was devil's water; to drink any was worthy of flogging, to sell it worthy of death.

"Hush," the Lily said again. "The mouths of the ghouls are the most rancid of any creature on earth. I know it hurts, but this will cleanse you. This will allow you to recover.

The pool was in a courtyard of the temple, surrounded by pillars which looked like newer, un-eroded versions of the Pillars of the Moon. Their capitals were elaborately carved in the shapes of leaves and berries; the marble fluting was chiseled by expert hands. This whole complex seemed recently built. It lay here in the midst of the desert: like Tadmor, an island of comfort among the treacherous elements. Outside there were sandstorms, jackals and hyenas; here there was comfort: a pool to bathe in, and fish to eat.

"What is this place?" Yara said, still bracing from the pain. She couldn't help her curiosity. She had never seen such a temple. She'd heard of them in history books; how the ancients would sacrifice humans, how they'd engage in ritual prostitution. Yet here she was, in the middle of the desert, finding sanctuary in one of them.

"This is a restoration of the old religion," the Lily answered, "a monument to the Goddess of the Moon. A place of healing and isolation within this troubled world of ours... A place where her hand reaches down from heaven, healing the sick and the wounded..."

Words such as those would arouse a mob in Tadmor; before nightfall the crowd would descend on the family—drag them out from their home before the clerics. The Thul would sentence them to death in public, in the most excruciating manner they could manage. Here, in isolation, these pagans didn't have to fear their blasphemy. They didn't have to worry about justice.

Hearing her speak irked Yara, despite the pain. She remembered the stories she had been told. Child sacrifice. Degradation. Disease. And now it had risen again, from the ashes of destruction: paganism, a pagan temple, a pagan sisterhood.

"You worship this pagan goddess," Yara said, "and yet have you witnessed any of her healing or miracles? Or is she just an image? A fraud?"

The Lily regarded her with a glare. One of her attendants began to wrap her arm in cloth, and with each tightening Yara was taken with a spasm of pain.

She didn't cry out. She gritted her teeth. She wanted to seem tough before these pagans.

Where, she wondered, had this newfound piety come from?

"I was once like you," the Lily answered. "I believed in nothing. But now I see her everywhere."

Did Yara truly believe in nothing? In a way it was true. But though the clerics called her an evildoer, no one called her a pagan. No one even suspected her of it.

The Lily's servant at last finished tying the bandages.

"I don't want to be here," Yara found herself muttering. "I want to go back to Tadmor. Back to Mother. To Father."

"You were running from something," the Lily said. "Whatever you ran from in Tadmor, little Yara, it has surely grown worse. What you were you running from?"

She didn't have to tell the Lily anything. But the question percolated in her mind, as the pain began to grow less intense. She had joined the caravan, she had fled the caravan, because of that night in the marketplace. If she had chosen to stay at home, the truth would have spilled from her mouth. Her parents would have found out. Soon all Mahara would know.

She didn't want to go back to that night. She didn't want to think about it. She resented the Lily for causing her to dwell on it.

But it was true she didn't want to be here. She wanted to return. She wanted to go back to Tadmor, to the protection of Mother and Father. She was too young for this. She was too young to be out here alone, in the midst of this temple, injured by a creature of the night.

"What was that thing?" Yara said. She could scarcely make out its features in the darkness. "That creature that bit me?"

"A Son of Darkness," the Lily said. "That's all you need to know for now. Sister Zara will be taking you to your sleeping cultures."

On the mattress, there were handles and an iron frame

supporting it. The shadows of more Sisters appeared.

Chapter Fourteen: The War Begins

The battle lines had been drawn. The die had been cast.

Javan, Wazir of Tadmor, had done what neither he nor his ancestors dared to do until now: to declare war on the clerics, to announce his opposition to Mazda's religion, to risk the wrath of the mob.

Three days later, he watched from the palace balcony as fighting continued in the streets. The kabakhs had been seized, the clerics expelled from the city; but vigilante stabbings continued and open war waged on in the city's outskirts.

The conflict had been as bloody and internecine as he'd feared.

All around the city square, buildings had been burned to ash and bodies interred in mass graves.

"What have I done?" he said.

He felt a hand touch his shoulder.

His wife Marit had secluded herself for weeks. This was the first time she'd ventured out of the comfort of her grief. Perhaps the tragedy overtaking the city had caused her to see past the much greater tragedy of Yara.

"A king is supposed to love his people," Javan continued, talking mostly to himself.

"You are a wazir, not a king," said Marit, "and this was an act of love."

As he surveyed the smoldering remnants of what had been confectioneries, blacksmiths, tinkerers' shops and homes, he doubted his sweet wife's words. Thousands had been killed.

And yet, thus far, he did not doubt the righteousness of his decision. Mahara had lived in fear of the clerics and their mobs for centuries, ever since the worship of Mazda took root here. What he doubted was its wisdom. Support for the clerics was even stronger in the country. No one would doubt, anymore, the title of "The

Blasphemer Wazir."

The zealous shepherds would take up arms; the date farmers would beat their hooks into swords. But once Javan assumed full control, the power of the clerics would be broken. The people would no longer live in terror. A great weight would be lifted off the shoulders of all Tammuri. This could only be achieved by blood.

~

The halls of the palace seemed empty without the cavalcade of warriors and emirs. The bright marble floors and the sunshine emanating from the windows soothed Javan's soul. He sat down with Marit on one of the couches. He laid his hand in hers. In an instant tears began to form.

"I thought I had cried all I could today," she muttered.

Yara. Javan didn't want to utter the word. If he spoke it aloud, he'd break down too. He would be distracted by his grief when his people needed him the most. "Hush," he said. "It's okay."

"She is dead… I know it. She wouldn't leave for this long." Marit's hand was trembling. "She wouldn't leave us worrying. She wouldn't leave us like this. She is dead… may Mazda have mercy on her."

In grief, Javan's wife had found comfort in the darkness: in Mazda, whose clerics took a scourge to anyone who questioned them; in Mazda, whose clerics set up laws alongside the wazir's, who demanded fealty and power and the wealth of the people.

"She is not dead," Javan said. "You don't know that yet." As soon as he spoke, he was weeping. Where, indeed, had she gone? He would not lose hope. She had run away. There was no reason to think she'd been killed.

And yet, in those few times when she'd run away, she always returned before the sun set. What did it say now, that she'd disappeared one night and never returned? His heart sank and he folded. He began weeping alongside Marit, just as potently. He didn't want any harm to come to her. But if she had gone, and hadn't returned in all this time, how could she possibly be alive? How could she explain it? How could this long absence have any reason to it, without her death?

~

In the late afternoon, his emir returned to the throne room.

"Victory," Rashad said. "The clerics have retreated to the countryside. The stabbings continue, but they are manageable. Mahara is free."

Javan wondered if Rashad disagreed with the mission. How many emirs paid heed to Mazda? How many who, according to their martial code, obeyed the command of the emir, but regretted attacking the mob? It didn't matter. Mahara was a free city now. The power of the clerics was broken.

"And the Thul is gone?" Javan said.

"He has fled the city," Rashad answered. "We believe he has taken refuge in Adwar."

Adwar was a strange place to take refuge, with no wall or fortress protecting it. But Javan would not interrupt his enemy in their error.

For the first time since he'd wept with Marit, he returned to the palace balcony to survey Mahara.

The sounds of war had ceased. The fires had largely been put out. And in Mahara's city square, a group had brought torches, and begun dancing.

Chapter Fifteen: A New World

In the village of Adwar, Ahram had washed his face, cut his hair, scrubbed his body with soap and eaten the largest feast he'd had in years.

A villager had taken him in out of the kindness of her heart. Her name was Rubia.

He had left her, now, and stood in the center of the square as the sun set.

He was in Tadmor. But he still did not feel safe.

The memory of Zathustra's death was still heavy. The King of the Dark was greater than anyone in Tadmor. No one here was safe, not Ahram, not Rubia, not even the wazir himself.

A little before sunset, the sound of galloping horses echoed through Adwar's city square.

About a dozen riders on black horses were headed Ahram's way. In the center, surrounded by them, was a man in a black hood.

Behind them was a ragtag collection of warriors, some holding knives, others daggers and swords.

A horn blew, one Ahram recognized as a call for religious rituals.

These were clerics of Mazda, and following behind them were common believers, with swords and knives and daggers. There were angry looks on their faces. They wanted blood.

A chant began rising through the ranks: "Death to the Blasphemer Wazir! Death to Javan! Death to Marit! Death to his family!"

What outrage had the wazir committed, Ahram wondered, that warranted these militants storming Adwar? Had he partaken of Devil's water? Had he bedded a woman not his wife?

As the column continued, pouring into Adwan, he realized the mob was not composed of just hundreds but instead thousands. They were women and men, even zealous children—all holding whatever implement of violence was available to them. This was an army of the faithful, angry and enraged to the core.

What had happened, Ahram wondered again. No minor transgression could cause such deep outrage.

They assembled in the village square, and Ahram ducked back in the shadows as he watched one of the village elders approach. "Greetings," the elder said. There was fear in his voice.

Neither the mob nor the riders responded. Their burning anger remained.

The rider in the center, wearing the hooded cloak, spoke, and his voice carried throughout the entire village: "The Blasphemer Wazir has declared war on the clerics and the faithful. He has driven the pious from Mahara. It is here we will seek refuge."

"We welcome the faithful," the elder replied, but his voice reflected his fear. Neither he, nor the majority of Adwari, wanted them here.

Ahram slinked away. He knew how dangerous the clerics and their pious mobs were, how much violence they caused, how much vengeance and hate they could harbor. This would not end well for the Village of Adwar. Such things never did.

Adwar, laying on the very edge of the desert, would suffer interminably because of this. Ahram planned to stay out of it, as far as possible.

He remembered the command of Zathustra: that he appear before the Wazir of Tadmor, and tell him to flee for the coast.

~

Riding a mule which Rubia had given him out of the kindness of her heart, Ahram trotted as quickly as he could away from Adwar. Though he was in Tadmor, amid the lush greenery, the sound of the desert storms began with nightfall.

The King is near.

Dawn was breaking when Mahara appeared.

The grass in Tadmor was green, and irrigation canals were dug everywhere, allowing the earth to burst forth with wheat fields, pomegranate orchards, watermelon patches and date farms.

Located in the middle of the desert, Tadmor was more bountiful than Bezakirah or any city on the coast. Its soil was rich and dark, perfect for life.

Birds were singing, and the horrors of the prior night became a distant memory to Ahram. The air was sweet with the smell of flowers. In the sunlight, farmers were working in their fields. A rooster was crowing. This beautiful earth was the source of Tadmor's wealth. It was the source of Tadmor's splendor. Without this rich soil, the famous monuments of Mahara could never have been built.

In such brilliant sunlight, in such fresh and sweet-smelling air, it was easy to forget the danger that Tadmor was in.

As he passed through Mahara's gate, he recalled Zathustra's promise of ten pounds of gold.

Surely, if it had any ring of truth to it, that money was waiting in Mahara's city treasury.

Evacuating Tadmor could wait. He had earned that gold, even with Zathustra's death. He had stayed along, guarding him in the midst of the desert. That gold was his.

But how could he prove it?

~

In ancient times, gold was kept safe in temples, the only places that no one dared attack. With the coming of Mazda and his faith, the practice died down. Now all money was stored in the Royal Treasury of Tadmor, from which loans and other transactions were procured. Everything was processed through the City Mint. Ahram had spent his adult life robbing graves; those who tried robbing the Royal Treasury never lived to tell the tale.

And yet when he walked the streets—vaguely familiar to him, still—he realized doing anything now would be a daunting proposition. There were signs of destruction everywhere: homes burned to a smoldering ruin; even traces of blood remained in the road, though the bodies had been moved and buried. "The Blasphemer Wazir" as he was called had indeed waged war on the clerics, driving them from their places of worship. To some, roused by piety, this was a sacrilege of incomparable magnitude; but to the majority, Ahram suspected, it was a relief, though they dared not admit it. How long had they endured the Law of Mazda, living side-by-side with the law of the world? How many had been flogged and beaten? How many had been rounded up and forced to recant their improper beliefs? The Law of Mazda was instilled in all, at the end of a scourge.

How many would rejoice to be free of that weight? But Ahram knew as well as anyone that the danger remained. The Faith of Mazda permeated the land. The Maharans would be considered idolaters. Violence was the inevitable result. Ahram prayed it would end well for the wazir, but he couldn't be certain. How could an army and the rule of law stand against an onslaught of such hate?

In the center of square, rebuilding had already begun; masons and stoneworkers were laying the foundations for new buildings and houses, made from Tadmor's famous white limestone.

The palace loomed above, its onion domes gleaming in gold, its white turrets and towers as unblemished as the mountain snow. The Royal Palace was a symbol of Tadmor's wealth and might, and a sign of its past. Such beauty and ostentation would never have been tolerated by the clerics; its founding had been centuries before the Law of Mazda ever arrived.

At the gate of the Royal Palace, the Royal Treasury was a fortress unto itself, guarded by a thick double door of heavy oak. Soldiers stood guard there, wearing headwraps over their faces and leather jerkins on their chests. They bore wicker shields and scimitars. Long before Ahram asked, he thought he knew the answer: "I have gold stored here. May I come in?"

"No one is allowed into the Treasury until the wazir says otherwise," one answered. "And there is a curfew in place after dark. If you are a visitor, find lodgings…"

~

On the edge of town, a caravan post remained open and undamaged by the destruction.

Built of stone, its gate was thick and built of heavy oak. It was as well fortified as any caravan post in the desert.

Within, the scent of pipe smoke overpowered Ahram and he began to choke.

The smokers reclined throughout the main hall, their eyes red from indulging in their pastime.

The post master approached Ahram. "Two pieces of copper, or anything equivalent, for a night's stay."

"I have nothing," Ahram answered.

The post master nodded and smiled sadly. "You may stay. The streets are dangerous. Soldiers are being stabbed. Common people, too. Anyone the Black Hand suspects of supporting the wazir."

"The Black Hand," Ahram muttered. It was clear as day what the group was: zealots, or at least people devoted to the clerics, who were taking the law into their own hands. If the Wazir of Tadmor wouldn't institute the Law of Mazda alongside his own, then they would. The bloodshed would continue. For how long, how could anybody know? The Black Hand was here to stay.

He left the choking smoke of the main hall into the sleeping quarters, where all the residents had been bunched into bunks and simple mattresses. Ahram was shown a mattress on the floor, stained with pipe smoke, with feathers emerging from slits in the fabric. It was the best the postmaster would do.

He partook of bread and water, and spent the night in the

caravan post.

Chapter Sixteen: The Night Brood

For days, Yara remained in the infirmary, fed whatever her body could handle at the time, as the wounds from the ghoul bite began to heal. Saboo—the so-called Lily of the Valley—brought her bowl after bowl of boiled vegetables and anything she could tolerate in her ill, fevered state. Eventually the illness broke; the chill receded and she began to feel herself. The open wounds, once red, raw and oozing, began to seal. By the time ten days had gone by, she had recovered, and for the first time stood up and decided to walk around, to take stock of the Temple of the Moon.

She soon realized the tiger wandering near the pool wasn't alone. Not long after she left the infirmary, she ran into a white tiger with black stripes and pink eyes. The tiger's name, she learned, was Snow; and she was a girl. She allowed Yara to scratch her behind her ears. She purred like a house cat.

"She likes you," said Sister Zara, walking by.

Here, among pagans, Yara had found sanctuary, a respite against the spreading darkness. How strange she would find such comfort and acceptance among the enemies of Mazda and his worship. Yet she had never felt so accepted anywhere else, besides home.

She passed through the door and entered the courtyard, where the waters of the pool were surrounded by dozens of columns. She dipped her toes into the cool waters. For the first time in weeks, she breathed easy.

She began to cry. The pent up travails of the long caravan journey, the emotions she had managed to hide just beneath the surface, the betrayal, the knowledge she'd been taken as a sacrifice, all hit her at once. She didn't want to appear weak among these bandits, but she couldn't help herself. She tried to sob quietly, but she sobbed nonetheless.

She felt the soft impression of teeth on her hand.

Ruby had taken a hold of it. Her bright emerald eyes indicated she wanted to play. Yara jerked free from her fangs. Her tears stopped. She grew calm. She would endure. She was safe, now, in this valley of women. There was no male in sight. Even the tigers were her sisters.

~

Stretching from the temple's roof was a towering observatory. At dusk, the Lily took Yara by the hand and insisted she come and see it for herself.

Yara, still shaken by these months' events, was hesitant. But she went along with it just the same. There was no point in angering the Lily.

The tower was built from the same gleaming white marble as the temple, with slabs fit so neatly together it looked like carved alabaster.

Up a winding set of stairs they walked, carrying torches, for what seemed like an hour; then they stepped out into the observatory, into the bright sunlight.

From here they could survey the desert.

Far in the distance, Yara could make out the Pillars of the Moon. In the opposite direction, toward the north, the rocky barren earth stretched into the horizon. Beyond the undulating hills, somewhere, was the altar she would have been sacrificed upon, all to appease an angry god.

"Where were they taking me?" she said, mostly to herself. "Why were they taking me there?"

Saboo walked up to her and laid a hand around her shoulder.

She jerked her away from the northern horizon, toward the west.

Far away, beyond canyons and dunes, there was a black river she'd never seen before. Had it burst forth from some mountainside? Had the underworld burst open one of its springs? "What is that river?" Yara asked. "What is its name?"

"It is not a river, Precious Yara."

Precious Yara. Only her parents called her that. How did she know?

"Take a deeper look," the Lily continued. "Do you see the blackness moving and jilting? That is an army, Yara, headed toward Tadmor."

In a flash, the stew of negative emotions returned, the terror, the fear, the anger. "Mother and Father are still there," Yara cried.

"Tadmor is doomed." The Lily turned to Yara. Her black eyes were gleaming. "Be glad you are in the Goddess's sanctuary, safe from harm."

"I will return home," Yara said. "I'm going to tell Mother and Father to flee…"

"Stay here," the Lily answered, "and I will show you the way of a warrior. I will teach you the way of the saber. I will let you take vengeance on that army, and on the darkness and its king."

~

The next day, at dawn, Yara was led outside the temple into the cool of the morning.

The Lily was carrying something, hidden under cloth wrappings. The birds were singing as she unwrapped a saber, laying it bare before the sun. The metal blade gleamed like silver. Jewels were inset along the blade: rubies, sapphires and emeralds. The steel was forged in intricate patterns, and the hilt was trimmed with gold.

Yara ran her hand along the cold metal. This object was priceless.

She took it by the hilt and lunged, sweeping sideways in a broad slash.

This sword meant freedom. It meant independence. It meant she could defend herself against the Rafizes and Hirazes of the world. She did not have to rely on the protection of her betters.

But could Yara, daughter of the wazir, take up with pagans and ne'er-do-wells? What would Mother and Father think?

For now, she couldn't afford to think of them. They would remain happy memories until she returned, triumphantly, to save them.

The Lily beckoned her closer. "Follow me," she whispered, and Yara obeyed.

~

For hours, they hiked through the desert, until Yara was drenched in sweat and every inch of her was wet. She stopped in the shade of a tamarisk tree. She was panting and out of breath. Her waterskin was still not empty. She took a deep gulp and then sprinkled the remainder over her hair and face.

"We are getting close," the Lily said to her.

"Close to where?" Yara answered. "You won't tell me anything." The desert heat was deadly for anybody, but even more for two people so ill-prepared.

The sun was blazing on the dry earth. Only green scrub brush broke up the monotony of brown earth and rocks. Yara could tell they were ascending; the air had grown crisper, and a cool wind was blowing.

~

Late in the afternoon, they reached the foot of a mountain. Near the summit was a dry creek bed overgrown with weeds and grasses.

The mountain was tall, taller than the observatory or even the tower of Magdala back home.

Yara didn't want to do this. But she followed the Lily's lead, up the mountain and its winding, treacherous path.

The sun had set, and the night emerged, when they at last reached the peak.

Nearby was a grotto. Its waters were bubbling.

All along the rock walls, alcoves had been carved, and within those alcoves were silver figurines, forged in the shape of a woman.

Near the babbling alcove was an altar, with a blackened burn-mark and charred bones and ash nearby.

This is what the ancients did, before Mazda and his law arrived. These bandits, these sisters in the desert, had single-handedly revived all the practices the modern Tammuri despised.

What would the clerics think now? What would Mother and Father think?

If the mob heard, they would destroy the city in their demands for Yara's blood; but Father wouldn't give it to them.

She walked up to one of the alcoves, etched into the rock wall, and grabbed a figurine.

Carved of white silver, it resembled a woman with a bushy head of hair, carrying a jar in one hand and a sheaf of wheat in the other. Such exquisite silverworking was unknown in Tadmor. She set it down, back in its place.

"How long has this been here?" Yara asked.

"The figurine?" the Lily answered.

"No. The shrine."

"Come with me," the Lily said, and again, Yara followed.

Another short climb later, they reached the absolute peak of the mountain, and Yara could see for miles around. Somewhere to the south lay the Temple of the Moon. Somewhere, far to the east, was the trading post of Kish and the impossibly distant kingdom of Cathay. She inclined her head to the west, and see the last ghostly trail of the army, continuing west. It was emerging from the north and heading toward the dunes and, eventually, the blessed land of Tadmor.

The Lily walked up behind her. Yara could not see her, but

she could sense her.

"Don't look at what troubles you." She pulled Yara to face her. She was so beautiful. "This is the sanctuary of the Goddess. For five years it has stood here, ever since the Sisters built it."

Yara tried to jerk back away, to look at the army marching through the desert, to see the terror that threatened her home.

"In time, you will learn the Goddess's wisdom. You will be filled with her peace. Now come… fill your waterskins. We camp here tonight, on the roof of the world."

~

That evening, Yara practiced with her saber, lunging full on at the Lily, who was so confident in her own skills she didn't require wooden swords and weapons.

Five times they had a mock battle, each ending with the Lily's saber at Yara's throat. They fought until Yara was out of breath and utterly spent. But she felt she had learned something. The next time she faced a ghoul or a creature of the night, she wouldn't be quite as helpless as before.

The Lily had brought, among other things, bread and dried meat, and a cask of pomegranate juice.

Against the silence, she detected a noise: a distant chant, so far away it was scarcely audible.

She got up and turned again toward the mountain view. She could scarcely see anything, but those chants were louder than she was liable to hear. They had come close.

"They are near," Yara said.

"Go to sleep." The Lily didn't believe her.

Yara's stomach was full; she had immersed herself in the grotto. She was refreshed and ready to sleep, but the thought had awakened her entirely. If they were nearby, Yara and the Lily were in terrible danger.

But she acquiesced.

~

The following morning, a bad feeling followed her all the way across the desert. She didn't know why, but for some reason, she didn't want to return to the Moon Temple at all.

Late in the day, when the Moon Temple appeared with its alabaster-white pillars and slanted roof, Yara breathed a sigh of relief to see her sanctuary. For the first time all day, she was glad to have left camp on the mountain. She would bathe in the pool and eat fresh fish for dinner. All was well.

When she entered the sanctuary, passing through the doors, she heard loud screaming and shouting and the whimpering of a tiger.

Together, Yara and the Lily sprinted to the pool. There, Ruby lay mortally wounded, bleeding profusely from a gash.

One of the lesser Sisters was screeching: and Amala is dead!

The panic overtaking the Lily indicated Amala's importance.

Indeed, she was the deputy to the Lily of the Valley, the second in command entrusted with all sorts of privileges and responsibilities.

Yara followed the Lily as she ran through a series of doors and hallways until at last she reached Amala's sleeping chambers. Sisters dressed in blue were huddled around her. Their sabers were sheathed and clipped to their belts as they doted on her.

When Yara finally managed to take a look at Amala, she saw a corpse, pallid and bloodless, stiff as a statue. There were no signs of any wound, no blood or cuts at all. She was whiter than marble. All her blood was gone.

"Out of the way!" the Lily shouted, with more than a little emotion in her voice. It was uncharacteristic of her.

The Sisters cleared away from Amala and the Lily was given a wide berth as she began to examine her dead friend.

It was clear the Lily was on the verge of tears, in a state Yara had never seen her in before.

To Yara, Amala was someone she barely knew, someone whom she had little knowledge of. She watched, with little emotion, as the Lily undressed her. In time, Amala was completely naked. With her skin bare, the Lily searched every inch of her for the wound.

At last, she called her Sisters over, pointing at a tiny bump the size of a pin prick.

"This was the work of a stridge," the Lily said. Her eyes were watering.

Yara had heard of stridges, blood sucking birds who dwelled in the deep desert. The drained the blood of camels and horses. She'd never heard of them touching humans.

"Stridges don't—" a Sister began.

The Lily hushed her. She walked up to the window, with its pane of hammered goat-horn. Part of it had been cut away, as if by a knife. The stridge clearly had a handler.

"This is an assassination," the Lily said. "Someone intended to kill Amala. Me, no doubt. This was the work of the Night Queen and her brood…"

The Sisters seemed to know who the Night Queen was. Everyone did, everyone except Yara.

Their faces had turned ashen. For the first time, Yara sensed fear spreading in the room, a gut-level fear in every sister's heart.

"A brood must have taken root nearby," the Lily said. "It must be expunged or we will see more death by morning. Torches, everyone. Torches and sabers. We will root out this problem just as before."

~

Ruby's wounds had been patched up. She was whimpering in

the corner, licking her paws. The stridge was no match for a tiger's wits and speed. She had pounced and overcome the enemy. The sight of her gave Yara strength as she stood there with her un-lit torch. Yara's stomach was twisted to knots at what was to come. The fear of even the brave Sisters made it clear the danger Yara was going in.

The Lily brushed up behind her. "You are not ready, Yara. Put away the torch. The Lamia would destroy you…"

"I want to come," Yara said. "I want to fight with you… with my Sisters."

"You are not a Sister. Not yet." The Lily smiled. "This fight is not your fight."

The Sisters were gathering with sabers in their hands. Sister Zara had Snow on a leash. The tigers were obedient like dogs.

"Goodbye, Yara," the Lily said. "You will be safe in this sanctuary."

After the Sisters left, and the door was secured, Yara dipped her toes nervously in the water. The stars were visible in the courtyard. She had never felt so utterly alone.

She wandered up to Ruby and took a seat beside her, scratching her fur. Poor Ruby was still whining, feeling sorry for herself. Yara knew she had a nasty temper. She carefully avoided her wound, scratching near her neck and cheek.

Thoughts began racing through her head. What would happen if the Sisters were slaughtered, if the Lamia or whatever they were called won the day? What if they were unable to purge the brood and save the Moon Temple?

Yara had her saber, now in its sheath, clipped to her belt. She drew it and looked on admiringly as the moonlight gleamed off the blade. She stood up.

Ruby had begun to growl.

The tiger was too weak to stand up, but her ears had perked

up, and her eyes were focused intently on the other side of the pool.

Yara focused on the shadows beyond the pillars, in the open door. The sound of slapping skin echoed through the pool. A shadowy figure was crawling toward Yara. It was Amala, awoken with new life.

But this was not Amala. Her eyes had turned pink, like a rabid animal's. Foam was trickling from her lips. Despite her obvious discomfort, she began to cackle. She had become possessed, a ward of the one who slew her. But she was weak and pitiful. One arm wouldn't move, and her legs were useless.

Yara approached her cautiously. As trail of foam had followed her from her bedchamber.

"Who are you?" Yara snapped.

"Amala," she mumbled. Her red eyes met Yara's for the first time. They were not the eyes of a human but of an animal, of a creature of the night.

"You are not Amala," Yara replied.

She walked up behind the creature which had possessed Amala; in vain she tried to scratch at Yara.

Yara fell upon her, striking her head with the pommel of her saber.

"Who are you?" Yara snapped again.

Still she mumbled "Amala" but she sounded dizzy, dazed. She was losing life.

"Who are you?"

This time there was no answer. Yara beat her again with the pommel of her saber. Then, raising it up, she swung down and beheaded the possessed Amala in one slice.

Whatever spirit indwelled in her left. Now she was lifeless.

~

Yara, sleeping next to Ruby, was awoken in the middle of the night to the sound of screams and running feet.

The Sisters had arrived, their torches having burnt away. They were wet and panting.

The Lily of the Valley looked shaken.

It was clear whatever mission they had embarked upon had failed.

"Where is Snow?" Yara said. Instantly, she knew the answer. A grief settled into her heart, deeper than what she'd felt with Amala's passing.

She had to get out of the Moon Temple. She had to escape this trap.

"The brood has been exterminated," the Lily said. "The brood mother has escaped on foot toward Kish. In time she will return, when she lays her hatch. For now the Moon Temple is secure against the desert. We are holding firm. No one should worry. You are all secure."

But she sounded uncertain.

The Lily gasped, turning to the beheaded corpse of Amala. "Yara… what have you done? Defiling a body is a grave sin…"

Yara turned, seeing the body and its head, both bereft of blood, separated from each other. Despite the lack of gore, it remained a grisly side. "She had come alive," Yara explained, "as if possessed."

The Lily nodded as if she understood. "The body must be burned. The dead who return to life will never die again."

~

Outside the temple grounds, in the midst of the cold desert night, the Lily and Yara laid tar and bundles of wood upon the body of Amala.

The Lily muttered some incantation, invoking the name of the Goddess: "Isdar." Then she took a flint and tinder and set the corpse alight. As flames engulfed the body, the Lily beckoned Yara to follow her, and walked away.

But Yara idled, watching the flames crackle, watching the

inferno consume the possessed woman and devour her whole.

87

Chapter Seventeen: The Grave Robber

Javan, Wazir of Tadmor, surveyed his city in the morning light.

Against his instincts, he allowed the kabakhs of the clerics to remain, though they'd become a focal point for devout worshippers and for a possible insurrection. Javan was not pious, but destroying kabakhs would be a sacrilege beyond even him.

The streets were quiet. Martial law had been imposed, and a soldier stood on every street corner.

The stabbings continued. Vigilantes, full of piety and zeal, were knifing soldiers in the back in "defense of Mazda and his holy law." These vigilantes called themselves the "Black Hand," the long arm of the Thul in the "pagan city of Mahara."

And yet paganism had not been established, nor would it be. No longer would the Law of Mazda exist side by side with the Law of Man.

"Your Worship!" A court page had come up behind him. "There is a man who wants to speak to you. He is very insistent. He has been begging for three days…"

Javan turned to face the page. "I will not reward beggars," he said. "Is he a subject of the Crown?"

"He is not a Tammuri," the court page said. "He is a grave robber."

Javan laughed. "A grave robber. An outlander. I will not speak to this man. If he confessed to grave robbing, he should be hanged anyway…"

"He says he has information on the clerics," the page continued.

For information on the clerics, Javan would listen to a grave robber and an outlander. He was not a Tammuri; he was not a son of the Land of Date Honey. But he would be useful.

In the throne room, the hairy, bearded savage of a man fell prostrate. He had a distinct odor and clearly had not availed himself of the city baths. Yet he was muscular, and clearly a warrior. He would be deadly in combat.

"Rise," said Javan, and the man—"Ahram"—rose to a kneeling position.

"What information do you have to share?" Javan examined the grave robber, an outlander, a savage desert wanderer. It is said the Tammuri were tall as the royal palms of Mahara and had tongues as smooth as date honey. But this man, a giant among giants, was not noticeably foreign. His white clothes would fit in among any weekday market. He had a rugged handsomeness to him. And it was apparent he was straining to show the proper respect, unsure of the motions to go through. Clearly he had something urgent to say.

"The clerics and the Mob have holed up in Adwar…"

This "Ahram," whoever he was, wasn't stupid enough to think Javan didn't already know. He had come for something else.

"And you must evacuate Tadmor. You must flee." Javan had let a madman into his palace. "The King of the Dark is coming… the ghouls are nearby. The Lamia!"

"Throw him out!" Javan shouted.

He kept screaming, shouting about ghouls and the "King of the Dark," as a pair of soldiers dragged him out of the throne room and through the door of the palace. It was a wonder they could restrain him.

Chapter Eighteen: Beaten

The warriors threw Ahram out into the street and tossed his sheathed saber out with him. The palace gate slammed shut.

Ahram had done all he could. He had demanded the wazir do what was best for his people. Now it was time for Ahram to fend for himself, to look out for his own interests. He would flee for the coasts. He would take a ship and travel into the heart of the continent. He would save his own life and purge all memory of the King of the Dark and his ghouls. He would foreswear grave robbing and become a pious man.

That afternoon he set out on a camel he'd stolen, traveling away from Mahara. He reached the southern village of Ophar before the sun set. Caravaners were heading north with disappointed looks on their faces.

A battalion of warriors stood there, swarming the village as they guarded the desert passage.

"Stop!" their captain shouted to Ahram. "The wazir has decreed no one may leave Tadmor until the storms pass. The road is closed."

Ahram urged his camel on, trying to evade the warriors as he desperately tried to flee. He was knocked over the saddle and tackled as binds were slapped on him.

"Thirty lashes for disobedience!" the captain shouted. "Take him back to Mahara."

Chapter Nineteen: Holy Men

Each morning, the Lily took Yara out of the temple quarters into the growing desert heat. They dueled with wooden swords, and as Yara grew better her body became pocked with bruises. She had learned to lunge, how to parry, how to press the offensive and how to withdraw. Her arms became stronger, and her muscle began to grow. The Lily promised that, if she continued her efforts, one day she would become a Sister.

The Lily never failed to take an opportunity to correct her, and she always did so with an edge to her voice.

One morning, Yara asked, "What are the Lamia? What is the brood?"

The Lily, still wielding her wooden saber, stepped back and relaxed her hands. Her face was covered in sweat. It seemed the mornings were getting hotter until it was too much even for a Sister of the Moon to bear.

"Lamia," the Lily said. "The Sisters of the Night. They wander the wastes, singing, laughing. Not long ago, there were hardly any; but now they seem to lurk in every forest and stagnant pool…"

"Saboo," Yara said, using her true name for the first time in a while, "I want to go home."

"The world is darkening. The end is near. The desert isn't safe for you, Yara, nor any of us. The Temple keeps the power of the night at bay. It will seize you if you let it."

Yara knew the truth behind Lily's words. She had made a terrible mistake crossing the desert, running from her problems, fleeing from her own despair and her own self. Now what would happen to Mother and Father, back home, as the desert encroached?

She would return home, one day, and hopefully soon. No one could keep her here forever, not even the Lily of the Valley.

~

That night, beset by dreams of home, she awoke to the silent temple.

She could not bear this anymore. No matter the danger, she had to go home. She had to go back to the place where she truly belonged, to her father the wazir, to her mother the wazira. As silently as possible, she began stuffing her things into her pack.

She crept through the door, down several hallways, into the pool with its white pillars. Ruby perked up.

But she left it behind, opening the double doors, wandering out into the night.

~

The Pillars of the Moon were only a short walk when you knew the way. And by now, Yara had become familiar with every bit of the terrain.

She rested against the pillars in the midst of the cold night.

She was ill prepared. The Land of Tadmor lay directly west of the Pillars. She could navigate by starlight.

She laughed at the thought, slumping on one the base of one of the pillars

She had no chance of lasting through the desert days, in their blazing heat. She did not know where to stop for water. She did not know the locations of the watering holes which Rafiz and his caravaners stopped along the way.

It was a dream, a flight of fancy. But it was nice to sneak out of the temple against the Lily's best wishes. It was like the good old days on the streets of Mahara, at midnight, before she met Hiraz. She had always been inclined to sneak out, to rebel, to disobey.

How good it was to be alone, in the moonlight, with her saber to keep her company. In the moonlight a white robe glittered; she could see the outline of a tunic or a shift, and a shadowy face to go along with it. Her first instinct was not fear, but curiosity.

Down a valley, the person or creature lay; perfect for the ambush. She would, at the minimum, identify her prey.

~

She caught him unawares, hiding in the scrub brush.

It was not a ghoul or a Lamia, or any creature of the night, but a man in a white robe, with a white beard. He had a great staff in his hands.

The man let out a shout, so loud that the ground underneath Yara's feet crumbled and some pebbles scattered. She tried to cover her ears.

The man was ranting like a madman. "The King of the Dark! The King of the Dark!"

He keeled over.

"What is your name? What is your name, old man?"

Yara saw that a madman had traveled here, to the Pillars of the Moon, but how had he done so with so little of an addled mind remaining?

The man flicked his hands, and fiery lightning jolted forth with a crackle, illuminating the night.

"Who am I? Who am I?

"Zathustra… yes, that was my name."

"Zathustra" looked up at Yara.

"Hello, little girl. Do not be afraid," he mumbled. He had a wild, unshorn look. But there was a glow to his face. He seemed healthy, lively even.

"I left my *quara* here, in the Pillars of the Moon. I was not expecting such savagery. What is your name, little girl? Tell me! I have no intent of hurting you!"

Not only was he a madman, he was a sorcerer, and would be marked for death in Tadmor.

All sorcerers are rebels to Mazda's name, the street preachers said.

They should be burned at the stake according to the Holy Law.

The man's white beard stood out against his dark complexion, his skin some shade of ebony. His clothing was white and unblemished, like he'd just purchased it from a tailor. There was not a single smudge of dirt or desert sand. It made no sense. But little made sense about this madman, bumbling about the Pillars of the Moon.

He was good for one thing: Yara's amusement.

"Tell me, Zathustra, where is your *quara*?" she said with a grin.

"My *quara*, my *quara*," Zathustra said. "I apparated here, so it must be nearby. Oh, gods, have you seen it, little girl? It's about this big." He twisted his fingers into the shape of a circle. "It's made of gold, and has a diamond in the center. And my Book of Spells? Where is my Book?"

Out of the corner of her eye, Yara saw it: a black smudge in the dark desert, rectangular in shape and far bigger than any book she'd seen, larger than the Book of Mazda's Law. How could anyone carry that thing, let alone read it? And yet this Zathustra couldn't find it, though it was as plain as day.

She crept around him and down to the valley floor, grabbing the book for herself. It was as heavy as she thought, and half her height. As Zathustra took notice of it, she opened a page.

"No! No! No!" Zathustra cried, but the deed was done.

The page was blank, bereft of any writing or symbols.

"You are a strange man," Yara said, "carrying a blank book through the desert. It looks awfully heavy."

Just ahead, half submerged in the dirt, she noticed a metallic gleam. A gold orb was buried there. Was this the *quara* that the madman babbled about?

"Here!" Yara said and threw the book to him.

He caught it but just barely, and it nearly knocked him over.

Yara grabbed the *quara*, a gold orb indeed, with a diamond in the center. She examined it in the moonlight and saw that runes and symbols had been forged onto it. This object would go for many talents of gold. But Yara wasn't inclined to steal, though she looked the part.

"Look out!" Yara cried, and threw the *quara* at him.

"Oh! Oh!" Zathustra mumbled and staggered backward, nonetheless catching it in his left hand. It was clear he did not exactly know where he was. He did not know who he was, either. He was just getting his bearings.

"The Pillars of the Moon… are outside Tadmor." He was talking himself through it all. "I seem to remember a man accompanying me there, not long ago. What was his name? I have forgotten. Have you seen a man passing through the valley? Tall, strongly formed… a beard of black. I'm not sure what his name is…"

"No one has passed through here for days," said Yara. "No one except you."

"And who are you?" Zathustra said. He began to examine her in the moonlight. "You are such a pretty girl. And yet you are tough. You have seen a lot, haven't you? A lot of turmoil. A lot of disruption."

This conversation was no longer fun. She was no longer teasing him. She soured on Zathustra. "I'm sorry to leave you, old man, but I have to be on my way…"

"You will leave an old man in the dark, by himself, alone without any help? The Sons of Darkness are everywhere."

"Where I am going, someone like you would not be welcome." No man was allowed in the Temple of the Moon. "Besides, you are more than an old man. You are a sorcerer. You could fry us all!"

She turned and walked away, into the darkness of the night.

~

She sneaked back inside the temple doors, shutting it without anyone seeing. Only Ruby knew that Yara had gone.

The next day, she practiced with the Lily as she used to, never overcoming her even in the weakest moments. She developed new bruises. She was hit in new places. But she was growing more confident in herself and in her ability to strike, to parry and to weave. She was becoming a warrior, something totally forbidden in Tadmor to a woman. Soon she would fight with the best of them. She would overcome the foes of Father and Mother, and rescue them one day.

She couldn't hold in the secret any longer. "I saw an old man in the valley. He was a sorcerer. His name was Zathustra."

The Lily stopped her swings and parries. "You're kidding. When did you see him?"

Yara kept silent. Her mouth had gotten her in trouble again.

"You sneaked out of the temple, didn't you?" the Lily said.

Her cheeks turned red.

"You are impossible to discipline, Yara," the Lily continued. "One day your curiosity and obstinance will get you killed, or one of your sisters…."

Yara looked down.

"Where was this man? This sorcerer?"

"He's probably gone… He was lost. I wouldn't let him in. He's a man… erm, in the Temple…"

"The Temple will always be a sanctuary against the darkness and its minions," the Lily said. "We do not let well-intentioned strangers to chance. Let's go search for him, and see if he survived the night."

Amid a growing sense of guilt, Yara wondered if she was responsible for Zathustra's death. She had thought men were banned from the Temple of the Moon. She would do her best to rectify the situation. She hoped to Mazda, and to the Goddess, if she existed, that Zathustra was alive.

~

They found him sitting on a rock amid the burning sun, not far from the Pillars themselves. He would not survive long out there. He was emaciated and pallid, clearly dehydrated. He was staring blankly ahead, muttering in some strange language. He took no notice of them. He seemed resigned to his fate, unbothered by the whipping dust and searing sun. His blank book sat at his feet, and he was twiddling his *quara* with his hands.

"Sir," the Lily said, but he kept mumbling to himself, either unaware or deliberately ignoring them.

"Zathustra!" Yara shouted, and he snapped to attention.

"Ah, you are the lovely girl I saw last night… and who are you?" His gaze grew fearful on the sight of the Lily. "And you are the bandits who guard this way… those which the caravaners were talking about. A den of veritable Lamia! Stay away from me."

"We are not bandits," the Lily said. "We guard the Temple of the Moon. We are the protectors of the Pillars which point the desert way… We only rob those who show ill intention."

"But you are robbers nonetheless," Zathustra said. "And the Temple of the Moon has not stood for more than a millenium."

"You are wrong," the Lily answered. "And I can show you."

"Leave me be." He dropped the *quara* and buried his head in his hands. He was trembling. "Leave me alone in silence, to wither."

Yara grabbed him by the arm and yanked him up to his feet. She was stronger than she thought. "You're coming with me, old man. I'm not going to let you die out here."

He muttered only weak protests.

"Lily, grab his book. He seems to like it. And that *quara* on the ground."

The Lily looked puzzled.

Yara led Zathustra toward the Temple of the Moon. It would be a long journey, but with the best company she'd had in months.

~

In the Temple of the Moon, the Sisters treated Zathustra like a precious child, taking turns washing and combing his beard, removing his white robes and giving him a silken tunic and pants. They fed him fresh-baked bread and fish from the temple kitchen, and gave him squeezed pomegranate juice.

And yet he did not stir from his strange trance. He was still mumbling. He still seemed exhausted.

Yara couldn't wait to find out what a *quara* was and what *apparating* meant. A sorcerer living to his old age was unheard of in Tadmor. He was a rare gem.

The only time he made any kind of effort at communication was when Yara spoke, or was nearby.

As nightfall set in, he declared, "I'm cold!" and blankets were brought to cover him. For a spare minute, he had made sense without Yara's coaxing. Yet he had a full stomach, and he was in good hands. He was safe, spared from the elements and the dangers of nature. He was in the world's best sanctuary and safe haven, the holy Temple of the Moon. He could ask for no better place.

In time everyone went to bed, but late at night, when Yara heard the others snoring, she sneaked out once more and crept back into the pool, where Zathustra sat, still awake, still mumbling. Ruby had crossed the distance between them and laid down beside him, an orange-and-black ball. The pool waters were glinting in the moonlight, and down below, in the deepest part, the dark shapes of the fish swarmed around. The night was silent, and only the cool blowing of the wind and the sound of Zathustra's muttering rose above it.

He had his *quara* in his hand. The book was on his lap. He was fidgeting.

Yara approached him quietly.

Like before, he brightened on the sight of her. With a smile, he said, "Hello… what was your name?"

“Yara.”

“Ah, Yara, have a seat. There is a cushion here for you.”

Ruby perked up, as if she knew they were talking about her. Yara laughed. Nonetheless she took a seat. She curled up next to Ruby. The night was cold, the air icy and biting. Yet the desert lands outside were quiet, and there was no storm for the first time in many nights. Huddled here with Ruby and Zathustra, in the solitude of the night, Yara should have felt safe but she still did not. She was in the company of a powerful sorcerer, who could protect her from the terrors that wandered the desert in the dark. But could she trust him? Did, he, too, hide a secret, like it seemed everyone who passed the Pillars of the Moon or traveled the sands did?

“Where are you from, Zathustra? Did you come from Tadmor?” Yara said.

He did not look like a Tammuri. He was darkly complected, with features she had never seen before, but with a handsome but old and weathered face. If he came from Tadmor, he was a foreigner. And he was not a golden-skinned Cathayan either. Yara had never seen a person like him before.

“Where am I from, I can hardly remember,” Zathustra said. “My memory has failed me since my apparation. But I was headed to Tadmor. I was sent to warn Tadmor of their coming destruction.

“And yes, I remember. I am from Indjar. But where that is, and what it is, I cannot remember… only that I was sent here. I was sent here to warn of the coming doom. To tell everyone who would hear me to flee.”

More than ever, Yara wanted to return home. “If we leave now, will you show me the way? I must get home to Tadmor… to warn my parents.”

“Tadmor is lost by now,” Zathustra said. “Its people are dead, rotting to bones. I cannot remember what the danger was, but I remember the face of a ghoul with a crown on his head, carrying a scepter and wearing a robe. He led legions of ghouls behind him. Like a king of the dark. Yes… the King of the Dark was his name. He was once locked in a prison, but the gods have freed him to scourge the world…"

More pagan beliefs. Yara no longer dismissed them out of hand. "If the gods, as you say, are good, why would they release him from his prison? If the gods are good, why would they let my mother and father die?"

"The King of the Dark was to slay the inhabitants of the desert," Zathustra said. "Ah yes, I remember, in the Land of Indjar overlooking the Tower, I resided among the monks! My leader sent me to spare Tadmor, and Tadmor alone… to condemn the rest of the desert to die, for they were the foes of us—of the holy men."

Few lived in the desert, in oasis towns and tiny villages near rare bodies of water. Why would they be worthy of death?

"You call yourself a holy man," Yara said, "but you would leave the inhabitants of the desert to be killed, and in such a cruel way?"

"Mazda's faith has spread across the world, even to Indjar," said Zathustra, "and my brothers have fallen to their swords and scimitars. I do not pity them now that the Ghoul King has awaken and broken free from his abyss. I have no remorse."

To speak of Mazda that way in Tadmor was unheard of. "The Tammuri adore Mazda," Yara said. "You are mistaken."

"Mazda's faith is a cancer… his law is against all mankind." Zathustra was defiant. "And yes, the Tammuri live under its sway… but the wazir is a good man. And he has accepted an audience with Indjar's emissaries. He plots to overthrow Mazda's men, or at least he did…"

Yara couldn't believe the words he was speaking. In truth, it made sense. Just beneath the surface, the hatred of the clerics burned in Father's heart, and it was apparent to anyone who knew him.

"I am the wazir's daughter," Yara said. "Now will you help me save him?"

"Tadmor is lost," Zathustra said. "Here is your best chance

for safety. Here, in this temple. I did what I could. I tried to aid your father and his kingdom. I must return to Indjar tomorrow."

Chapter Twenty: A New Order

Javan could sense his emirs did not entirely agree with him. As they began their march to Adwar, in the cool of the morning, he knew they, and their warriors, were halfhearted at best. They were loyal to their wazir, but were they not condemned to hellfire for opposing Mazda and his law? How could these soldiers face their deaths with bravery if eternal damnation awaited?

Of course, most soldiers did not take much stock in it. Most Tammuri despised the clerics underneath a façade of fear and reverence. But that did not stop the minority from weakening unit cohesion. A small portion but a very large number of Tammuri were zealous and devout, and would resort to violence to protect Mazda's name—as the efforts of the Black Hand showed. This would not be easy, even after the clerics were defeated and the chief cleric was dethroned. What would follow, in some ways, would be worse; years of insurrection and rebellion, of daggers in the backs of government officials, until at last the chains were broken, and the memory of the clerics was forgotten.

As they left the gates of Mahara, marching in columns, the people had gathered to send them off, throwing flowers in their path and wishing them victory—ironically, "in Mazda's name!" Of course, Javan, riding at the head of his troops on a white horse, had gone to great lengths to push that very fact, that he was the devout upholder of faith and the clerics, Mazda's enemies. It was a stretch, but many citizens of Mahara had taken it to heart. They watched their wazir exit the city, girt in armor, bearing a sword, on his white charger—the symbol of victory—and wished him the best.

~

Down the pathways of Tadmor, through its lakes and wells, its forests of date palms and fields of wheat, the army marched, giving

Javan appreciation for the bountiful and beauteous land he ruled. Most farmers, intent on their task, ignored Javan's men altogether, though some stopped to give him quizzical looks. No doubt, the army's efforts weren't widely known.

Few emirs, however, expected a surprise. The clerics would be ready, or as ready as they possibly could, for what was to come.

~

Hours later, the village of Adwar came into view. A makeshift wall had been built, cordoning off the village entirely. Yet the wall was flimsy, and crafted from wooden piles. It would take little effort to break it, even though the clerics and their Mob swarmed its battlements, bearing whatever tools of war they could afford. They stood there, glaring, holding swords and knives but also pitchforks and shovels. Their greatest weapon was their anger, and their zeal.

As Javan's army filtered out and began to surround them, a horn blew from within Adwar, and one whose sound and timbre he recognized: a religious horn, used for calling the faithful during feasts. They had taken it from the city's kabakhs before their destruction.

At its sound, the defenders on the walls fell to their knees and raised their hands. In unison, they shouted, "Praise Mazda!" and the noise of the multitude echoed through the air, frightening the horses.

Here would be the last stand of the zealous, the final fight to determine whether the Law of Mazda superseded all others. For centuries, that Law had ruled Tadmor, creeping in on the wazir's authority until the point they'd reached now, where Javan had little ability to stop it. Now, for the first time, a wazir had stood up to the clerics. For the first time, a wazir had looked into the eyes of the faithful Mob and not backed down. Javan had an army and all the strength of Tadmor; but could even they prevail against such hate?

The siege began before nightfall. The city fell. The instigators of the rebellion were put to death; but the Thul and his coterie had escaped. Justice remained far off for him.

In the morning, Javan surveyed the bodies and the destruction he had wrought, and wept.

Chapter Twenty-One: The Coast

Trapped. That's what Ahram was, and what even the Tammuri were.

He was trapped in this land of plenty, an island amid the desert, even as the King of the Dark and his armies approached. The people of Mahara, where he'd returned to, were concerned about the civil war underway and the "Blasphemer King." They did not know the danger that lurked just outside Tadmor's bounds.

On the streets, he'd tried to warn the people of Mahara, but they looked at him like a madman and one of the city's warriors gave him a stern talking-to about "public order."

Three days after his return to the city, it was clearer than ever. He had to flee, even by himself. The desert sands could take him, but a much greater danger was remaining here in the Land of Tadmor. He could leave the desert by himself, without a caravan's protection. A week's journey through the scalding winds and sand, and he'd reach the coast. He could take a ship to the Continent. At night, even far from the desert's edge, he heard the sound of the storms in his nightmares, and the steady pounding of drums.

Yet without any money, leaning on the generosity of strangers, the journey presented tremendous risk. Perhaps he could find a camel, but there was precious little food to last him the long days between stops.

I will deal with hunger, Ahram told himself. *I will find a way to leave.*

~

Relying on the kindness of Maharans never failed him.

A friend he'd met loaned him his camel, and offered whatever meager rations he could afford to give.

Ahram loaded the saddle with waterskins to get him through the worst of the desert.

The wazir's warriors couldn't stop him now. He would find a way to circumvent their orders. He would escape their dark grasp. And yes, Mazda willing, he would reach the coast, and flee the world he'd known altogether.

He set out once again, that morning, promising himself he'd not fail this time, that he wouldn't back away at the first sight of trouble.

~

The village of Mlaka sat at the desert's edge.

It was not a popular stop for caravaners, but it lay perched on the border, where the dunes began and the harsh desert sun beat fervently on the dry earth.

He got to Mlaka at dusk. He could already hear the winds in his mind, the shrill howlings like ghosts, and the sound of the King of the Dark's approach.

His nerves turned to jelly. He turned back toward Mahara. Then he cursed its, and Tadmor's fate. Why should the living have to fear the dead?

Mounting his camel, he headed due west, west toward the coast, west toward freedom.

Chapter Twenty-Two: Better Days

This morning, and for the past five mornings, Yara had led Zathustra on walks.

The old sage was only barely recovering his strength. He spoke often of his "fear of death," and how the apparating process had killed many a lesser sorcerer.

He took Yara's hand in his and they left the Temple of the Moon in the morning light. The Lily had prepared fish in their kitchen. They were well fed and satisfied, and yet Zathustra struggled to put one foot in front of the other. He was still weak. Many days after he appeared here near the Pillars of the Moon, he had reached a sort of sick stasis, neither improving nor relapsing.

"You are on the cusp of a breakthrough," Yara told him.

Zathustra laughed. "I am seventy years old," he said. "Perhaps a young bull could survive this. I am not so sure about me."

"You will survive," Yara said, "and you'll be stronger than you were before."

Yara led him off to the right, away from the normal path they took. Yara would lead them to the Pillars of the Moon.

In the morning light, before the heat of the afternoon, birds were singing, and the sagebrush cast a verdant note against the dry, rocky ground. Zathustra was private, perhaps a little addled, but Yara was determined to get to know him. She had never known her grandfather, and this sage from the Land of Indjar was the next best thing.

"Tell me, Zathustra," Yara began, "how far you had to travel from your home to get here."

The Pillars appeared in the distance, a worn and battered remnant of another age.

"To return home is a journey so far I don't want to think

about it. I worry I won't make it. In fact, I am old, and weakened. I probably won't." Zathustra sounded worse than last night.

Was he deterioriating?

"And yet," Zathustra said, "I must try to return to Indjar, to my home. I must make my report known. I must let them know the mission I'd undertaken failed… that Tadmor has fallen into the hands of the Gray King."

The Gray King was another word Zathustra used, which Yara had found was the same as the King of the Dark. It referred to his appearance as a lord of the dead, gray, withered, rotting, with a crown on his head. Yara hoped to the Goddess she'd never see him. But she had to convince Zathustra to take her home so that Mother and Father could be warned. Perhaps all of Tadmor would fall, and the earth would be dragged down to hell, but Mother and Father would carry on. They were still alive. Yara could sense it. She could feel their presence now, even so far away. But Zathustra remained obstinate. He would not go. "Tadmor has fallen," he would say.

But Yara wasn't so certain. The Tammuri were prone to luxury and plenty, it was true; they were the wealthiest land in the known world, but they hid a hardiness behind their soft exterior. If anyone could overcome the King of the Dark and his armies, the Tammuri could. If anyone could defeat him, Yara's father could.

"What is Indjar like, Zathustra?"

Zathustra chuckled. "Oh, Precious Yara, you are full of questions. And if you went to Indjar, you wouldn't be much impressed. A band of monks, living in caves, copying texts, studying the stars. We do not drink or do much rejoicing.

"We do not sing or dance to music. We commit our time to our labors… to building up the sacred libraries, to gathering knowledge, to predicting events. You would not much like it, Yara. And things have grown worse in my time here on this earth. The followers of the Law of Mazda call us heretics, and strive for our executions. The Law has taken root outside Indjar. And soon even

Indjar may succumb… Indjar, a sanctuary of light near the Land of Shadow, may also fall…"

"You make it sound so terrible," Yara said, "but I'd go with you anyway."

"I would not return if I didn't have to," said Zathustra. "I would remain here, near the Temple of the Moon, for as long as I could."

"As long as you could?"

"The desert will claim the Temple eventually. I am sure the Lily is making preparations already to leave."

At the Pillars, they stopped to breathe, sitting on the base. Yara had grown sweaty. The heat of the day had not fully kicked in, but the sun was blindingly bright. The desert remained oppressive, and they were far from shelter.

Yara rested her head on Zathustra's shoulder. With him, she felt safe from the blazing sun which sapped away life by day, and the terrors that walked the desert by night. Zathustra was a sorcerer, more powerful than any warrior in Tadmor.

"I am leaving tomorrow," Zathustra said.

Yara jerked up. "You can't be serious," she said. "You will leave me alone here, in the middle of the desert?"

"I must return to Indjar, as fast as I can, if it is at all possible for me to. That is what duty requires of me. Indjar needs me."

"And Tadmor needs you," Yara said.

"Tadmor is not my home. I did what I could. I am sorry, Yara…"

Yara had gotten to know Zathustra over these weeks and days. He was nothing if not stubborn.

But Yara was stubborn, too.

Her eyes were watering, her fingers trembling with grief or fear. She would not let Zathustra get out of this. She would force him to do her will, the best way she knew how.

At night, she packed her things. She grabbed her waterskin and stuffed her pack with waybread. She tied her saber, in its sheath, to her belt. Then, as her Sisters slept and Zathustra spent another sleepless night by the pool, she departed.

Zathustra gazed at her as she left, but he remained silent.

Yara continued out the Temple doors.

~

Disturbed, Yara was, and perhaps a bit betrayed by the fact that Zathustra did not jump to her rescue or even convince her to stay.

But she had made this path for herself. Shouldn't she at least continue it?

She would let Zathustra worry for a while, if he had any capacity. She would walk to the Moon's Pillars, and enjoy the brisk air.

The sound of drums were gone. The storms were far off. The desert lay silent.

She had not gotten halfway to the Pillars before a familiar voice called out: "Enough!"

She turned to see Zathustra standing there, garbed in white.

He was walking toward her. She backed away.

"You are beyond help," Zathustra said. He sounded legitimately angry. There was an edge to his voice she'd never detected before. "You do not understand the dangers of returning to Tadmor. You must look past your family, your familial bonds. You must see the darkness spreading through the desert. You must preserve your own life. You are safe here, among these Sisters, for a time…"

"I am safe," Yara said, "but Mother and Father aren't. Do not leave me, Zathustra. Come with me to Tadmor."

"Tadmor is lost. Its inhabitants are dead. Nonetheless I will return. I will go to Indjar, but as long as you remain here in the protection of the Sisters, you will see me again. I will go to Tadmor, or wherever you want to go."

Yara didn't have much of a choice. She could not go to Tadmor alone. The Lily would not venture there. "Very well. I trust you. I trust that you will honor your word…"

In the morning, when Zathustra departed, Yara wept. The Lily tried to comfort her, to no avail.

Chapter Twenty-Three: Years of Darkness

Marit, mother of Yara, wife of Javan, had secluded herself for months now.

She was still pained by grief; Yara's disappearance remained like a dagger in her heart. But for the first time in a long time, she stirred to life, leaving the privacy of her bedroom. She was garbed in black, in the colors of mourning. She was certain Yara was dead. She could sense her spirit already gone into the earth. Whatever afterlife, whatever spirit life lay beyond, Yara was there, and more and more, Marit had convinced herself to join her. In the fires of hell, she would clasp her daughter's face; she would press her lips to her daughter's cheek. In the life beyond, they would embrace once more. They would be together, Marit and Yara, forever, until the end of time.

But Marit knew she was deluding herself. And she had a higher duty… to the country, to the Land of Tadmor which she lived. That Land was darkening, even as her husband drove out the clerics. And it would darken until the dawn broke. But would the dawn ever break again for Tadmor, or the world?

As soon as she left the privacy of her bedchamber and entered the main hall, she was swarmed by a gaggle of servants.

"My lady, my lady, there is a horrific sight in the city of Mlaka!" one of the girls shouted. "You must see it for yourself."

"Your description will be enough," Marit said. "What is this horrific sight?"

"A man, headless, riding back from the desert. There is a message sewn onto his skin."

Marit needed no further description. She felt sick. And yet her husband was at war. She was the only official presence that could comfort the citizens of Mlaka.

And a message could only mean one thing: enemies were

afoot.

~

In Mlaka, she arrived in her carriage. She exited quietly, though the villagers were scrambling to have a look at their wazira.

The body was waiting for her. Both the rider and the camel were dead.

The rider, she recognized as the madman her husband spoke of. She could not recall his name. But his clothing was instantly recognizable.

She shuddered in disgust. Flies were buzzing around the headless corpse.

The camel was warped and twisted, lying on the ground. Its teeth were bared and foam was drizzling from its mouth.

One of the village elders approached Marit.

"My lady," he said, "We had to kill the camel he rode in on. It was rabid, kicking and biting. I've never seen a thing like it before."

Marit knew as well as anyone this was not normal. She'd never heard of a rabid camel. And this beheading was intended to send a message... but to whom, and where was it sent from? Between Tadmor and any semblance of civilization was a journey of countless miles.

"This is not normal," she said aloud.

A strip of vellum was sewn crudely onto the dead man's bare arms, bordered by torn flesh and dried blood. Marit wondered if it had been sewn on him alive.

She walked forward and the stench hit her. It was thick, nauseating, and almost a physical barrier. Still she walked ahead, seeing the man's quickly decaying arms. She grabbed the vellum writing and ripped it off, skin, flesh and all.

She recognized the Naamer letters, but she was no scholar. She could not decipher them.

The villagers were looking at Marit like she was a fiend, holding the bloodied vellum letter. But she had to find out what these letters meant and what the message was. Whatever the Mlaka villagers thought of her was fine.

"We will bury him and his camel at sundown," said the village elder.

"No," Marit said. "Burn them." She did not quite know why she gave the advice. For some reason, she feared that camel and that rider would stir again.

~

Scholars of Naamer writing were few and far between.

For centuries, the clerics had been killing them, believing the knowledge of Naamer civilization would entice the Tammuri toward their idolatrous past. But Marit knew where to find those who specialized in this ancient chicken-scratch.

The letter posed an even greater mystery. Of the tiny number who could write in Naamer, why would they communicate this way, and for what purpose?

A scholar of sorts lived near the palace. He was an old man, once an emir, who had taken to study in his older years and taught himself all about the clay tablets which sometimes made their way into Tadmor. He had served Javan's father with great dignity and loyalty.

Amal welcomed her into his home warmly.

He brewed her some tea and insisted on taking his time.

His home was vast and spacious, the equal of the palace, with white plaster walls and silken green curtains. In his dining hall, Marit sat alone. The clerics would have roused the Mob if they'd heard of her impudence, drinking tea alone with a man other than Javan. Thankfully, the clerics were no longer in Mahara, and the only trace of their power was the Black Hand.

The tea was steaming when he brought it over. He had served it in a painted porcelain cup, no doubt imported from Cathay. He took the strip of vellum, and when he touched it, he looked sickened. "What is this?" he said.

"It was sewn to a man's arm," she said, "a man who was beheaded and then set loose on his camel."

Amal gawked. Slowly, but surely, he ran his fingers along the strip of vellum and began sounding out the words. "*Ka-a na-ga o-ga-sha-ga…*" His voice became a whisper.

He looked up at her.

"It reads, 'A thousand years of darkness.'"

Chapter Twenty-Four: On the Gallows

The morning after the slaughter in Adwar, Javan was stirred from his sleep.

A servant had awoken him. It was still dark outside. Here, in the Royal Tent, there were certain protocols to be followed. Utmost respect for the wazir was to be shown.

"I am sorry, my lord… your warriors are frightened."

Javan stood up from his cot. "Leave me be. I will come with you in a moment."

He was still in his underclothes.

He began to dress for the day. An unease had settled in the pit of his stomach. Was he truly this worried about the clerics and their Mob?

He was roughing it, traveling Tadmor for the purposes of war, but he was the wazir and he would dress the part. When king's emissaries saw him in his purple robe, resplendent with diamonds, jade, and emeralds, they remarked in private on his effeminacy. But in Tadmor, wealth was the true sign of strength, not buckskin robes or a body tanned from the sun. He draped the silken robe over his body, knowing his warriors would respect him, knowing that his emirs would honor him. From his belt, his jeweled saber hung in its sheath. He wrapped it around his waist and clasped the gold buckle. To look the part of a warrior, he placed a silver helm over his head. It was forged with a gold crown, indicating his status as wazir. At last, he was able to present himself before his men.

~

He left the confines of the royal tent to see his armies massed throughout the village of Adwar. His warriors numbered thirty thousand, overwhelming the tiny settlement.

He left the front lines to find his emir Moktata standing near the village well, looking shaken. He had never seen Moktata like this, ashen-faced, tense, even during the height of battle. But here he was, a great emir, frightened like a small child.

"What is it?" Javan said.

"We slew the Mob, and hanged the clerics that remained… come with me, Your Lordship."

Outside the village bounds, near the edge of desert, lay the gallows.

Thirteen bodies hung on the various gallows. They had been torn apart, and mostly cleaned of flesh. Arms and legs were missing, and what bits of the body remained where gnawed to the bone. Something had eaten them, but no animal Javan had seen had ever been so vicious.

"Vultures?" Javan said.

Moktata looked at Javan like he was stupid.

Javan supposed that was warranted.

"Someone in camp said they saw *people* eating these hanged men… Have the Adwaris become cannibals?" Moktata didn't sound convinced.

Had some madness inflicted the warriors, some sort of terror inspired by their disbelief? Javan had to find out. "You're certain…"

Moktata seemed as confused as Javan.

"We must find out who did this," Javan said. "We can't continue the campaign until these sick people are purged from our army…"

Moktata nodded. "You are right, my lord."

By Javan's instruction, the emirs began to question their warriors, one by one.

It still seemed impossible to Javan. Why would a man eat the flesh of another when there was meat and bread available? No cooking had been done, no salt or spice to erase the taste and the conscience. Yet some madness had inflicted a group of warriors. Perhaps, seeing what they'd done to the clerics and the Mazdahi, the loyal followers of Mazda, their consciences had been strained to the limit, sending them into the madness.

Yet that made little sense to him either.

He looked out into the desert. Not far from the village of Adwar, the dunes began: a sand sea stretching from here to Kish. Could whatever ate those hanged men lurk out there? Was there something Javan did not know about the desert?

He had never ventured far into the desert; he had practically never left Tadmor. Was there a tribe of men out there, lurking, that he did not know?

It seemed impossible. The sun burned travelers by day; the moon froze them by night, and there was no water for hundreds of miles around.

Somehow, though it baffled Javan's mind, a small group of his warriors had taken to eating the flesh of men. He had heard of nothing like it before.

At dusk, the emirs approached, seven in all, with many thousands of warriors reporting to each of them.

One by one, they announced they couldn't find the culprits.

Then they came to Moktata.

"Your Lordship, the cannibals will all deny it, except under force of torture," he said. "We must not allow them to lie to us. As emirs, we have ways of extracting the truth…"

It was unconventional, but true. Why would the wrongdoers admit their crimes, except under the greatest stresses of pain?

~

One by one, those suspected were taken to the rack. Under enormous duress, they not only confessed but gave the names of all their conspirators.

Fifty-one warriors were sentenced to die; they were put to death at sundown, left hanging on the gallows.

The next morning, Javan received word that the Thul had been seen in Magdala. The army departed, leaving the corpses to rot and putrefy.

Chapter Twenty-Five: A Lost World

Yara did not want to join the Lily for their morning training. Zathustra had left, and now she felt she had lost everything: her parents, the land that she loved, and her only true friend here in the Temple of the Moon.

The Lily, however, wasn't having any of her impudence. "Get up," she said sharply. "If you want to be a Sister, you must learn to fight."

Grudgingly, she obeyed her harsh headmistress. What did she have now, except the Temple of the Moon? What did she have now, except this?

~

The Lily struck, and Yara parried. Yara's body was covered with welts and bruises, but she had become an expert at the dodge and the lunge. She knew how to strike and slash, and she knew how to back away. She could, for the first time in her life, defend herself.

In Tadmor, according to the clerics, a woman warrior was sinful, a symbol of the pagan past. How angry Father would be if he saw this.

Actually, he might be proud.

Yara fought more aggressively than she'd ever fought before. She drove the Lily before her, harnessing her anger at Zathustra's leaving. At last she struck the Lily's wooden saber so hard it flew from her hands.

She struck the Lily hard on the shoulder, and she fell to the ground.

Once the dust settled, the Lily looked up at her. She was smiling. "Congratulations," she said. "Tonight, you will be a Sister."

~

That night, underneath the mantle of the stars, beside the temple pool, all seventy Sisters gathered around Yara, with the Lily facing her.

"Precious Yara," said the Lily, "we have spent all these months getting to know you. We believe the Goddess sent you here to help guard her temple and sanctuary. But if she, the Goddess of the Moon, depends on you for protection… if she, the Goddess of the Moon, demands you become her agent in the world, then you must swear fealty to her and her alone."

"I swear it." There was no hesitation for Yara. Of all Mazda's works, which had been for the betterment of mankind? Hopefully, Isdar, goddess of the moon and of the fertility of the soil, would prove a better benefactor.

Sister Zeira was holding a jar of oil. The Lily scooped some of the oil from the jar and sprinkled it on Yara's head. "Welcome, Sister Yara." The Lily met her in an embrace.

Another Sister handed Yara her new clothes: silken garments of blue, a diamond necklace, and a silver moon pin. A saber, she already had.

Her eyes welled with tears.

This could not replace Mother and Father, nor the loss of the Land of Tadmor, but it was something. She was part of the Sisterhood of the Moon. She was a guardian of Isdar's temple and her holy places. She belonged to something which could never be revoked. And she was a warrior, brave and true. The Hirazes and Rafizes of the world would fear her from now on. No one could ever outmatch her strength, or betray her trust.

"And as a Sister," the Lily said, "you must perform each quest which is given to you."

Yara nodded. "Of course."

~

The next day, she did not practice outside with the Lily. She entered the temple courtyard dressed in blue, the diamond necklace tight around her neck, the silver moon pendant affixed to her shirt. She expected serenity in the cool of the morning, but instead the Sisters were darting this way and that.

After a bit of searching, Yara found the Lily near the observatory tower.

"What's going on?" she said.

"Nothing for you to worry about, Sister Yara." Nonetheless she had a stressed look to her face.

Yara wouldn't accept the brusque statement and move on. "What is it? Tell me."

"Come with me." The Lily stormed out of the room, and Yara followed.

~

The Lily led Yara through passageways she had never seen, through corridors and twists and turns and finally down a set of stone steps leading into the basement. At last they came to an iron door.

"You are a young Sister," the Lily said. "You are not supposed to see this. But the times call for stringent measures. Behold, our Goddess's shrine."

Using a bronze key, the Lily opened the door.

The room was dark, completely void of illumination, but the residual light from upstairs glinted on many gold surfaces. Even before the Lily lit the candle, Yara knew this room contained precious objects, priceless in value.

As the room took on light, she saw just how wealthy the Sisters were. There were silver candelabras, emerald-studded figurines, silver ceremonial swords studded with rubies and sapphires, and even bars of solid gold. But set against the back was something clearly more prized than the rest: sitting on a stone altar, small but catching Yara's eye, was an amulet, shaped in the form of a crescent moon.

In the light of the candles, it seemed to fluoresce, and the crystal it had been carved from began to glow.

The Lily walked over to the altar and clasped it in her hands. "The Pendant of the Moon," she said. "When the Temple was ruined for a millennium, lying in disrepair and abandoned, the Moon Pendant remained. It was a symbol of the Goddess in a world that had almost forgotten her…"

Yara gasped. The Lily placed the pendant in Yara's hands. It was surprisingly warm; a heat seemed to radiate from it.

"This is the Temple's most prized possession," the Lily said. "When the Temple was first destroyed, when its pillars were thrown down and a fire was set… the Moon Pendant remained. It survived the fire… and it survived centuries of degradation in the wind and sand.

"It is what gives this temple its sanctuary."

"And why are you giving it to me?" Yara said.

The Lily frowned. "We have heard word that a group of Lamia are moving towards the Temple… a powerful group like we've never seen. If we don't survive, we want to keep the sacred pendant out of their hands."

Now Yara realized the reasoning for the somber mood and the worried looks on the Sisters' faces. "And you want me to take the pendant… you want me to leave?"

"Sister Hatzor and you will be taking the Moon Pendant to the sanctuary in Kish. Above the town, in the mountains, there is a sacred cave which no one knows about. There, it will be safe from the Lamia, if they overcome us…" The Lily's voice was tinged with worry Yara never heard before.

It was clear the situation was grave. "I don't want to leave you here to die," Yara said.

"You cannot defend me, Yara." The Lily smiled. She brushed Yara's cheek with her hand. "But you can serve the Goddess in this way. You will protect the Moon Pendant and in doing so, protect yourself."

I don't want to protect myself, Yara wanted to say. *I want to protect the Temple.* But it wasn't entirely true. She didn't want to die anymore than anyone else did. With Sister Hatzor, she would flee the danger and enter Kish, the far-off town on the edge of the world. The Lamia wouldn't touch her.

"Sister Hatzor is an experienced traveler," the Lily continued. "She will not guide you wrongly. She knows the way to Kish."

They departed in midday, in the burning desert sun, leaving on camels. As Sister Hatzor drove the camels on from the front, Yara looked back wistfully as the Temple became a backdrop. The Lily and several other Sisters were waving goodbye. For the first time, Yara had regrets. Perhaps it would have been better to stay in the Temple and fight. In the daylight, the worst Yara had to fear was the burning sun and lack of water; but at night time they were all alone in the face of the terrors which wandered the desert.

Yara did not know Hatzor well. She knew she was an archer, that she favored the bow above the sword, and that she was an excellent shot by any standard. Yara had spoken to her only briefly before, but had heard about her in the gossip and rumor which spread throughout the Temple.

Hatzor, it was said, had it out for the Lily; besides her, she was the most senior Sister and, some said, felt herself deserving of the role. Hatzor, unlike the other Sisters, had been married before, but was driven from her village after being accused of adultery. Hatzor denied the charges were true, but other Sisters had expressed to Yara their doubts. Hatzor was a beautiful woman, despite being one of the oldest Sisters in the Temple. Yara didn't know who to believe.

The land before them was flat and dry, cracked and waterless in the sun. Sagebrush dotted the earth and in the distance there were mountains, but here to Kish was a journey of interminable length. Yara didn't want to think about how many days they'd be on the journey. She would face each day, with all its struggles, on its own terms.

By the time night fell, they had traveled many miles. The land seemed to stretch for eternity into the distance. As the air cooled and the skies turned to vibrant shades of rose, Hatzor dismounted and wordlessly began to set up their tent.

Seeing the snub, Yara dismounted as well and gave her camel Illa a scratch on her neck. Then she left Hatzor to her own devices and wandered out into the wilderness.

~

A desert fox bounded away from her. As dusk settled in, a screech owl began to sing.

Yara was further from home than she'd ever been, in a land she did not know. She had never been so far from Tadmor. Its comforts and wealth were only a memory now. It was gone; and she had become a Sister.

The clerics and street preachers of Mazda would call for her head. But no doubt they, too, had perished. She smiled at the thought. Though the Tammuri had been erased from history, their oppressors had not been spared. She reveled at the idea of the clerics perishing in terror, at the hands of the King of the Dark.

In the distance were rocky outcrops. To her surprise, she saw structures carved into them: pillars and lintels, scratched with symbols. There were at least thirty of them overlooking this valley. Yara had learned not to let her curiosity get the best of her, but she couldn't resist.

When at last she drew near, she saw the remnants of doors which had long rotted away, and entryways into pitch blackness.

Clearly these were tombs, but for whom? Who could live in such a treacherous place, void of water and soil? Who could endure this heat?

Hatzor's voice broke the silence: "Yara! Yara!" she was shouting.

With some reluctance, Yara returned to camp. A fire was going, and the camels were tied to a post. Hatzor had done all this work without Yara, and no doubt she had some resentment. There was an edge to her voice as she beckoned Yara closer.

The cold was setting in. Hatzor handed her some waybread, and it was as tasteless as ever. Yara nibbled on the dry biscuits as she sat there.

"Where have you been?" Hatzor said, eyeing Yara with no small bit of scorn.

"There are tombs out there…"

"Yes. The Naamer ruins. Haven't you seen them before?"

Yara could sense Hatzor's derision for her. No doubt she resented having Yara tag along. Yara was a young Sister, new to combat. Clearly Hatzor considered her a burden and nothing more.

And what value did Yara add to this journey? Clearly, the Lily had intended on preserving her life. Any other Sister, sent with Hatzor, would have provided better protection. The Lily was merely looking after her young ward, and nothing more.

Hatzor ate her waybread in steely silence.

Yara wished she was back in the Temple, back among friends. It would be worth it, despite the danger. She wouldn't be stuck in this company, with a woman who clearly despised her.

"Sister Yara," Hatzor said, "know that we are still in danger. Do not wander off again. The terrors still walk the desert. The night has taken far greater Sisters than you."

Yara bristled at the harsh words. Hatzor clearly viewed her as undeserving of Sisterhood. But it did not matter what she thought. The Lily was the Guardian of the Temple. Hatzor was not, and would never be… Yara would make sure of it.

"You must listen to me, Sister Yara," Hatzor continued.

"Enough," Yara answered. "Leave me be."

"Kish will not be much better. It is full of robbers and bad men."

"I don't want to hear it," said Yara.

Hatzor was glaring at her. "You are not the first Sister with a rebellious spirit. I remember many. All of them perished. They disobeyed their superiors… they fell, one by one, to bandits, to Lamia…"

"I thought the Sisters were equal… that we belong to one single Sisterhood."

"And yet," Hatzor said, "the best Sisters always knew their place. They rose up through the ranks and gained the respect of their elders… that is how I got to be where I am now."

"And you are not where the Lily is," Yara answered.

"If you do not make it back on this journey," Hatzor said, "I warned you." She got up from the fire and brushed the dirt from her clothes. "Good night."

Alone in the cold, Yara poked at the fire with her saber as the embers began to die and the heat began to fade. She didn't hear the ghostly howl of storms, but instead silence, interrupted occasionally by a screech owl. No doubt desert foxes and birds of the night were watching her, but Yara felt truly alone. The King of the Dark, with his army, with his spectral drums, was far away.

So why was she worried about it? Why did she feel vulnerable?

She stirred and drew her shirt tighter around her body.

The camels were calm. There was no reason to worry.

Except for those tombs… monuments of stone, overlooking the desert, the traces of a lost civilization. The clerics had taught that the Naamer were wicked, that they had waged war against Mazda and then received their due punishment. Mazda himself had destroyed their country; he had brought vengeance upon them and turned their fertile fields into a desert.

Even before Yara left Tadmor, she didn't put much stock in it. The clerics had been wrong before. Like everything else, she had viewed the claim with a skeptical eye.

So what happened to the Naamer? Would the mystery one day be solved?

Perhaps Yara could solve it. Perhaps if, in the cover of night, she ventured to those tombs, and searched them for clues.

Packed amid her things was a torch, tied tight with cloth and soaked in oil. She searched in the darkness and found it in one of the camel's saddlebag.

In the tent, Yara could hear Hatzor snoring. She was sound asleep. Yara wouldn't awaken her. Besides, Hatzor was not her mother. She had no right to boss her around. Yara was coequal. She was independent; she was a full Sister.

A short way from camp, with a flint and tinder, Yara sent a spark flying and set the torch ablaze. With the torch in her left hand, she drew her saber and returned the way she had come, toward the hills, toward the Naamer tombs.

~

In the darkness, with a renewed focus, she paid careful attention to the masonry of the tomb before her.

The pillars which flanked the pitch-blank entryway were unlike any in Tadmor.

In Tadmor, pillars had rich capitals, carved with leaves and berries and foliage. These pillars were plain, almost square, with simple capitals.

Etched above were letters and runes she did not know.

The rusted-out remains of metal hinges clung to one side of the entryway.

As Yara took the first step into the pitch-blackness, the scent of must and old, dank air overpowered her. No human had been inside in centuries, clearly.

The sound of a screech owl broke the silence and Yara fell forward; she collapsed on the crumbled staircase. The entire first step had worn away; she almost lost her grip on the torch. She nicked her knees on the hard edge of the next step.

She was not meant to be here.

Still she steadied herself, standing up once more, and watching each step carefully, she began to descend into the Naamer tomb.

The corners of the staircase were covered in cobwebs. She cut them away with her sword, and black bulbous spiders scurried away.

When she reached the end of the staircase, there was rubble.

The must and sickly air had become very heavy. The staircase had opened up into a vast antechamber, with walls of stone. Against the wall was a sarcophagus; the stone lid had been opened and thrown across the floor, broken into two distinct pieces.

Around the room were casks. Once they had been filled with gold and precious objects, but they were looted and completely empty. Grave robbers, a constant nuisance in the desert, whom Yara's father had punished severely, no doubt found these Naamer tombs. Someone had grown very rich at the expense of the dead.

She peered into the coffin, seeing there was no body, no skeleton, no trace of the buried. But there were scratch marks: scratches so heavy they had eaten away at the stone.

Did the Naamer bury their dead alive?

It didn't make sense. But these scratches looked recent. Yara didn't know why, but they did.

In this tomb, had the King of the Dark awoken a vengeful ghost? Had an ancient Naamer king been returned to life as a wraith, as a phantom of the night?

Goose bumps were appearing on Yara's skin.

With her saber, she could slay desert bandits and wild animals, but she could not slay the dead.

She wished she could read the Naamer writing, but it was beyond her. She wanted to know who this was, and if he—or she—walked again. But instead she found herself backing away.

She felt she had realized something important, but she didn't know what?

All these tombs, overlooking the desert valley, had given up their dead. Had the desert offered its victims to the King of the Dark to serve as his foot soldiers? Had everyone who perished in the sands been raised to a new state?

Yara didn't know. Perhaps she never would.

She turned to leave when a gleam caught her eye: the sparkle of metal, the glint of silver.

Amid all the rubble and ruin of the tomb, beneath some debris, she saw the source of it, in a corner.

She walked over and brushed off the dirt and pebbles.

A figurine lay there in the darkness, forged of silver, and no doubt forgotten for centuries. The grave robbers hadn't touched it. Yara wondered why.

She sheathed her saber and stooped down, grasping the object in her hands. It was expertly forged in the shape of a woman. In place of a face, there was a skull, and a tentacle emerged from its mouth. Clearly this was some religious fetish, an idol of the Naamer. How could they worship something so horrific? Was this a goddess of death, or some sort of demon like the clerics warned about.

Yara had lost track of how many times the clerics spoke of the punishment awaiting unbelievers. Demons with forked tongues would lash the adulterers; demons with barbed skin would flay the liars; and demons with horns on their heads would boil alive those who questioned the clerics or disobeyed their commands.

Whoever and whatever the Naamer were, Yara doubted they had such superstitions.

No, this figurine she was holding, this creature with the

skeletal face and the worm-like tongue, was one of their gods.

She pocketed it in her robe. Hatzor didn't have to know. The figurine was slender, and lightweight. But it was also valuable. Someday, somewhere, Yara could sell it. She could turn this idol into profit. She was a grave robber after all.

~

They left camp before sunrise. Hatzor, at the front of the camel train, led the charge. She said nothing. She acted normal. She had no idea that Yara had slipped away in the dead of night, or that she had robbed a Naamer tomb.

Chapter Twenty-Six: Sundown

The town of Magdala was surrounded.

Its walls and fortifications were manned by the Mob, the desperate but zealous of the Mazdahi. No doubt the Thul had promised them absolution and entry into paradise. No doubt they despised their Blasphemer Wazir.

Javan didn't want to harm them. He wanted them to lay down their knives, their swords, their farming implements, and accept his rule. Surely, deep down, they knew this wouldn't end well for them. They knew they stood no chance against Tadmor's armies. But the Thul, ever the great manipulator, had stirred up such hatred within them that they stood firm.

Javan heard word that the Thul had holed up in Magdala's tower. From there he was giving his Mob their cryptic commands. Surely he knew his time was up, too, but had put all his hope in the anger of the Tammuri.

He had good reason to hope. Many Tammuri were devout; for the poor, faith was all they had. Their entire lives, they had been promised great reward in the afterlife if they obeyed the clerics to the letter. Javan did not want to take them there, and see that bitter disappointment for themselves. He did not want to kill any Tammuri, not even the clerics. The Tammuri were his children; this sacred land, in the middle of the desert, was his to protect.

Javan's army began to blow their trumpets. In response, the Mob stamped their feet against the battlements and invoked the prophet Mali. Mali, the "blind teacher," had been a great destroyer of kingdoms and empires centuries ago, when the faith itself emerged from the desert sands. In those days, Tadmor worshipped the Goddess of the Moon, Isdar, and laughed at the thought of the desert nomads overpowering them.

But the nomads did overpower them, and the Faith of Mazda spread, at the end of the sword, to Tadmor. The Tammuri armies were overpowered; and the Law of Mazda was set up, coequal, to the law of the land. Tadmor's sovereignty had never been restored, all these endless years later. Only Javan dared do something about it. Only Javan dared fight.

He rode up to the wall, riding on his white charger.

"Here is your last chance!" Javan shouted. "Your last chance to surrender."

The Mob began to pelt stones at him. The choice was made.

For a day, and the following three days, the Mob held the army back.

On the third day the gate was breached; the armies poured in and swallowed Magdala whole.

Soon, word reached Javan that the Thul had once again escaped.

"He has fled," the emir told him. "He has fled into the desert. Surely, the sun and sand will claim him…"

But Javan knew better. The Thul had escaped greater dangers before.

That night, as his warriors buried the mob, Javan looked out into the growing dusk.

"Where are you?" he said to the Thul, now absent. He was somewhere out there, amid the storms, amid the growing night.

Chapter Twenty-Seven: Desperate Measures

Marit watched the sun sink beneath the horizon.

On the palace balcony, a cold breeze was blowing. A cup of hot tea was in her hands, and a pitcher next to it.

Despite her comfortable seat and her silken bedclothes, she was straining to relax. Her mind kept returning to that vellum, sewn onto the headless body, and the words in foreign writing: "a thousand years of darkness."

What did it mean? And of all the scholars who knew the writing of the ancients, why had they chosen that script, and why had they beheaded that grave robber?

To send a message, it was clear. But why would they choose that language? And what kind of sick, demented mind would send a headless rider back to deliver it? She had never heard of any bandits afflicted with such madness. There was something to this message, something Marit did not understand. Her friend, the translator of the letter, offered no clues.

Late in the night, Marit wracked her mind thinking, trying to understand what the letter was, and what it could mean.

"A thousand years of darkness…"

She wished her husband was home. To this day, the stabbings continued, the Black Hand trying to reassert the power of Mazda among the common people. To this day, to this night, and to this hour, Marit wondered if her husband had made a mistake, if—in his zeal to free the Tammuri from the Thul's yoke—he had acted too hastily. But against the armies of the wazir, the clerics and their Mob stood no real chance.

Victory, she did not doubt; lasting victory, she was certain of. Unrest, she could foresee far into the future.

Yet her greatest worry was that strange letter and what it

meant, how it had been sewn so artfully onto the headless rider's skin.

Despite herself, she set the tea on her table and re-entered her room. She had placed the strange object inside a jar so that she wouldn't have to look at it.

She opened the jar, took out the note, and headed back to the balcony.

Sitting down, she peered over it once more. The last bits of sunlight were fading. In the horizon, the ever-present dust of the desert was filtering out much of the light. This note came from there, this vellum, this piece of writing.

Around its sewn edges, traces of flesh remained which Marit's fingernail couldn't remove. Being several days removed from its host, it had acquired a smell.

The writing of the Naamer appeared strange to the eyes of the moderns. The characters were wedge-shaped, as if each one were imprinted by a stylus.

Javan was wiser than she was. Would he know the secret? There were limits to his knowledge, though she loved him as much as she did on her wedding day. In his absence, and in the wake of Yara's death, she'd never felt so vulnerable. She was alone with her thoughts… alone with this horror she was holding.

Someone knocked on the bedroom door.

Marit turned, wondering whether she should answer it. Her servants knew not to disturb her, especially after sundown. She paused for only a moment, but her loneliness and building dread pushed her away from the chair.

She hid the note in the jar once more.

She crossed the room. She opened the door.

Standing there was her servant Tigra, clearly worried of how Marit would react. "I am sorry, Your Excellency… I thought I would mention… I thought I would say…"

"Don't worry," Marit said. "Come in."

In normal circumstances, Tigra's fear would be correct. But

Marit was gone from her husband; left alone, she spent all her time worrying about the future. She was wazira, the luckiest woman in Tadmor, but it often didn't feel that way. Tadmor was a land in turmoil, and the palace was a nest of vipers. She wasn't sure who she could turn to, or who to trust. A lowly servant like Tigra seemed a good bet.

"Come in," Marit said again. "Sit." She shut the door of her bedroom and locked it.

Tigra had been born in the palace. Her parents and grandparents had served the wazirs for countless generations. She knew the palace inside and out; she knew every task and chore.

Marit was not so lucky. Her father had been an emir, a man of some import, but nowhere near as wealthy and powerful as Javan.

Javan's parents had been enraged at the marriage of someone so lowly born, but had at last relented. Javan remarked often how good a decision he'd made, how his determination and iron will had overcome his parents', and the Council of Elders', resistance. Two thousand years of precedent had been erased by Javan, all to marry Marit.

Out on the balcony, Tigra sat on a seat of her own.

Marit poured Tigra a cup of tea. "What is it?" she said.

"I was in the market today," Tigra said. "I saw a merchant… he said he was from the Spice Cities, carrying cargoes of dried fish… but for a moment one of the crates were opened.

"There were swords…"

For a moment, the mystery of the note was not her greatest fear.

The Spice Cities, a far off land whose merchants nonetheless frequented Tadmor, were known for their treachery.

Their leaders, the Mercantors, were known for their immorality and greed; nonetheless, Marit wouldn't put it past them to aid the Mazdahi for money. What were the lives of the Tammuri compared to cartfuls of desert gold?

"You must show me," Marit said. "Why didn't you tell someone before?"

"I don't trust some people," Tigra said. "I… I worry…"

"What do you mean?" pressed Marit.

"People in the palace… people I know… people I trusted…"

Marit put a hand on Tigra's shoulder.

"They have begun calling you a blasphemer, a heathen," Tigra continued.

Marit gasped. In the palace, in her own household, there were traitors. What did she expect? Did she think Javan could change centuries of history, that the faithful would not fight back?

She felt ill.

She wondered if she could tell anyone in the palace the news and if they'd do anything about it. Were the emirs against her too? Could she trust the army, the heart of Javan's support, or were they also against the wazir, also plotting, also scheming?

"Perhaps, Tigra, you should leave me…" Her mood had soured. This tea would only compound her nerves. She grabbed the cup and stood up, then tossed the hot liquid into the garden many fathoms below. She braced herself against the railing. She was showing weakness to Tigra, but she could trust Tigra. Couldn't she?

She wanted Javan to be here.

He had made his choice to challenge the clerics; she had fully consented. Side by side, they would triumph or perish together. Why did he have to leave her, even if it was for a little while?

"Tigra," she at last said, firmly, without any trace of wavering of weeping, "you must tell me where you saw this."

"In the marketplace," Tigra said. "I don't know where."

That couldn't help. Where could Marit begin? Would she seize every cargo that entered the city and search?

Yes. That is what she had to do.

In the morning, she gave the order.

The stunned city administrators did not quite know how to respond.

"You mean... you want every cargo in Mahara seized?" one said.

"Yes," Marit answered. "Every cargo. Every crate. Every barrel. Every jar."

No doubt the religious judges that remained would express their outrage. The Mazdahi in the city would know exactly the purpose of Marit's searching and scouring.

Marit could expect more violence, more burnings and more fire tonight. But it was worth it. She had to neutralize the threat. Her husband would return in peace.

Chapter Twenty-Eight: Desert Ways

The third day of their journey from the Temple, Yara let out a scream so loud she could hear it echoing across the bluffs and canyons.

Hatzor, at the top of the camel train, looked back at her and glared. "What are you doing, Precious Yara?"

She said "precious" as if it were an insult.

"How much longer until we get to Kish?" Yara said bluntly. The heat was getting to her. She'd only been on the road for three days and the waybread, the dry tasteless morsels, made her want to retch. There was no pomegranate juice or wine to drink, just water delved from the desert's rivers and streams.

Hatzor jerked herself ahead and uttered a string of curses.

It was clear traveling with Yara was getting to her. Her hatred was plainly written on her face.

This journey wouldn't end well, if it ever reached its conclusion.

If Yara had her wish, she would have stayed in the Temple, come hell or destruction, if she could just avoid this journey and Hatzor. The more Yara spent time with Hatzor, the more she thought the rumors were true, that she was an adulteress, in addition to a thief and a cheat. Spending the journey with her, alone, had never been a good idea. Surely the Lily would have realized how much Hatzor despised her. She was ever the young Sister, ever the neophyte and never worthy of her respect.

Yara would have to get used to it. She would have to tolerate Hatzor's presence. She had to remember she had a sacred mission; and that the Lily had placed the Moon Pendant not in Hatzor's care but in Yara's. It was in her pack that the Moon Pendant rested, safe from the terrors of the night.

Up ahead, plodding along on her camel, Hatzor continued her lecture: "My Precious Yara, you have much to learn. It is not only at night that you are in danger… bandits are here, and caravaners seeking to rob us."

As dusk settled in that day, they reached an oasis, overgrown with reeds and palms. In the waters, bright red fish were visible darting back and forth. Near the muddy shore, bushes bursting with berries grew in abundance. Hatzor began plucking the bright red berries and popping them in her mouth, one after the other.

"We are alone," Yara stated the obvious.

Hatzor eyed her. She could not hide the fact she was as surprised as Yara.

"Have some berries," she said.

Yara gladly obliged. The tangy, sweet juice filled her mouth with flavor. After days of tasteless waybread and water, this was like a divine feast.

The camels shifted through the green brush. They would take shelter in the trees. As night approached, frogs had begun croaking. Up in the treetops, colorful birds, red, yellow, blue, had nested and were flying about. Here, amid the sameness and desolation of the desert, a tiny bit of paradise was found.

Hatzor tied the head camel to one of the trees.

Then she began to set up camp, not far from the shore.

~

Not far from the edge of the water, Hatzor built a raging fire. Before dusk, she had caught a wild hen and now roasted it, in a spit, in the flame.

"I've never seen Saar empty before," Hatzor said. "We are completely alone."

"Saar?" Yara said. "That is what this place is called?"

Hatzor nodded and pulled her blanket tighter. It had grown

cold.

"This is a popular route to Kish," said Hatzor.

Her words said it all. She did not understand why the oasis was empty, why caravaners passing along the way were missing.

"And I… I think… I thought there was a village here," Hatzor said.

Goose bumps formed on Yara's skin, like she hadn't felt since she entered the Naamer tomb. Hatzor got up to leave. "Watch the hen," she said.

The meat, dressed and cut up into all its various parts, was dripping into the open flame. Suddenly the meal Yara looked forward to with relish didn't seem as important.

Hatzor departed, disappearing into the greenery and the brush.

Yara knew of the terrors which wandered the desert, but there were also wild animals to worry about. Could tigers or other great cats be lying in wait among the reeds, hungry enough to pounce on Hatzor, or on Yara?

Amid the crackling flame, the tender meat on the makeshift spit was dripping grease, which sizzled on the embers. Their meal, long awaited for, was almost done, seasoned with cumin, salt and pepper. This would be the best they'd eaten since the journey began.

And yet, she was no longer hungry. She waited, looking out into the darkness, eager for Hatzor to return but not seeing her. She could no longer hear her rustling through the bushes and weeds; she was distant.

The moon arose, white and full, supreme among the stars' mantle. The hen was fully cooked, and Yara removed the breasts, the tenders, the wings, each into equally divided bowls.

She got up and grabbed some berries from the bushes, and dribbled them inside to add flavor.

Her stomach growled. But food was the last thing she was thinking of. It seemed like Hatzor had been gone an hour. Where was she?

Yara could not make the journey to Kish alone. She was trapped. If Hatzor died, she'd die too. She let the bowls alone, hoping no animal got to their food, and left to search for Hatzor with a hand on her saber's hilt.

~

The oasis was not very big, but in the darkness, Yara had no idea where she was going or where she could find Hatzor. The date palms and scrub trees formed ominous shadows as she tried searching round the lake. The waters were still, and the frogs were deafening in their croaking. Yara had never felt so vulnerable.

She stumbled through the reeds and the vines, not knowing where she was or where she'd come from, in the pitch darkness. A snake slithered by her and she screamed.

"Yara?" Hatzor's voice echoed through the oasis. She was nearby. She followed the voice, stumbling through the brush, staggering through the reeds, and fell with a splash into an irrigation canal. She emerged from the cold water wet and muddied. A dark shape appeared: "Hatzor."

"Are you all right, Sister Yara?" she said. She stooped down into the canal and helped Yara up.

"I am," Yara said, and tried to brush off some of the mud.

Hatzor was looking at her patronizingly.

Yara deserved it, so worried, so terrified to be left alone. She was a Sister; emotion was supposed to be beyond her. But in the end, she was still just a girl, in an increasingly dangerous world. She could not fight the terrors of the night and the plagues of the day by herself.

"Saar is gone," said Hatzor. "Follow me."

Through the jungle of weeds and bushes, Hatzor navigated a

path, until at last they came to a village.

The houses sat empty.

Near a pen, a starved lamb bleated nervously. All the humans were gone, but the beasts were left alone.

A starved dog approached them, perhaps begging for food. In Tadmor, dogs were often regarded with suspicion, but Yara stooped down and scratched its ear, wishing she could offer food but having none… at least, not here.

The dog slobbered on her as Hatzor tepidly approached the village square. "These animals are scared," she said.

Not far from the houses was a chicken coop. There was food aplenty; perhaps that wild hen Hatzor caught had escaped.

Yet Yara, and surely Hatzor, felt they needed to leave, and quickly. Whatever had driven the villagers from Saar into the embrace of the searing desert would surely stalk them, too.

"Should we leave?" Yara said. Her voice indicated her fear.

"No," Hatzor said. "At least, not yet."

The village square was empty. Carts lay abandoned, filled with rotting fruit now swarmed by flies. It was as if Mazda reached down from heaven and snatched the people of Saar into the sky.

Mazda. Some habits were hard to break.

"Do you think," Yara began, wondering if she should utter the thought, "this has something to do with what's happening in the desert? With the King of the Dark?"

She did not want to draw his attention. Would saying his name do so?

"All things are interconnected," Hatzor said. "Your life and mine… this dog's and the villagers of Saar."

It was still panting at Yara's feet, searching for food and love. She wished she could care for it and take it with her. These animals would all perish, in the worst way. Hunger and thirst would gnaw at them until their deaths… all because the people of Saar had vanished into the night.

In the stillness of the air, against the backdrop of the frogs, Yara noticed a faint but putrid scent. She looked up at the trees and saw an inky black cloud obscuring the stars.

Flies.

She looked down, sickened, and noticed, for the first time, blood dropping like rain in the village square.

"The people… they're in the trees!" Yara screamed.

"Lamia," Hatzor said calmly. "We must leave, as quickly as possible. We are not alone."

Hatzor ran briskly. Yara bolted after her in a panic. As she walked, she looked across the lake, seeing a shadow half as tall as the trees, like a goddess of old.

The forest seemed to come alive.

Soundless lightning was flashing; a flame of light with no thunder, always in the distance or behind her. The camels were grunting so loudly and jerking their ties so tightly Yara could hear the commotion from a long distance.

"They feed on fear," Hatzor said. "Try to stay calm."

But staying calm was not an option; it was utterly beyond her. In a full-fledged panic she began to run ahead of Hatzor, though she did not know the way.

Voices began to call out from the treetops: a thousand voices, like a ghostly choir, speaking in a language she did not know.

"*Kaaaa gaaa yaaa maaa shaa…*"

"Don't run so fast!" Hatzor shouted. The fear was rising in her voice. "You might trip!"

At the thought Yara stumbled and almost fell-face first into the grass.

She recovered, sprinting just behind Hatzor, as the camp came into view.

The trees were shaking. Shadows rose in the distance, shadows the shape of women, like giants of the earth. One shadow was smiling, and her eyes burned like yellow beacons.

Hatzor cut the ropes that bound the camels. They stampeded away.

Yara followed just behind, managing to scoop up the bowls of chicken, which, happily, had not been disturbed.

~

The sounds of thunderous cries and the flashes of lightning in the night consumed the oasis. But soon Yara and Hatzor were gone. She looked back, and saw the Lamia had not followed them. They remained in Saar, where they had committed their massacre. Yara was still shaking, still panicking, still breathless, but she remained on her saddle, managing even to clutch the bowls of chicken which—despite the long time elapsed—still emitted a crisp, spicy scent. Some things were more important than a timely escape, and the first good meal in weeks was one of them.

Late into the night, when they stopped in the middle of the desert, Yara was still shaken and out of breath. Hatzor, despite the late hour, began to set up the tent. Yara could not bring herself to dismount or do much of anything.

She breathed in deeply and tried to focus. The Lamia were gone, or so it appeared; but couldn't they have followed Yara and Hatzor here? Couldn't they be right behind them? Yara wondered if they'd put her in a tree like they'd done to the villagers of Saar. Was there anything the terrors of the night could not do?

Yara dismounted, balancing the bowls of chicken with her hands. She stumbled and fell. The bowls hit the ground, and out from the folds of her shirt the silver figurine slipped away, tumbling toward Hatzor.

The silver figurine, which she'd snatched from the Naamer

tomb, was gleaming in the moonlight, and Hatzor was looking at it.

"What is this?" she cried. Leaving the half-erected tent alone, Hatzor stormed over and snatched the figurine from the ground. "This is an idol. Where did you get this?"

"From the Naamer tomb," Yara admitted, with an edge to her voice. Hatzor wasn't going to make her feel guilty.

Hatzor picked it up from the ground and brushed off the sand and dirt. "This," she said, "*this* is a talisman of evil."

Yara looked away from her harsh, overbearing gaze. "I am sorry, Sister Hatzor," she said at last, hoping it would be the end of the matter.

But Hatzor continued. "Yara, Yara, Yara," she said. "Why would you take this from the tomb? Why would you take something that even the grave robbers wouldn't touch?"

"I thought I could sell it in Kish." Yara's honesty, perhaps, wouldn't serve her well. But she spoke the truth anyway.

Hatzor shoved the figurine toward Yara. Its figure—a woman in a billowing gown, with a skeletal face and a worm-like tongue— unsettled her like never before. Perhaps the recent worries of the Lamia were weighing on her; perhaps she feared that the figurine had drawn them there.

"You fear the followers of Mazda," said Hatzor, "but do you not know that whatever crimes the Mazdahi have committed, the Naamer were far worse? Do you think the Naamer era was a golden age? No, it was a world of evil, and the King of the Dark would not be here without them…"

Hatzor dropped the figurine on the ground.

"And you would take this idol, which even the grave robbers fear, to sell in the markets of Kish." Hatzor cursed. "All for gold and silver. Are you greedy, Sister Yara? Weren't you the daughter of a great man… the daughter of a wazir?"

"Don't talk about my father," Yara snapped. "I'm sorry I'm not superstitious. I don't fear idols. I don't fear charms."

"Perhaps, you don't fear the Naamer gods," Hatzor said. "The hags and the Night Sisters do not bother you. But perhaps you could have, at the very least, some respect for the dead."

Yara managed to bite her tongue.

"These idols are feared by everyone who knows them," Hatzor continued, "by anyone who fears what they represent. Take it away, Yara, as far as you can go. Bury it in the sand and hope it never emerges."

Yara grabbed the idol, wanting to say something curt. But she kept quiet. She headed out deep into the wilderness, and with her hands, dug a hole, placing the idol inside. Somewhere, someday, the idol would be found. The sand always gave up what was buried underneath.

As she covered the idol with dirt, she looked up. She thought she saw an old woman standing there, wrinkled and white haired, but as she looked closer it vanished, turning into a mirage. She wondered if she had just imagined her, staring, leering, but quickly abandoned the thought. She returned to camp shaken. Hatzor had already gone to bed.

Chapter Twenty-Nine: Trust

Marit had ordered every cargo entering Mahara searched. She had waited a day, and a night. Now, in the darkness, she had grown impatient, worried about the unrest she might have caused, and worried about the den of vipers the palace had become.

She had fixed herself a pot of tea. She was ready to sleep and put the troubles of the day behind her. Then, there was a knock on her bedroom door. She knew who it was before she opened it.

Tigra stood there, the servant whom Marit had befriended, the servant who had gained Marit's trust. With her favor and good treatment, Marit had turned her into an excellent spy, serving as her eyes and ears around the palace and beyond.

Marit welcomed her in.

"I have tea ready," she said.

Tigra smiled. In her life, she wasn't used to the wazira doting on her.

Until these past few weeks, she had been unnoticed by the wazir and wazira. Now, Marit had use for her. Marit had begun to trust people less and less. Tigra had spoken of open insurrection in the palace, of the cook speaking out against the wazir's "blasphemy," and of old friends turning against her after her husband's war on the clerics.

She had begun to learn whose loyalties were true, and whose were not—who valued the clerics, and who valued Javan.

"I am waiting," she said as she and Tigra moved out toward the balcony. "I told my husband's warriors to raid the city's cargoes."

The air was pleasantly cool, and a wind was blowing, bringing up the scents of the city, the garbage, the refuse, the smoke, and the spice. Marit poured her little spy some tea from the pitcher. It was still hot and steaming as it filled the porcelain cup.

What other servant was treated so well, Marit wondered. What other servant had the ear of the wazira? Tigra was a lucky girl, but it was all for a purpose.

Tigra sat down at the table and removed her headscarf, laying bare her long black hair. She took the cup in her hands and had a sip, peering into the vast darkness below. Silence had overtaken the town ever since Javan proclaimed a curfew; and yet, night after night, the stabbings continued—the work of the Black Hand. Freedom fighters, they called themselves, waging war against a "heathenous and blasphemous regime." Every night, suspected members of the Black Hand were hanged in the city square, but the violence continued, threatening to spill into open warfare. The city was like a pit of dragon's tar; a single spark threatened to ignite widespread violence.

"What news have you brought, Precious Tigra?" said Marit. She had begun to use the very words of affection that once belonged solely to her daughter.

Oh, Precious Yara. Precious Yara. She had tried so desperately to distract herself, but it wouldn't work. A piece of Marit was gone forever, and she could never have it back.

She turned to Tigra, and seeing her innocent face, wondered if she'd slip away one night and disappear into thin air.

Was she focusing all the love she had for Yara on this Tigra? Was she looking for a daughter? She could ask Tigra to take up sleeping in her daughter's room. She laughed sadly at the thought.

"News," Tigra said. "I have none. I only wanted your company."

It would be inappropriate for a servant to speak of her wazira like a mother or a close friend. But Marit was forgiving to Precious Tigra. At least, she was for now, in a palace where so many wore masks, where they spoke of Javan in unending platitudes and then cursed him quietly behind his back.

"Tigra," Marit said, "you remember my daughter, Yara…"

"Of course," Tigra said. "She was unforgettable. I thought she was destined for great things…"

The pit in Marit's stomach seemed to grow, now that they talked openly of her. "Do you have any reason why she would leave? You knew little of her. But you saw her around the palace. You might know why she left... and why she's gone..."

Tigra was staring at Marit blankly.

"I know she liked to leave," Marit said. "She had gotten frustrated and left the palace before..." She began to cry. Weeping slurred her words. "I don't know why she didn't like it here. Perhaps, if I'd been more welcoming, more loving, she'd still be alive..."

"Yara was a spitfire," Tigra said. "She was bold and brave. A tomboy. Nothing you've said or done has anything to do with it. I am sure you were loving... I've seen it myself."

But that much wasn't true. In public, Marit had shown little affection. A nursemaid had fed Yara. Servants cared for her, day to day. Only in private did she admonish her out of love, or hug her, or kiss her. Yet now, she was gone—a piece of Marit, irrevocably taken from her. Tigra could never replace her, nor could anything.

"And now she is dead," Marit said.

"Why are you so sure?" Tigra said. "Do not give up hope. Until you see her body, until some witness comes forward, there is hope... she may still be alive."

"If she was alive, she would come home," Marit said. "She is brave and ornery, but she would always come home. She is, at heart, still a vulnerable girl. This world is too dangerous for her."

"Perhaps, you do not know her as well as you think," Tigra said.

Marit stared at her in silence. Her words were too impudent, even for a woman she called "friend." "Perhaps you should leave me," said Marit. "I must get ready for bed."

There was a second knock on the door. Marit left the balcony, leaving Tigra alone.

At the door was a city official she recognized as Tammuz. This was the man who had taken charge of the investigation, of the search and seizure of cargo.

"My lady," he said. "Everything has been searched and seized. Not a weapon has been found. And no cargoes from the Spice Cities have been located."

"Not a weapon? Not a single sword? Someone is lying." She wondered who. She did not trust Tammuz. She did not trust anyone. And the swords and daggers could already be distributed, waiting for the beacon or clarion call to vault them into action.

She turned and saw that Tigra was approaching, tying her headscarf once more around her hair.

She bade them goodbye and shut the door. She would prepare for bed. She would hope and pray for Javan's swift return. She would not sleep for hours.

Chapter Thirty: The Sword of Mahara

One by one, the towns had fallen. Adwar. Magdala. And now, the last holdout of the clerics and their Mob was being run through.

Javan watched as his warriors cleared out the city of Wazra. The walls and fortifications had been stormed; the kabakh, the second-holiest in the Land of Tadmor, was cleared of the holdouts.

It turned out the grip of the clerics and of the Thul was less ironclad than they wished to express. Pillars of fire did not rain from the sky, as the clerics threatened. The warriors of the wazir did not turn to plumes of salt. The warnings and threats of the street preachers and the hateful Mob proved as worthless as the wind.

As Javan stood in the city square of Wazra, his emir Moktata approached. He was the oldest of the emirs, and his half-silver hair was done up in a lengthy ponytail. He wore his leather breastplate long after the Mob had been slain and the clerics, purged from the city. He bore his spear like a walking staff.

"A little bird came to me, my lord. There's been an outright rebellion in Magdala. Bloodshed. Burning buildings." Moktata didn't seem surprised.

But Javan had not expected this. The clerics and their Mob had been utterly subdued, killed to the last man. Had the people of Magdala, whom he had left in peace, risen up? Was their faith in Mazda that strong? Was their hate for their wazir and the Land that intense?

He wondered what "little bird" told Moktata this, some messenger or warrior who had escaped the bloodshed.

"They've overcome your warriors, my lord," Moktata continued. "They fled the city last night. The rebels have taken up shelter in the tower."

Javan looked out into the streets of Wazra. Its mudbrick homes and shops were silent, exactly as peaceful as Magdala had been. The people of Wazra had shown deference to Javan and his emirs; but how many were zealous? How many were devotees of Mazda, waiting for the proper time and hour to overthrow the warriors of Tadmor? If such betrayal could happen among the famously worldly citizens of Magdala, how much more could it happen among the Wazarene?

"We must leave a garrison here to keep an eye on things," said Javan.

"We are already stretching our warriors to the limit," Moktata answered. "I'm not sure that would be wise."

"And I do not intend to put out fires… to continually allow villages to slip into the hands of the rebels." Javan's tone left no room for argument. "We must leave a hundred warriors here, in the least. Otherwise we will incite the zealous to rebel…"

Tadmor, for all its ancient wealth, was a small land. There were not many hundreds of miles to cover. It lacked the vastness and breadth of the Continent, though its people were wealthy and well fed. If Javan kept some of his troops out of Mahara, they could cover Tadmor.

And yet he saw Moktata's point. There was only so much his warriors could do. Mahara, a city of many thousands, deserved greater protection from the rest. Mahara was the crown jewel of the Land of Tadmor, the sum of all its wealth and dreams. Could he relinquish its protections for the sake of lowly Wazra?

"Two hundred warriors to Wazra," Javan demanded. "Two hundred to Magdala. One hundred to every lesser town. Mahara will have to do with fewer. We must secure the Land of Tadmor in its new future."

Moktata nodded. "As you wish, my lord!"

It struck Javan, as the sun was setting, that the warriors he had sent were not protecting the people, but instead law and order. The threat to the new way of things, without the clerics, came from the Tammuri themselves.

They will bristle, and they will fight, Javan told himself as the darkness settled in. *They will rise up and do battle. But one day, they will submit to this new future. They will forget the memory of the clerics and the street preachers… they will taste life, and love, and wine again, like the ancients did.*

Perhaps, one day, these rioters and rebels would not see Javan as a blasphemer, but as a reformer, as a leader and a "father of their country."

~

He rode all day and well into the night. Long after the sun had set, and the moon appeared among the stars, Javan and his cavalcade arrived at the City of Mahara. In the darkness, the city—under a heavy curfew—did not take notice of its wazir's arrival. Javan passed by streets he knew, which he had supervised his whole life, in total anonymity and silence.

In the palace stable, the hostler took his white charger away into the stall.

He returned to his home, but not before visiting the palace kitchen, and bringing home to his wife a plate of candied oranges and lemons, smothered in date honey.

In their room, Marit was sleeping and snoring, tossing and turning in bed. Even in the moonlight, he could read her face: she seemed to have grown weary, and worried in his absence. He questioned whether he should wake her up. No doubt she had not slept well since he'd left her here. She needed rest. But he couldn't resist.

"Javan," she mumbled after he poked her. "Is that you?" Her eyes widened and she leapt from bed, fully awake. She embraced him so hard he nearly dropped the platter of candied oranges and lemons. "Ah, ah, thank Mazda for you… Thank Mazda you're home." She began to weep. "It's been so hard without you… without Yara…"

At the thought of his daughter, Javan joined in her weeping. Precious Yara was gone, but at least he was here, at home, with

Marit… here in her company, with the woman he loved most.

Eventually, her weeping trailed off. She took a step back. "Look at what you've brought me," she said.

The platter was silver, forged along the edges with shapes of monkeys and elephants. Marit, still weak with emotion, managed to pluck a candied orange and plop it in her mouth. "I will make tea," she said.

On the balcony, Marit and Javan sat, sipping the best Cathayan tea they had. Marit had awakened fully and begun expressing her displeasure with the day-to-day running of the palace, with servants who couldn't be trusted or couldn't be counted on to keep everything clean. She had gotten back to herself, back to the woman Javan loved.

It was late, perhaps later than Javan had ever stayed up, but he was wide awake, and as comfortable as he'd been in many days.

"I am worried," Marit at last said. Something had been bubbling just underneath the surface. "I've heard reports… people in the palace—our own household!—calling you a blasphemer, taking the side of the clerics."

"Don't worry," Javan said. "There was bound to be some tumult as we ripped those savages' power away. They will learn to love and trust us again."

"And there is something else," Marit said. She left her half-eaten candied lemons and entered the bedroom, returning moments later.

She returned with a vellum parchment that had bits of shriveled flesh attached to it. Javan recoiled in disgust.

"Do you remember that madman who came to the palace? The one who spoke of 'the King of the Dark' or whatever feeble-minded madness?"

Javan looked up into his wife's eyes, which had the look of horror in them. "Ahram," he replied. "His name was Ahram."

"He tried to flee Tadmor," Marit said. "He returned from the desert, headless. His camel had gone rabid."

Javan had never heard of a rabid camel.

"He had this attached to his flesh, sewn in like a piece of fabric."

Javan looked at the gruesome writing in disgust. The flesh, infinitesimal in size, had wilted and shrunken.

He did not want to think of Ahram, the madman, that way, even though he was a grave robber and a criminal. He could not imagine Marit's horror at the sight of him, riding back, headless, on a camel. Marit had never seen the true horrors of war before—and nor had Javan, truly, until this year. The Land of Tadmor had been at peace for centuries. Its peace was the greatest reason for its prosperity, the greatest reason for its triumph. In a matter of weeks, that had all changed; Javan, Wazir of Tadmor, had witnessed the death and destruction many hundreds. He had witnessed his warriors turn their swords and spears against their own people. He had seen kabakhs leveled, and clerics hanging on nooses… all at his command. The bloodshed had been his doing. For the first time in centuries, a wazir had stood up to the clerics. For the first time in centuries, a wazir had overcome the Mob.

"You need to get rid of this," said Javan.

He took it from his wife's hands, preparing to throw it from the balcony. In the moonlight, he caught sight of the writing. These runes were foreign. He recognized them. They were ancient. He had seen them in ruins, on stone tablets. They did not belong to the modern world.

"What kind of writing is this?" he said.

"Naamer," Marit said. "I was told it said, 'A thousand years of darkness.'"

A chill ran up Javan's spine. The number of Tammuri who could read this writing could likely be counted on one hand; and those who could write it, even less. Whoever wrote this, whoever intended to send a message, was a strange man indeed.

Chapter Thirty-One: A New World

The road continued, through canyons and gullies, between mesas and painted rocks. Kish grew closer with each passing day. Each hour, braving the burning sun, each day in waterless valleys bereft of life, drew them close to their end goal. Kish became a paradise in Yara's mind, a place of bounty and plenty where her troubles would, at last, cease.

She and Hatzor had worked out an uneasy truce. They spoke little during the day, and in night, at camp, they afforded each other the respect they both deserved. But in these weeks of journeying, they had not grown close. The incident with the Naamer idol only seemed to further poison Sister Hatzor against Yara. Now she was not only the young, overbold and haughty young Sister, but a reckless and careless one too.

In the ensuing days, a recurring dream had inflicted its way into Yara's psyche: a dream of old women, usually in groups of three, bearing staffs or swords of silver. In their eyes the light of the moon seemed to glow. They seemed to stare into Yara's heart, seeing her vulnerabilities and her flaws. She dared not bring it up to Hatzor, who remained cold and judgmental.

She had begun to understand her life as a Sister: her solemn vow to protect the Goddess's shrines from destruction. Some nights she still wept at the thought of losing Mother and Father, but this was her new life. She had a new purpose. She was a new person now. She was a woman, now, not a girl. She was a warrior and a protector of the Goddess's shrines. The Land of Tadmor, now gone forever, was a memory… an afterthought. She had a duty, now.

After a stretch of many hot days, and nights whose coolness did not help relieve her, Yara and Hatzor were headed through the desert in what was supposedly the final stretch.

Supposedly, somewhere beyond that endless blue horizon, the Heavenly Mountains would arise… the barrier to the green, lush land of Cathay.

One night at camp, Hatzor had told Yara: "Cathay would make Tadmor's greenery look like barrenness."

That night, Yara had questioned herself. She had wondered whether she should abandon her sacred oath and venture beyond Kish. She wondered whether she could become a maid to some rich Cathayan family and forget the terrors consuming the desert altogether.

Hatzor's words had braced her from that possibility. "Cathay is in trouble, too," she had said. "Wars without end. Invaders. Unrest. Perhaps, one day, even the Dragon Emperor will fall."

As dusk settled in, Hatzor and Yara pitched their tent beside a mesa. Its ochre color glistened in the light.

In the desert near Tadmor, there had been caravans, occasionally spotted, every few days, but here, in the long stretch between the Pillars of the Moon and Kish, they were utterly alone. Occasionally they would hear the howl of a desert dog, or the sound of a fox skittering away, but never the sight or sign of another human. Here, they were in true desolation. If they got in trouble, they would have no help. The terrors of the Lamia and the King of the Dark were gone, but other horrors had replaced them: hunger, thirst, a brutal journey, and the company of Hatzor.

Some scrub brush and a few scrawny trees allowed for the first fire in days.

Hatzor bunched the kindling and positioned the wood she had found, lighting it with a flint and tinder.

For dinner, they had once more the dry, tasteless waybread which had begun to sicken Yara's stomach. They had eaten nothing else since their visit to Saar. The memory of that chicken, seared with spices, was like a lost glimpse of heaven.

As the fire began to burn, Yara wanted to ask Hatzor how far off Kish was. She had remarked that they were close. But she bit her tongue, knowing she'd receive an acid reply. She nibbled her waybread.

As the light began to leave the sky, a screech owl began to sing. She thought of the three ladies she'd seen in the vision.

"Sister Hatzor," she at last decided to say. "I have been having a nightmare. Three old ladies, with the moon in their eyes, staring at me…"

In the dream they had been nude, with sagging bellies and breasts, wrinkled and old. Yet despite their innocuous appearance, Yara had sensed something eerie about them. They were more than women; they were dark goddesses, or demons from the dark beyond.

"I have never been much of a good counselor," Hatzor said. "I'm sorry your dreams are troubled, Yara."

"But didn't you say something about the Naamer… hags or something else?" Yara wondered if it tied back to that idol she had found, which now lay buried in the sand, waiting for another victim to claim it.

Hatzor peered into Yara's eyes. "Don't worry about it," she said. "We have enough troubles here, in the desert. Kish is still far off. And when we get there, we will have troubles all its own. The people of Kish are not known for their good morals."

Still far off. Hatzor had promised that their arrival was near at hand. Was she merely trying to soothe Yara? Was she trying to calm her down? Was she lying to her?

And Yara knew the reputation of Kish as a haven for bandits and lawlessness. She'd heard rumors that the Lord of Kish was a bandit himself, that he robbed guests and took a hefty price from each caravan unlucky enough to pass his way.

And yet the thing that bothered her the most was the nightmares, the dreams of the three old ladies, nude and unclothed in all their hideousness. Yara felt Hatzor knew more than she was letting on, but refused to comfort this "young and brash Sister."

Were Naamer gods, lost from history, now beckoning Yara

their way? She would not follow them. She would not heed their call.

The Naamer are evil, Hatzor had said. Their spirits remain to this day, in the desert, in the land they were born in. They are to be never admired, but to be feared.

The heat of the day had begun to wane. Their camels were thirsty and there was little water to spare. Hatzor obviously knew the way. Some oasis or watering hole had to be nearby. And yet, it seemed, with each passing day, Yara grew weaker. The waybread could not sustain her. She feared the sun and sand would claim her life.

"Hatzor," she said, "where are we?"

"We are in the middle of the desert," Hatzor answered with more than a little annoyance, "and we have a long way to go."

~

After dark, Yara left the fire, wandering away from camp in the darkness of the night. The moon was a poor lamp, and her eyes strained to see, but she wanted to fight something to eat… something, anything, besides the waybread she was sure was killing her. Even a lizard would be preferable. She had never tasted a lizard before. Back home, in her privileged life in Mahara, she'd heard of the very poor and destitute eating lizards, picking them apart bit by bit. A poor boy once told her they tasted slimey and gamey, like goo. Yet even that descriptor sounded better than the waybread, which now turned her stomach at the thought. Even the poor in the slums of Mahara ate better; they did not eat the same thing, day after day, for weeks. On holy feasts they'd sometimes get to eat the sacrificial lamb. Yet Yara, daughter of the wazir and wazira, born into riches and power, stood here, in the middle of the vast desert, lacking food, willing to eat anything and everything.

How had it come to this, she wondered. Did the Goddess's worship and protection demand such hardship? It seemed so.

As she began to stray further from camp, she began

overturning rocks, searching for lizards but never finding anything more than bugs. Mesas, like stone monuments, loomed in the distance. How had the Naamer existed in such a god-forsaken land? How had they endured the heat and desperation? Dry creek beds perhaps provided an answer, but even then, the land seemed too harsh. Even if there was water bursting from streams, and greenery everywhere, wasn't this land inherently cursed? Wasn't this land naturally destructive to life, under a harsh and hateful sun?

She found no lizard or any animal. She went to bed hungry, and continued on, wearily, as before.

~

Three more days passed, three long days in the sun, through gullies, beside canyons, between mesas, and through long stretches of desert with no shelter. The water had begun to run dangerously low, but Hatzor insisted an oasis lay nearby.

In the extreme heat, the air itself seemed to waver. The camels had begun to grunt. Even they were straining.

At dusk, they reached a salt pan: bright white, a sheet which stretched into the horizon. Yara had begun to become delirious: sightings of greenery and her hoped-for-oasis seemed to stretch into the distance, ever visible but never appearing. Twice Hatzor cried out, snapping at Yara that she was only viewing a mirage. Yara, too tired and weak to object to her harsh words, only plodded on, spending all her energy and focus on trying to stay in the saddle and not slip off. She had become numb.

"Hatzor," she mumbled, "I think I am dying."

As the dusk twinkled in the distance, the sun giving up its last dying embers on the horizon, the salt pan was behind them. Up ahead were mountains, taller beyond words, their towering peaks capped in white.

"The Heavenly Mountains," Hatzor said. "Kish."

It had been weeks since the journey began. Yara had lost count at fifteen days. She began to weep with joy. At last, they had found their destination. At last, she could rest.

~

In the foothills of the mountains, in the light of dawn, as the ground began to rise, there were streams and ponds in abundance, green scraggly pines appeared at first in clusters and then in a verdant forest. The sun's burning heat did not seem so oppressive in this land of running water.

At last their camels joined a road which was winding itself steadily upward toward the mountain pass and the fortress town of Kish which guarded it.

As they ascended, the skies became cloudy. A drizzle began, and then a harsh and heavy rain.

In Tadmor, rain was greeted with jubilation. Yet Yara felt no such thing; she only wanted to be indoors, to enjoy the comforts of civilization. The long journey was over. It was time to celebrate.

As the morning progressed, they passed travelers on the way, men and women in foreign garb. The men wore conical caps of green and brown, and the women wore their hair naked and uncovered. They did not acknowledge Yara. Instead of camels, those who rode, rode on horses. Their aloofness reinforced the fact that Yara was a Tammuri who did not belong. She began to dread the arrival at Kish.

Birds were singing, and occasionally she'd see one perched on the branch of a pine. Yara had never seen a place so green, so bountiful, so full of life.

Following Hatzor up the ascending mountain road, Yara secretly checked the folds of her robe, feeling the warmth of the Moon Pendant and ensuring it was still there. Who knew if one of these men of Kish, notorious bandits, had snatched it from her when she passed them by?

The road took them high, up on the roof of the world, where she could see the desert stretching into the interminable distance far below. Tadmor was too far to see, but beyond the white salt pan were the mesas and red monuments of natural stone which had become Yara's companion. She had never been so glad to leave the desert, but she knew the journey back would be just as long, and could prove dangerous.

~

The sun was baking when the road ended. A gate stood before them, and a towering wall of stone where archers stood, wearing the same conical caps as the people on the road.

The gate's giant wooden doors were open, allowing people to pass in and out, but men in iron breastplates guarded the way, wielding tower shields and hand-axes. Yara had seen such thickly-forged armor, sold by caravaners who came from Dwemer. They were embossed in gold, with designs of hawks. The people of Kish were tall, and they stood halfway up Hatzor's camel.

Hatzor stopped before them.

"Where do you come from?" one said.

"Saar," Hatzor said.

It was a total lie. Yara wondered why Hatzor's entry required deception.

"The Dogo of Kish demands everyone entering the city must have their belongings searched," the soldier continued. "Please dismount and remove all your saddlebags…"

"I come with myrrh and desert gold, to spend in your marketplaces," Hatzor said. "I will not enter if you touch my things."

The soldier looked at her for a while, and smiled. "Go on."

Hatzor urged her camel on, toward the city.

Yara tried to follow her, but was stopped.

The soldier was looking at Yara in a way that reminded her of Hiraz and Rafiz. She shuddered. She was not a vulnerable girl anymore, but she felt vulnerable again.

"And where are you from, young girl?" he said.

She shuddered.

"She is my maidservant!" Hatzor snapped. There was a cutting edge to her voice that seemed to cause him to recoil. "She comes with me! She is my property! Leave her alone!"

The soldier backed away, scared.

As bells rang in Kish, declaring that the hour was noon, Yara entered the mountain city, and exhaled.

~

Perhaps two-fifths of people in the streets of Kish were Cathayan merchants going this way and that, secluding themselves and avoiding the others. They stood out by their silken gowns, which even the men wore, and their eyes. Their wealth was evident compared to the natives of Kish. They seemed aloof, set apart, perhaps arrogant.

The buildings of Kish seemed to be carved from the very rock itself, and between streets there were wooden lattices, turning all of the town into a network of tunnels.

In the dimly-lit street corners, every few feet, there were merchants selling cargoes, and a dozen customers for every merchant, shouting and haggling, creating a cacaphony. Homes were carved into the stone, above the street level. The air was moist and cool. Candles and oil lanterns were burning on each doorstep as merchants eagerly hawked their wares: ivory statuettes, works of gold, vials of sacred oils, potions, Dwemer weapons, silken cloth and more.

Worried she'd get lost in the crowd, Yara kept near Hatzor,

trying at all times to stay close. The air was thick with the smell of spices and incense. Yara could tell, for all its cleanliness and gizmos for sale, that Kish was ancient, perhaps just as old as Tadmor.

"Hatzor," Yara said loudly, confident her voice would not carry above the crowd, "why did you lie to the gatekeeper?"

Hatzor turned her head, and for the first time in this endless journey, smiled at Yara. "Ah, my sweet, you have much to learn. If I'd let the gatekeepers search our things, at least some of it would disappear. The Dogo may lead Kish, but he is a robber at heart… as greedy as any bandit.His men are bandits, too. You must always guard yourself in this city… in this den of thieves!"

The street opened into a circular town square, where the sky was bear, revealing a cloudy firmament. The rain continued pattering down, but every inch of the square was nonetheless packed with people.

Music was playing: a plucking lyre and cascading dulcimer. A few women of Kish were dancing and laughing, their hair and faces uncovered. The clerics hated music, but they hated dancing even more.

A few young men were idling by them with piping hot drinks; Yara could smell the alcohol on their breaths.

What joy, what happiness: everything that Tadmor lacked. Perhaps one day, in better times, where life was more peaceful, when the cleric's yoke was not so heavy, Tadmor had been a place of happiness.

Up above the market, high above the buildings, was the slope of a mountain. There, carved into rock, was a giant stone entryway etched along the edges with runes. It seemed too large for human use, like a giant's lair.

Yara pointed, and before she asked, Hatzor said, "That is the Dogo's home, inside the mountain."

Yara could not believe human hands built a door so large. It racked her mind to think of it. How could man's hands build such a monument? How could they carve such a large space, such a large opening?

A road led up to the slope, barely visible from Yara's vantage point in Kish's town square. It was made of gravel, empty and silent.

~

In the town square, there was an inn. As they approached, Yara saw candles lighting windows on the upper stories, giving a warm, hearty glow.

A servant rushed up to them as they reached the door. "I shall take your camels, my lady! Welcome to the Mountain's Heart Inn!"

Yara dismounted. Hatzor followed, a step later. She began unloading the saddlebags, one after another, and the servant seemed annoyed. Some of the saddlebags jingled as Yara joined in—full of coins of silver and gold—while others contained the last bits of waybread. *Tonight*, she thought with relish, *I will eat good food, and sleep in a bed.* Her quarters would be as luxurious as hers in Mahara. She could not wait.

To her surprise, Hatzor, burdened with saddlebags, turned away and headed back into the heart of the town square. After gawking a while, Yara followed.

On the edge of the town square, just a street down, a building with a golden dome called itself the Safehouse of Kish.

"This is the only safehouse I trust," said Hatzor.

It was clear Hatzor loved this place. Where Yara felt out of place and perhaps insecure, Hatzor's mood had clearly improved. She had been here before, in this place of plenty. She thrived here. She had never treated Yara so kind.

They made their deposit for a small fee. This, according to Hatzor, would protect them from the Dogo's thieving hand. Yara wasn't as certain as her compatriot, but she didn't raise a fuss.

~

The room was cold, and the stone floor colder, but Yara—having taken a bath and wearing nothing more than her underclothes—counted herself lucky. There were two feather beds and her stomach was full of spiced chicken. For the first time in weeks, she could rest easy. For the first time in weeks, she could enjoy the comforts of civilization.

Hatzor had returned to her cold self, not speaking to her at dinner. The euphoria of her entry into Kish had perhaps worn off.

"Where will we take the Moon Pendant?" Yara said. "Where is the shrine?"

She had returned to her old worries. Despite this comfort, she was not here to enjoy herself. She had a sacred duty. She was here to protect the Goddess and her mortal possessions.

Hatzor was looking at her darkly, with a glare reminiscent of the darkest moments of the journey. "Don't worry about it, Sister Yara." Her voice was acid, caustic. It seemed her annoyance and derision had burst into open hatred.

Yara, hurt, had no one to turn to, no one to find comfort in. The Lily, who respected her, was not here to protect her. She was lonelier than she'd ever been.

To the Goddess, she said something like a prayer. Then she climbed in bed, blew out her candle, and tried her best to sleep.

Gray clouds were shifting across the moon, visible from Yara's window. The wind, blowing through the window lattice, was icy and cold, colder than anything Yara had experienced in the desert. Straining to sleep, she wondered about the streets below her, about the town outside. Even late in the night, there was the sound of voices and footsteps. In Mahara, the clerics demanded everyone stay in home past sundown, under punishment by the religious courts. Here, in Kish, there were still people wandering the streets, in darkness, like Lamia.

How far was she from home? She was across the world. She had never been this far, and neither had her father or mother or anyone she knew. The Tammuri were wealthy and wise; why would any of them have any reason to see the outside world? After all, that is where the foreigners live.

Now she saw, in her small, insular world — tiny island in a sea of sand — that she was wrong, that there was much the world had to offer. There were riches, and sights, and great monuments, far beyond what lay in Tadmor—though saying such a thing would be blasphemy back home. There were roads, and networks of roads, north and south and east of Kish; Yara wondered, if she followed them to their farthest extent, where would they take her? What sights would she see? What splendid kingdoms would she encounter? It was too bad one day she would return, to the terrors of the desert, to the troubled Temple of the Moon, sitting alone amid the darkness.

She fell asleep, dreaming of an old woman, naked, with the moon in her eyes.

~

At dawn's light, Yara was up. The main hall of the inn was full of people, and on the tables, patrons were feasting on sausages and drinking flagons of beer.

To this day, not a drop of wine or fermented drink had touched Yara's lips. To her, it was still forbidden, still taboo. The clerics' admonitions against "Devil's water" remained inexorable. She was a rebel, but not that much of a rebel.

She couldn't see Hatzor in the crowd. Where had she gone? Had she left her unannounced? Yara had never known her to be so inconsiderate.

Remembering she was in a den of thieves, Yara reached into the folds of her shirt and felt the warmth of the Moon Pendant's crystalline surface. The robber Dogo of Kish had not yet stolen the Goddess's most prized possession.

One of the inn servants approached her.

"My lady," she said, "we have fat pork sausages in the style of Xia and as much ale as you require."

Not knowing what else to do, or where else to sit, she found the only place available to her—between two boisterous merchants, caravaners by the look of them. They were dark, smooth skinned, wearing light white shirts and pants, laughing and talking boisterously. There were women among them, with their hair covered in colorful headscarves of red and pink. These were people of the desert; if not Tadmor, then some oasis town.

To their credit, they took no notice of her, understanding her plight. They spoke of the "good winds" which favored them in their desert, of their plans of a journey to the Cathayan cities of "Dongwo" and "Ul-Jian", and of jokes with one another.

Eventually a servant slid Yara's meal before her: a silver platter of more sausages than she could eat, a bowl of steaming hot rice, and a flagon of ale.

Dare she drink Devil's water, what the pagans and the foreigners guzzled on to "fuel their immorality?"

She started with the "fat pork sausage," spiced in ways she'd never tasted before. Soon, before she knew it, she had devoured every last link, and gone on to the rice. Thirsty, she eyed the flagon of beer, still resistant.

The folk of the desert, bunched around her, were openly drinking from their flagons. She would not be alone. But she would cross a threshold she had never crossed before. She would be condemned to eternal hell, the clerics would say, and if by chance they discovered her immorality, she'd be condemned to death, by stoning, by hanging, or by some other cruel means. Devil's water meant just that: water meant for a devil, for a heathen, for a disruptor of Mazda's will.

She grasped the flagon by the handle, raised it to her lips, and took a deep sip.

She almost spat it out.

But instead she braced against the unusual taste, unlike anything she'd ever had before. It was strange, bitter, almost doughey. Why did the heathens risk eternal damnation just for this?

But as she continued eating the rice, she found herself sipping from the flagon steadily. Before long, it was gone. She had become dizzy, and absent minded.

The woman sitting across from her, wearing a headscarf, was smiling. "Are you all right, young girl?"

She spoke the desert tongue. She sounded like her neighbors back home. "I am," she said. "Are you from Tadmor?"

She had spoken out of turn, perhaps inappropriately. Was it a cause of this flagon of beer?

But the woman took her uncouth words in stride and smiled. "We are all from Tadmor, young woman."

For some reason, it surprised Yara that she did not know this woman, even though Tadmor was home to hundreds of thousands of people. Yet she felt an instant connection. In this foreign land, she had likely neighbors.

"Where in Tadmor?" said Yara, intent on having them become fast friends. "I am from Mahara."

"We are from Mahara as well," the woman answered.

Yet Yara had never seen these people. She had never encountered them in the streets. She had never seen their faces.

"We left from Mahara thirty days ago," the woman continued. "I've never made such a fast journey. Everything seems to have lined up."

Thirty days. That was well into the time that Zathustra had been at the Temple, insisting all of Tadmor was destroyed. Why had he lied to her? Why had he deceived her to her face? She couldn't believe it. Mother, Father, still alive… She could have returned home. She could have warned them of the King of the Night and the coming darkness.

Had it been some fevered manipulation to keep her in the Temple? Or was there a darker, more nefarious motive? Had he intended to keep her there for some evil purpose?

None of it made sense.

But one thing was clear: Mother and Father could still be alive. If the darkness had not gotten to them, if the King of the Dark had not claimed them, she could still ferry them off somewhere to safety…

But now she questioned everything Zathustra had told him. Was there truly a King of the Dark? Were the terrors which haunted the desert truly dangerous?

Yes. She had seen their evil. From the observatory in the Temple, she had seen the dark king's armies. It was all real. The danger was true.

Had her best chance slipped away, unbidden from her hands?

"You had no trouble on the road?" Yara continued.

Collectively they became calm, perhaps somber. Despite the raucous crowd and the sounds of clinking flagons and plates, Yara had caused a grim mood among the travelers. There were four of them in all, two women and two men. Women were almost always forbidden to be caravaners; Mazda's law demanded punishment for it.

The woman Yara was speaking to gave her a sad smile. "We are not going back to Tadmor," she said. "I fear for its future… but in Cathay there is trouble—trouble like it has never seen before. Who knows where the road will take us?"

Clearly they were fleeing. Yara had seen firsthand the horrors. Had this woman also seen a Lamia? Had she begun a journey to Cathay, anticipating a return, but then deciding to never come back? Who knew? It was not Yara's task to find out.

She left the table, as abruptly as she had joined it. She wanted to curse at Hatzor for leaving her alone, in a city she did not know. What if something happened to her? Yara would never make her way back.

She stepped outside, onto the porch of the inn, shocked again by how crowded the town square was. She had thought Mahara was a big town. It was certainly the greatest of the cities of Tadmor.

But what Kish lacked in beauty, in white pillars and colonnades, it made up for in size and activity. Like a swarm of bees, the crowd was: yelling and urgently buying this ware or that. This Kish was a hive of commerce, and a place where everything under the sun was for sale.

Yara had never felt so homesick. It was cold here, up in the mountains. She did not know this place. The people were foreign; they were strange to her. They did not talk like she did; they did not dress like she did. Their women wore their hair long and uncovered, and did so with relish.

The men of Cathay, all dressed in splendid silk suits, seemed to keep the people of Kish at arm's length, but they too were different from the Tammuri, perhaps even more so.

Here Yara was, at the edge of the world, and there was much more in Varda than she ever dreamed of. The roads intersected. They went east, north, west, and south. She could go in any direction, and end up in a place she never thought possible.

There were dozens of languages being spoken. Here was the crossroads of the world.

Yara ventured further.

Stalls had been set up, around the perimeter and within the square itself. One woman was selling elephants of ivory, with emerald eyes. Another to Yara's left sold medicine: bowls of crushed herbs, organs in jars, and potions in glass vials.

Where was Hatzor? Had she gone far? Surely she would not

have left her here on purpose. Perhaps she thought Yara would be sleeping. She certainly thought that little of her.

She pressed on through the crowd. With each step, she grew less confident that Hatzor could be found. Perhaps she had gone somewhere far away, nowhere near the town square.

The gongs struck eleven o'clock. Yara pushed past more strangers.

A Cathayan man sat on a stool. His trained monkey was striking cymbals. Amused passersby were throwing coins into his collection bin.

Yara could sense something bad happening. There was a raw energy to this crowd which she couldn't explain, which she didn't like. She heard the sounds of shouting and argument. Trusting her instincts, she made her way back to the inn just as violence broke out.

She began to sprint away as the two factions converged. There was the sound of shouting and fistfighting, but as she reached the inn's doorway, she heard the sound of drawing daggers.

The innkeeper slammed the door shut as Yara bolted in, panting. "What was that?" she said.

The innkeeper said nothing, instead electing to duck away. She probably didn't speak Tammuri, anyway.

The woman from before was looking at her. "Come here, young woman."

Yara reluctantly assented, taking her seat.

Outside, despite the thick stone walls of the inn, she could hear the fight: the ring of steel against steel, the shouting, the savage blows. She couldn't believe such a battle was raging just outside, in the town square, a place of peace.

"One day this civil war will be resolved," the woman said. "What is your name, child? You look familiar to me…"

If the woman had seen Yara before, it wouldn't surprise her. She had appeared, on occasion, with her father on state visits. But she would not put them, or herself, in danger. "Hizra," she answered.

The woman did not seem convinced. Yara had always been a terrible liar. Father and Mother could always tell when she made a fib.

"You will find this city is a dangerous place," the woman continued. "But you may always count on me. I am Maryám. I and my party will be here for the next few days."

In truth, Yara did not want to keep Maryám's company. She did not trust anyone here, in this city of robbers, not even a Tammuri. Especially a Tammuri.

"The Cathayans hate the Kish folk, and the Mazdahi hate the Priests of the Stone God."

At Maryám's words, a shiver ran up her spine. There were Mazdahi here. The religion of Mazda had spread even to Kish. It was not at all surprising, but she would surely be a target: a young woman wearing her hair uncovered, in light silk garments. She would attract the outrage of the pious.

For some reason, she had not thought about it. She'd guessed Kish was like the Temple of the Moon—safe from Mazda and his laws, safe from the clerics and the Thul, and safe from the zealous Mob. She had been utterly wrong. And now she felt even more vulnerable than before.

It made sense. Mazda's followers were everywhere across the desert. That they had spread here was unremarkable. What was remarkable was that Yara—having removed herself from their overbearing power—had forgotten the true extent of Mazda's followers and their law. She had become accustomed to liberty and freedom. In just months, some of the horrors of the Thul and his clerics had been washed away. Now, her heart was racing. Would the black flag of the Mazdahi be raised over Kish, soon?

Maryám laid a hand on Yara's. Perhaps she could sense her terror. "Be calm, young girl," she said. "You are safe."

But Maryám could not calm her. No one could calm her. She wondered if anyone in this room was a follower of Mazda, if he noted her Tammuri origins and then that her hair was uncovered. She could only wonder. She would never know.

The sound of the shouting and battle died down. The innkeeper opened the door and Yara got up.

In the center of the square, there were bodies, bloody and beaten. The guards of Kish, soldiers of the Dogo himself, had not bothered to intervene. Instead, they had allowed the massacre to occur. Yara had never felt so vulnerable, or so alone.

Chapter Thirty-Two: The Awakening

Marit wished she hadn't told Javan about the parchment she had found, sewn into the body of the headless rider. Their brief, life-giving reunion had been shattered. The next morning, he had departed, vowing to find out who had beheaded this "Ahram" in his bid to protect the country.

Marit once more had begun secluding herself in her room. She sat on the balcony. She had given orders to her servants to bring her food and tea throughout the day. She had become a recluse, like she had in the wake of Yara's vanishing. She had withdrawn totally. Her husband was off on some new adventure, trying to save a land that could not be rescued; and she sat here, on a chair, on the balcony, viewing the city she loved in the light of sunrise. Her cooks had made her a breakfast of yogurt and fruit, orange slices and candies made from date honey, but she had lost her appetite. She was too fearful for her husband and for this land, Tadmor, which seemed doomed to slip into darkness. Still she picked apart the orange slices and sipped occasionally at her tea.

She did not know what the future held for Mahara or for the Land of Tadmor as a whole. She only knew that the stabbings continued, night after night: vigilantes, whether filled with self-righteousness or some selfish desire for power, were causing chaos in the streets. A week ago, the wife and son of a warrior had been slain in their beds, and on the wall, the sign of a black fist had been painted. The Black Hand continued to exert its deadly grip over the city, and each night it seemed the violence increased, and their numbers grew. Soon, it seemed, all of the impoverished and the lower classes would join in, taking up the mantle of piety, seizing on a righteous cause while looting and robbing.

Yes, times were tough; and Javan had gone off again in search of an enemy he would never find. Whichever bandit or brigand sent that gruesome message would never be found. Whichever bandit, learned enough to write in Naamer script to send the grisly letter, could easily evade capture. He posed no true threat to Tadmor. The threat, as always, came from within, from the zealous and easily-impressioned masses.

Javan had driven the clerics away, for their own good, and this is how they answered him?

There was a knock at the door.

She had already been served her breakfast. Everyone in the palace had been warned not to bother her. Still she stood up. She would answer this disobedience with a lashing of the tongue.

She pushed through the curtains into her bedchamber.

At the door, she hesitated. She could shout from afar, and belittle this person without showing her face.

She twisted the knob, seeing the figure of Tigra.

Could she truly say no to this earnest soul?

The young woman had donned a turban.

The black strips of cloth had been tied around her head in a ball.

She had never worn such attire before.

Marit, normally receptive to Tigra's presence, found herself balking.

"It is Ascension," Tigra said, perhaps sensing Marit's unease.

But her words built it only further. The Feast of Ascension was not celebrated except among certain sects, and among those sects, only the truly devout put on any display of piety. Celebrating the rising of the prophet Mali into heaven on a winged horse, festivities were underway in some villages all this week… at least they had been, before Javan declared war.

Tigra's newfound devotion struck Marit as odd. She gazed at her a while, but Tigra, taking advantage of her action, pushed on through, into the room.

"I did not know you were so devout," Marit said.

"Does it bother you?" Tigra said.

Marit would not tell her the truth.

This servant girl, so pampered, so spoiled, had the arrogance to barge into her wazira's bedchamber. She needed a stern talking-to, and perhaps something harsher.

Marit, Wazira of Tadmor, would not be treated so. "You must leave now," Marit said sternly. To her surprise, there was fear rising up in her voice.

In a panic she stumbled backward, grabbing a candlestick. She screamed "Help!" as Tigra unwound the strips of fabric in a single tug, releasing a dagger from hiding.

Tigra leapt upon her and stabbed just as warriors came in, shouting, from the hall. They grabbed Tigra from behind and ripped her from her assassin's perch.

Tigra was screaming about Mali and the prophets and about piety. Marit had never witnessed such hate in anyone's eyes. A blind rage had consumed her.

She had hid her true self so well.

The dagger lay bloodied by Marit's side. She was bleeding and a pool was gathering on the floor.

In a moment, she was swarmed by servants, like honeybees swarming their queen. There were screams and amid some, weeping.

She could not feel any pain. She could not feel anything at all. "Kill her!" one of her servants shouted.

"No!" she answered. "Keep her alive."

As blood gushed from the wound and frenzied servants brought forth a stretcher, they heeded her call. She still could not believe what happened. She had trusted this woman, a servant she had known from girlhood. She would wring the truth out of her, whether she resisted or not.

As she was hauled into the stretcher, a servant pressed a gauze to her wound.

With pained faces, they followed her as she was hauled toward the infirmary. She was here, among people who were still devoted to her. She had misread Tigra, not knowing she was a viper. Tigra had told her about all manner of conspiracies, all while concealing her true intentions. What words of hers could be believed?

She had no time to think. Her wound had begun to hurt and throb in earnest. She cried out in pain.

What would Javan think? How guilty would he feel that he had left her here?

She tried not to cry or show her anguish as she was ferried across the hall, across the marble tile which had been carried in from far-off quarries, beyond gold-lined pillars, symbols of her great wealth. But what worth was wealth at a moment like this?

She was old. She wondered if her body could survive the trauma. She wondered if Tadmor's best physicians could cure someone like her.

~

Late at night, Marit could not sleep. Still lying on the cot in the infirmary, she noted that the bleeding had been stopped, but the pain continued. She uttered prayers to whatever god or spirit would hear her, to her mother's ghost, now long in the grave, to the ancient spirits, to the Naamer, even to the Dark One, Shemesh, himself. She did not beseech them to save her life, but instead to wreak vengeance on these wicked sons of serpents: the clerics, who had made war on the Beautiful Land, and brought it so low.

Chapter Thirty-Three: A Hasty Departure

Javan's wife had given him an earful when he left.

"You cannot solve this!" she had said.

"A bandit, alone, in the desert, isn't worthy of attention!"

Perhaps she was right.

He stood on the edge of the desert. Here, where he stood, there was grass and mixed shrub trees. Just yards ahead, there was sand, and in the distance, dunes. A sand sea surrounded Tadmor, harsh and unforgiving in its nature. Only the greatest preparations and the most advanced knowledge allowed caravaners to travel it. The desert was the great killer of old. It had claimed countless lives throughout millennia. Only those who respected her, and feared her, could survive her.

The day's heat had almost reached its apogee. The sun was midway in its journey across the sky, bearing down on Javan and all unlucky enough to be in its path. The sand seemed to glisten. It was hard to look, hard to breathe, hard to stare.

Two of his emirs, Rashad with his saber and shield, and Moktata with his spear, stood just behind him. They awaited his orders. But against such a strange enemy, an enemy who posed little threat to Tadmor, was investing the army the right decision? He knew what Marit would say.

But Javan had an inkling that this letter was not innocuous; that it meant something more. Who wrote in Naamer script? Who knew that dead language, in the world of the living? Who would write it, in the modern day, and attempt to communicate a message? There was some mystery Javan had to solve, some secret he had to uncover. "Where is the closest place a bandit might take cover?" he said.

Moktata stepped forward. "Seven miles out, there are caves, with water and springs," he said. "Bandits are known to haunt them from time to time… and criminals passing along the way."

The journey would take a day in the blistering heat and sand, at best. It would be an investment in water, in food, and perhaps in lives. And it could amount to nothing.

He turned to Rashad.

The emir was among his youngest, with a handsome face, a short cut beard and trimmed long hair. Yet those who accused him of effeminacy were wrong; he was among the bravest men Javan had ever met, and he had never backed down from risk or combat. Javan had absolute faith in him. He was the equal of Moktata. It did not matter what people said; Javan knew his worth.

"Take as many men as you think you need," Javan said. "Go with them to those caves. Kill anyone you see there. Search their belongings. Bring everything back…"

"Will you go with us, my lord?" Rashad said.

The thought had not occurred to him. It was unthinkable. It was risky. If he died, Tadmor would fall into further chaos. But Javan was not a coward.

"Do not go, my lord," Moktata insisted. "We need you here."

Courage or foolheartedness prompted Javan's words: "I will accompany you, Rashad. In my absence, Moktata, you are commander of the armies…"

The next day, the soldiers gathered, one-hundred in all. Moktata had departed from Mahara. Javan questioned his actions, whether he had made a mistake. He knew full well that the bandits may have left, or may have never even hid in the caves at all. But no other sanctuary from the desert dryness and heat was close enough; no other made sense. Whoever had beheaded Ahram and sent him back as a message-bearer was close. Fate had given Javan a dice, and he would roll it.

Chapter Thirty-Four: Statues

Yara had spent half the day wandering idly through the tunnel-like streets of Kish.

On every corner there were wares from every corner of the world: whalebone carvings from what the merchant called the "Icy North" in addition to blubber and seal-skins; spices of every kind from the Far South, as well as rubber and indigo; arms and armor forged in Dwemer and hauled in by ox-cart; and porcelain, silk, and every precious commodity that could be found in Cathay. In her cautious walk, she had seen no trace of the Mazdahi: no black-robed men in turbans, no zeal-filled followers or preachers shouting on the street corner.

The conflict in the market had been between Cathayans and Kish folk. But Yara remained certain that the Mazdahi were here. They were watching her. They were everywhere.

Gongs were striking noon as she re-entered the inn. She could not believe the gall of Hatzor, leaving her here, alone. Here, in a city she did not know, with endless days of desert between here and home, Yara could not truly fend for herself. She did not know the ways of Kish. Many could not even speak the desert languages. Here she was isolated. She was alone.

When she entered through the inn's doors, Maryám was thankfully gone. The inn's servants had begun tying blue and gold ribbon's around the walls and in between the windows. The scent of sweets and baking was omnipresent. The heat from the kitchen's fires had seeped into the main hall.

The innkeeper stood behind a desk. She was a Cathayan woman, as it seemed a great many in Kish were.

"What's going on?" she said.

"The Moon Festival begins at sundown," she answered.

Yara nodded absently. She knew little of Kish's festivals and holidays. Though the Mazdahi were undoubtedly here, the vast majority of Kish folk were unbelievers. She took comfort in the fact that the clerics and the Thul and Mazda's so-called law had not taken root. But as the faith had spread since its inception, it would continue. The goal of the clerics was not piety, but to spread its influence, until the whole world would rule under the Law of Mazda, until "the decrees of mankind are null and void, and the rule of kings are irrelevant." That is what the street preachers said in Tadmor.

At dusk, Hatzor appeared, meeting Yara's gaze.

She did not look regretful about her inconsiderate actions. She did not seem guilty or bothered.

Yara stormed up to the inn's doorway and met her, biting her tongue. She would try her best not to spoil what was left of her fractured relationship, not when she was a foreign land and in danger. "Where were you?" she said. Some of her hostility escaped, and Hatzor sensed it.

"Am I your keeper, Sister Yara?" she said.

She was toting bags, no doubt filled with precious commodities and foodstuffs. She had left unannounced, just to browse the market stalls. She had put her own greed and avarice above Yara.

"I am alone, here," Yara said. She was fighting back tears. "I don't know my way around here. You abandoned me."

"Don't make a scene," Hatzor growled. "And I thought you were made of sterner stuff. After all, the Lily said *you* should be the caretaker of the Moon Pendant… something far beyond your status."

There were a thousand things Yara wanted to say to Hatzor, a thousand ugly things. She bit her tongue again. She wiped her eyes and stormed off, taking a seat in the shadows of the inn.

~

Hatzor did not emerge from their room, but Yara was not

inclined to join her. She stayed in her seat as the main hall once again began to fill. She saw Maryám and tried to duck away into the shadows, but she was not invisible.

The woman had donned a headscarf embroidered with flowers and a rose-colored gown that would be far too tight for the clerics back home. Thank the Goddess, she took no notice of Yara and left her alone. Yara was free to enjoy her solitude, and stew.

At dusk, a meal was served, but still Hatzor did not emerge. Perhaps she had called for her food to be delivered to the room.

Musicians had taken the stage: Cathayans, playing sitars.

Almost everyone here was a foreigner: from the desert, from Cathay, from elsewhere.

As great silver platters of pork dumplings, emerging hot from the kitchen, were carried to various tables, servants brought forth pitchers filled with wine and began to pour them into patrons' cups. Yara had ventured to drink a tall glass of ale; would she complete her entry into heathendom, and drink what clerics across history despised most of all?

Beyond the pork dumplings, more feasts were carried in, sometimes on hot plates, other times on trenchers: pastries of all kinds, cookies, cakes, and candies; roast duck with all its accoutrements; steaming hot vegetables and more. Clearly, this was a feast day, and one which the owners of the Mountain's Heart Inn took seriously.

What would the Thul, back home, with all his imperious decrees, think of this pagan feast? What would they think of the wazir's daughter participating in it? Yara no longer cared. It did not matter what he thought.

As music rose up, and Yara began eating the pork dumplings with their various sauces, some inn patrons stood up and began to dance about. They were men and women, dancing; Cathayan maidens in bright silk gowns, desert folk in their light white clothes, even Maryám in her modest veil, prancing about sensually to the tune of the music. If music was anathema to the clerics, then dancing was the

Devil's work, and men and women dancing together was worthy of the worst damnation. Still, Yara did not feel stirred. Lethargy had set in. Her glass goblet, filled to the brim with wine, was untouched. For now, she was away from Hatzor, safe in a shadowy prison of her own making.

She watched Maryám and the men and women with her march across the room to the beat of the music. There was a sprig in their step as the speed of the music intensified.

This was the Moon Festival, apparently an excuse for dancing and disollute drinking.

Yara took a sip of her wine. She puckered, amazed at the intensity of the flavor. She didn't entirely like it. But she found herself sipping more and more. Outside, the sky was darkening. Torches were brought in to light the room. Out of the corner of her eye, Yara saw Hatzor descending the staircase; their eyes met and a look of rage seized her face. She walked over, pushing past the dancers, to sit just across from Yara.

"What are you drinking?" she snapped just as she sat down.

"Wine," Yara answered, "and a lot of it." She smiled mockingly at her.

"Devil's water…"

"You sound like a Mazdahi… have you abandoned the Goddess, Hatzor?"

Hatzor slapped Yara. She winced at the pain. Tears formed in her eyes. Again, Yara was a little girl, vulnerable and alone. She realized, despite how much she despised this harridan, she was dependent on her. Hatzor held Yara's life in her hands.

"I am your senior, Sister Yara, even if the Lily does not act like it…" Hatzor grimaced. "And Devil's water, it may not be… the Goddess may allow her followers to drink it. But it is not good for you. It causes the mind to become porous. It causes morals to become loose. No woman should drink it; nor any man."

Hatzor was not Yara's mother; but Yara would not win this

fight. She pushed the wine goblet away and said meekly, "I am sorry."

She wasn't sorry, of course, but Hatzor had broken her.

Hatzor laid a hand on Yara's. "I am sorry, too, Yara…"

"I am far from home… I didn't ask to be a Sister… I didn't ask for any of this…"

"Hush," Hatzor said. "It will be all right. I will take you home soon enough…"

~

When Yara entered the inn's main hall the next morning, Hatzor was waiting for her. She had donned a pair of boots which she had evidently purchased yesterday, and clutched a walking stick in her right hand. Wrapped around her body like a mantle was a fur coat. Tins filled with water dangled from her shoulders on a strap.

She had purchased all those items yesterday for the journey ahead. Yara should not have been so cynical. Lying next to her, on a table, was another, smaller fur cloak and another walking stick. They were up to Yara's specifications, for her slighter build.

Hatzor was smiling.

"Go on and don your clothes, Yara," she said. "It's a hard journey to Whistle Gorge."

~

The cloak was bracingly warm indoors, but as soon as Yara stepped outside, into the cold mountain air, she was glad to be wearing it. The walking stick she clutched would help her balance among unsteady mountain roads. She slipped her hand underneath the cloak and touched the Moon Pendant to make sure it was there. She could not afford to journey to the Goddess's sanctuary and then be empty handed.

She felt its crystalline warmth and breathed a sigh or relief.

The Goddess's pendant, the sign of her love and warmth in the world, remained safe in Yara's possession. It would return to the mountain shrine, where it belonged.

Together, Hatzor and Yara wound their way through Kish's dark, tunnel-like streets, avoiding the shouts of overeager merchants. It seemed everyone in Kish had one goal in life: to make a profit. But Yara paid them no mind, and Hatzor had grown adept at avoiding their cries. No one accosted them while Hatzor led the pack. On and on they walked, until they reached the East Gate, and passed beyond, onto a packed-dirt mountain road.

The wind hit them as soon as they left the shelter of the city's stone walls and tunnels. The wind was bracing; it was harsh, and icy in temperature. For a moment, Yara couldn't breate. She quickly got a handle on things.

The path wound its way through the slope. The pine trees provided little shelter. Whistle Gorge, Hatzor insisted, was not far away, and they would get there before nightfall.

The path opened up into a large vista, and as a pelting rain began, Yara took a gander at the vast expanse of desert below. It stretched beyond her vision, and the bracing heat, the dryness, the mesas and canyons, seemed a world away, though she could see them now. Somewhere out there, beyond countless miles in the harsh heat, lay the blessed Land of Tadmor. Despite Zathustra's warnings, it was still there. Yara had a chance of seeing Mother and Father again.

But she had a duty now. She doubted she would ever return. It was her solemn oath to protect the Goddess's temple and sanctuaries, to revere her power and her wisdom. It was Yara's duty to keep the Temple safe from the darkness which threatened to surround it.

She turned away from the breathtaking vista and went on their way, up the rocky slope, as the dirt path made its way upwards.

Up the arduous path, a meadow opened up, overgrown with

grass and bright purple wildflowers. The sun had begun to shine through the clouds as the rains dwindled. The air was fresh and sharp with the scent of pine. Here Yara was, on the roof of the world. For the first time since she'd left the Temple of the Moon, she was happy. She had set out on this journey, with a perilous goal, and here she was at its terminus. She was almost at the so-called "Whistle Gorge" and the shrine of the Goddess whom she served.

Birds were singing, and every once in a while one would flitter this way and that, displaying their brown and black feathers. Hatzor kept a relentless pace, a pace which Yara would never have matched before her months of training as a Sister.

As the ground ascended, the wind blew colder.

The sun was growing low in the sky when—after an exhausting hike up a steep patch of road—the ground opened up far below them. Between two snowy peaks was a deep rift in the ground, a canyon covered in green pines with a blue river at the bottom.

"Whistle Gorge," Hatzor said.

The climb down was steep, a harrowing descent down many hundreds of feet. One false step and Yara could injure herself severely.

Something had changed about the light. The silvery clouds now covered the sun. A wind was picking up. It had grown slightly darker. Yara drew her saber.

~

At the bottom of Whistle Gorge, the sound of the river was omnipresent, gushing against the rocks. A deer had scurried away just as they made their descent. Here was a land full of life, full of plenty. It was a fitting place for the Goddess's sanctuary.

Yet as for people, she saw no sign of them. She and Hatzor were alone.

The road wound through this bright green forest as lightning struck ahead, and thunder rolled. A storm was beginning. Had Hatzor brought shelter?

She did not halt her pace as the winds and rain began. She pressed on through Whistle Gorge, and Yara followed her.

At the end of the road, a door had been carved out of the mountainside. The door was immense, as large as the palace door back in Mahara. The stone itself was etched in brick patterns, to make it look like an arch. Yara wondered if modern man could still do such wonder-work, or if only the ancients knew how. Clearly the stonemasons in Mahara would not be capable of such awe-inspiring height and breadth. An elephant, outfitted with a war tower, could easily pass through the entryway.

A few yards before the opening, Hatzor stopped and removed her pack. From it she drew two cloth-wrapped torches. She lit one and the oil-soaked fabric burst into flame. She lit the other and handed it to Yara.

"Remove your boots," Hatzor said. "This is a holy place."

Bare-footed, feeling the mountain path turned to mud, Yara scurried in through the doors of the mountain shrine.

The light, purging the darkness, revealed a giant chamber with a vaulted ceiling. Set against the wall was a statue of surprising smallness.

It was the size of a woman, carved from marble. The nose and the eyes had been chipped away. Some of the fingers were missing. Time had not been kind to this image of the goddess, but she recognized the outstretched hand, the long hair, tied in braids. Once, this had been a beautiful imagining of the Goddess, sculpted by an ancient architect.

In a way, it was disappointing to see such a remarkable entry, just to see a statue degraded and partially destroyed.

"Who did this?" Yara said. "How could they have so little respect?"

The more she viewed the white marble, the less she thought

time had been the destructive force behind it. Deliberate destruction had wounded this structure, but by whom?

"The Prophet Mali, when he spread the religion," Hatzor began in a hushed tone, "he overran Kish. The Law of Mazda ruled the town for fifty years. Every image was to be smashed. Eventually one of his footsoldiers discovered this shrine. He tried to chisel it away, but he was sent away blinded. He returned to Kish a cripple, with no memory of what came before.

"Now the Dogo protects the shrine. He has no time or favor for the Mazdahi… It has been protected by his forebears for centuries now."

Yet if the Dogo was the warden for the shrine, Yara did not have a lot of confidence in him. By all accounts, he was a robber and a bandit.

"Is the Moon Pendant safe here?" Yara said.

Hatzor grimaced. It looked like she was ready to strike her. "So impudent, so untrusting… what did the Lily see in you? Give me the Pendant!"

Yara had begun to realize why Hatzor despised her so. Yara, the youngling, unproven among the Sisters, was honored with carrying the Moon Pendant. Not with Hatzor, with all her experience, who was aging. Hatzor was one of the highest ranking Sisters… but all the duties had been given to Yara.

"No," Yara said. It was the boldest thing she'd done since the journey began. She sheathed her saber and drew the Moon Pendant from the folds of her clothing. It gleamed in the torchlight.

"You are rude and spoiled," Hatzor said. "Give it to me. That Moon Pendant is far too valuable for you to handle. You are a youngling. A novice!"

"No!" Yara shouted. For once, she had asserted herself. For once, she had stood up to Hatzor's harsh words, her harsh glare.

But if her show of strength felt empowering, Hatzor was having none of it. Angrily she dropped her torch, which quickly extinguished in the wet, hole-ridden floor. She drew her dagger. "Give it to me," Hatzor roared, "or I will cut you!"

Yara wouldn't back down now. She dropped the Moon Pendant and stepped in front of it. "Come and take it!" she roared back.

Hatzor was not herself. She was not thinking. She had become something altogether nonhuman, an avatar of inchoate rage. Screaming, she charged Yara with the dagger. Jealousy had overcome her. She was not a Sister anymore.

Yara knew Hatzor intended to kill her. She was serious.

Yara dropped her torch and drew her saber, right in the nick of time to parry Hatzor's thrust. Then she slashed hard, opening a wound in Hatzor's chest.

As Hatzor fell, bleeding, Yara winced at the sight of what she'd done. She had cut down a Sister before the statue of the Goddess.

Was that statue leering at her? No. It was warm.

Hatzor was crying out as she bled on the floor.

Yara pitched back her saber with both hands, and delivered the mercy strike. Tears formed in her eyes as she witnessed the savagery.

Over these months, she had changed irrevocably. She was no longer Precious Yara. She was a warrior. And now a killer.

Weeping, she dragged the corpse away, which still bled out onto the porous stone floor. She dragged it out of the darkness, out of the shrine, and into the woods. Would she bury the body of Hatzor? No. She would let the vultures eat it.

When she returned to the cool and darkness of the shrine, her torch remained burning. The water had not gotten to it. The Moon Pendant glistened in the warm light.

Tears were streaking Yara's cheeks. She had committed

murder in a holy place, in a temple; was that not much worse than entering with sandals? She had defiled this place.

She picked up the torch from the ground.

She eyed the Pendant of the Moon, wondering if she still had a right to touch it, to be its caretaker.

But she had not come here for herself. She had not even come here for the Lily.

She had come here for the Goddess, a being she still did not entirely know or understand.

"I am sorry," she said to the statue, hoping the Goddess would hear her.

But the statue remained still. The broken fingers did not reach out to her for absolution. The head, marred by a chisel, refused to move. It was as still and lifeless as it had been, carved millenia ago.

She cried out again, "I am sorry, Goddess!"

She stooped down and grabbed the Moon Pendant which she did not deserve to guard. She approached the statue and, with one hand, laid the Pendant around the Goddess's neck.

Here the Pendant would remain… here, in the Shrine of the Moon in the region of Kish, where it belonged.

Chapter Thirty-Five: Visions

Marit lay in bed, as she had for many days. Each morning, afternoon and evening, the palace physician came in to check on her. He scanned the entries in his medical tome and examined the wound, which—early in the day—he had declared with delight: "It is healing! No sign of infection."

But Marit, now alone in her bedroom, knew what a toll the wound had taken on her. She was weaker than she'd ever been, and had never felt so unsafe. If Tigra could betray her, who else could?

And Javan was gone.

He had been gone for days, and there were varying reports of where he was: that he had gone to quash a rebellion in a village, that he had discovered the Thul hiding out in a desert oasis and had ventured to go kill him, or that he had gone searching for bandits in the desert. None made sense, but his absence only increased Marit's vulnerability. She was not herself, and she was growing more fearful by the day. She had begun to think she and Javan should leave Tadmor altogether: an astounding idea, one which the wazir and wazira would never embark upon.

But she had become consumed with fear: fear about this land, about the enemies within Tadmor, and increasingly without. She had dreamed dreams in her pain: vivid nightmares of the dead rising again from their crypts, of shadows as tall as date palms, of rapacious monsters feasting on the flesh of humanity. All of it was a product of her disturbed mind, of her terror. She did not want to rule the Land of Tadmor anymore. She wanted to run. She wanted to flee.

But where could she flee to? And how could she? How could she abandon Tadmor? She was the wazira, the premier woman of the Tammuri people. She was Tadmor. She was anchored in this land. She was its figurehead. She could not be moved, not any more than the very earth itself.

This Land, blessed with fabulous wealth, was under siege. But though the true threats were the Black Hand and the Mob, she wondered if there was a greater enemy. Her thoughts kept going to the border, to the shadowy desert which had always threatened to encroach. Was there a greater enemy just beyond this bounteous land?

"Javan," she murmured, "come back soon."

Part Three: Truth in Shadows

The Wazir of Huddin sat still in his throne.

"My lord," one of his warriors said, and beat his spear into the marble tile of the throne room. "The Thul of Tadmor wishes to speak to you…"

"No!" the Wazir thundered for the third time. The Thul had camped outside the palace gates like a beggar, demanding he be allowed to speak.

But the Wazir of Huddin wanted no part of the Thul. He would grant the clerics no more power than they already demanded. His people, and all the people of the Coastal States, lived in fear of them and their Mob.

He'd heard word that the Wazir of Tadmor, Javan, had outlawed them altogether and razed their kabakhs to the ground. It was bolder than the Wazir of Huddin would dare, who clung still to some semblance of religious faith. Pushing back against the cleric's encroaching power, yes; but declaring war on the religion itself, and living in opposition to the Mazdahi? It did not seem wise.

As his warrior turned to deliver the stern news, he shouted, "If the Thul asks again… kill him!"

Chapter Thirty-Six: Moons

Yara did not cry or weep as she ascended the road, as the darkness set in.

She had slain Hatzor. She had committed an egregious act, even before the Goddess's own statue.

Yet Yara knew, in her heart, that she'd had no choice. She'd had no other option. In that moment, she either had to kill Hatzor, or be killed herself. Hatzor had become a creature of consummate rage; she had become murderous.

Though Yara was now lost, with no way of returning home, she remained calm as the darkness settled in. With luck, she would return to Kish and not get lost.

The rain began to die down. Still, Yara was soaking wet as she left the valley. It would be a long night, a hard battle and a difficult journey.

~

In the middle of the night, Yara passed through Kish's East Gate. On the stone-paved roads, she no longer had to worry about her shoes getting muddy. She relished the thought of returning to the Mountain's Heart Inn.

From Hatzor's coin purse she had recovered many silver coins, worth several pounds. If it was robbery, she'd have to beg the Goddess' forgiveness. There was no other way out for her. And it would not last forever. Sooner or later, she would be on the streets.

Down the tunnel-like streets she walked, in pitch blackness. There were no guards to protect her from robbers. If one got to her, they would take all she had.

Ducking away at the sound of voices, trying her best to avoid the open streets, she at last made it to the town square, where torches remained burning and small crowds still lingered late into the night.

A woman grabbed hold of Yara and she screamed. She was emaciated and looked sickly. Her gangly hand was covered in sores. "Are you lonely, young girl?" she said.

Yara pushed her away as hard as she could.

The prostitute fell over on her back. Yara took off at a sprint and didn't stop running until she passed through the open doors of the Mountain's Heart Inn.

To her surprise, the hearth was still burning, and a few were gathered in the main hall. Servants were attending to them: patrons, huddled together in the shadows.

Yara was shivering.

Her fear had awoken her. She did not want to sleep. She only wanted to flee from her fears, from robbers, from Mazdahi, from the situation she had found herself in. What would she do? How could she survive?

She sat as near the hearth as she could. In the warmth, the chill began to fade. Like a blanket, the heat soothed her. Forgetting about her worries, forgetting about the future, she sat there, slumped against the stone. She shut her eyes. Soon enough, she was asleep.

~

She woke with a start, exhausted, seeing the main hall was deserted and the fire in the hearth had burned to twinkling embers.

She headed to her room, though the further she got from the hearth, the colder the air grew.

That night, wrapped in sheets of linen, she slept well for the first time in months.

~

She spent the following day in the main hall, plotting her next move. She wondered what on earth she could do. She could not navigate the desert herself. She did not know where to go. To travel such a hellish world, one had to know where the oases were, where they could fill up on water amid the parched landscape. Yara did not possess the know-how or the skills to do it.

And so she found herself in a prison of her own making. She counted the silver she had, and found that she had only six more days in the Mountain's Heart Inn before all her money ran out. She could sell the camels, perhaps, at a loss, but even that would only sustain her for a short period of time.

Could she rely on the goodness of the people of Kish? If she held out a silver platter, would they be inclined to drop coins within? She had doubts about her long term survival.

Perhaps the Goddess demanded blood for the murder of Sister Hatzor.

As the day wore on, she became more withdrawn. She had become convinced of her impending death. As the cooks brought forth their pastries and various meats for the evening meal, yet another day in the Moon Festival celebration, Yara had all but lost her appetite.

She was startled to look up and see Maryám walking toward her.

She was bold enough to have a smile on her face, though Yara had lost all capacity for one.

"Hail!" Maryám said.

It was remarkable, in all this time, she had not learned Yara's name. Yet this full grown woman, perhaps thirty years old, somehow seemed drawn to Yara. If their paths crossed, she had to approach her, even when Yara wanted to be left alone—like she did now.

Yara managed to lift her head and wave weakly at Maryám. Yara did not want to eat; she did not want to drink. She did not want to talk. She wanted to sit and stew in the darkness, and ponder her fate. There was nothing else to do but accept it. She would become a homeless vagrant, or perhaps she'd end up like that woman who'd approached her, pock marked with scars, selling her body to whoever passed by.

The thought made her want to recoil.

Maryám took a seat in front of her. Surely she could tell how Yara felt, how she wanted to be left alone. But it didn't seem to bother Maryám. As one of the scullions came scurrying out of the kitchen, she snapped her fingers. He set two goblets of wine on the table, one in front of Yara, the other in front of Maryám.

If there was one thing Yara wanted less than Maryám's attention, it was wine. Devil's water. The one drink, the one thing, all Tammuri were forbidden to have.

In ancient times, before the arrival of Mazda's Law, there was a vine in every yard, and wine enough to "get ten kingdoms drunk." That period of history had been demonized by the clerics. Every year, on the Feast of Ascension, the Thul preached on that topic, declaring hellfire and eternal punishment for drunkards and any who partook of Devil's water.

Perhaps he was right. The Goddess failed to protect her. She had brought Yara this low, just days from her doom.

Another scullion came by with a piping hot metal trencher, on which rice and seared duck had been ladeled.

Over these days, she had been eating like a queen. This food, cooked in the style of Cathay, was almost as good as the palace back home.

But she pushed the trencher away.

Maryám was looking at her, examining her. "What is wrong, young girl?"

"My name is Yara," she answered. "And I am a killer."

~

Almost an hour had passed before Yara had told Maryám

everything—Maryám, this woman she hardly knew and certainly couldn't trust.

Maryám's food had grown cold, and of course Yara's had too.

Yara cursed herself for trusting this stranger, for baring her soul to her. She had left out the parts about the Goddesss and the Sisterhood to which she belonged. She had managed to keep quiet about her heathendom.

But at the end of her talk, she was on the verge of tears. She looked weak, pathetic. She had put herself at Maryám's mercy. It was unwise. It was foolish. Maryám had no need to know Yara's problems. Maryám did not deserve Yara's trust.

But she had told her of her predicament, and, fighting tears, began to eat her duck.

"I have good news for you, Yara." Maryám was smiling. "I and my party are headed back to Tadmor… well, briefly. We are stopping there. We have decided Cathay and elsewhere have become dangerous… just as dangerous as Tadmor."

Yara smiled, for the first time in a long time. "Well, Maryám… I don't have to tag along the whole time. I only need to go as far as the Pillars of the Moon…"

She was a Sister. She was not the daughter of the wazir, anymore. She was not the royal brat. She would not return home. She would go back to the Temple, where she belonged. She had done as the Lily wished. She had returned the Moon Pendant to its shrine, where it belonged. And she had killed one of her own. If the Lily saw fit to punish Yara, then so be it. She would live or die by the decrees of the Sisterhood.

"Thank you," Yara said. "Thank you so much."

~

With a great weight lifted from her shoulders, Yara spent the evening drinking and eating, even dancing to the tune of the sitar. They left in three days. The Moon Festival would be enjoyed to the fullest.

Chapter Thirty-Seven: The Stranger

It was dark when Javan's party reached the caves. Screech owls cried as they approached this watered sanctuary in the midst of the desert.

The journey had been harder than any Javan remembered, but perhaps he was growing old. The heat had been insufferable, the sun bright and glaring, and with each stride of the camel's legs it seemed the sand and dust got into his lungs.

He had left the luxury of Tadmor for this. It was an uncertain fate. The bandits who sent Ahram as a messenger might not be here.

As he drew closer, he became convinced that they probably weren't. Bearing torches, his men scoured the caves. Near the edge of one, there was a burned-out fire pit, full of ash.

Someone had indeed taken shelter here. But whoever had was gone.

"Spread out!" Javan told the one-hundred warriors he had brought along. "Search everywhere…"

They ventured off into their various directions, some entering caves, others going further away, toward a spring.

Javan eventually found himself standing alone, amid the bracing cold air. Thankfully, there was no wind.

He turned to the fire pit, seeing it was cold, probably days old. Waving his torch, he saw signs of prior habitation. The contents of a pack were strewn about: flint and tinder, and shredded bits of rope. "How long," he muttered to the unnamed bandits. "How long ago were you here?"

It was a wild venture to think bandits sent that note. But here was the only place Javan could reasonably think it was sent from. No other shelter was nearly so close.

He looked ahead, and saw, in the darkness, a figure standing still, far away, almost a mote of black. He was on the edge of the desert.

A less sharp eye, a less focused mind, may not have been able to tell it was a person lurking out there, dressed all in black. But Javan was focused on the sight ahead of him; he had nothing else in his vision except that.

For a moment panic seized him. His muscles became stiff. He did not want to move. He did not want to approach this figure before him.

The man, or woman, was wearing pitch-black clothing. Even from this far away, Javan could sense he, or she, was staring at him.

Javan's sword remained buckled to his side. He drew it, and the gold enamel on the hilt sparkled in the moonlight.

Yet the stranger, on the edge of the desert, did not buckle or run. Instead, he remained still. It seemed he was goading Javan on. Perhaps, under that veil of darkness, he was smiling, laughing.

Javan turned to look around, seeing he was utterly alone. He could wait until Rashad appeared. He could wait for warriors to assist him.

But then, the stranger might run.

And the wazir was supposed to be a fearless lion, unbowed in battle.

Showing no fear, trying to put a face of boldness on, he walked ahead, toward the darkness, toward the stranger.

The stranger did not move. He did not flee, or buckle.

Yet as Javan drew near, it was his own guts that were becoming twisted, his own fear rising up within him.

~

The brightness of the white moon shone down on him: a tall man, dressed in a black cloak. A hood obscured his face. His sleeves were so long they hid his hands and drooped down to his rope-cinched belt. He was immobile.

But despite the darkness of the hood, Javan could sense he was smiling.

A presence seemed to exhude out from this person, an aura that caused goosebumps to form on Javan's skin, and for his hairs to stand up on end.

Alone, standing before this hooded figure, it dawned on Javan how vulnerable he was. He was separated from his warriors. The only thing that could protect him from danger was his own skill with the sword. The Wazir of Tadmor could fall in this fateful moment, and the Beautiful Land with it.

"Greetings, Javan." His voice was gravelly, as if his throat were half-filled with grave dirt. He reached out his hands; they were white and thin, with skin stretched tight across the bones.

But Javan did not hold those hands, as politeness demanded. Nonetheless, he sheathed his sword. This man in the hood was not armed. There was no dagger at his side, no weapon for him to reach.

"Who are you?" Javan responded.

This man spoke in fluent Tammuri, with a diction that implied high birth. But he was not from Tadmor. He was different. Javan could tell by his clothing, and by the dark aura he exhuded. It was like he was a puppet, and someone else was speaking through him, in the dialect that Javan wanted to hear.

"A thousand years of darkness," he said.

Javan stepped back and drew his sword. He wanted to run, but he stayed firm, gritting his teeth together.

The stranger had begun to laugh. "A thousand years of darkness," he said again, "is what you will have. The King Who Has No Equal will offer mercy to you and to Tadmor, if you will only bow before him, and kiss his ring."

Backing away, Javan caught sight of shadows beyond. There were more figures behind him, which he could not make out.

The Stranger was not alone.

"Would you rather perish in the light?" the Stranger said. "Or would you rule in hell?"

Javan had come here, seeking the answer to the mystery. He

had come here wondering who had written the Naamer writing and pierced it to Ahram's flesh. Now he had an answer. But that answer was graver than he'd thought; it was something beyond his ability to comprehend.

"Here, in these caves," the Stranger said, "where the ancients performed the sacrifices and devotions, there is an altar.

"Go to the altar, and cut your hand with your sword. Spread your blood upon it, and the King will save you. You will live on in fealty to him, together with your power and your kingdom."

Javan did not believe it. He did not want to believe it. He could not comprehend the offer. He only knew that his heart was pounding, his breath had become short, and fear was welling up inside him, becoming full-blown panic.

"You have thirty days to accept my offer," the Stranger said. "If you refuse, then you, and Tadmor, and all you hold dear, will perish into the night."

Chapter Thirty-Eight: The Return

After days of pain and illness, Marit had begun to walk. A message had been conferred to her, that Javan had returned from some expeditions in the "caves outside Tadmor" and that his arrival in Mahara was imminent.

She did not feel safe when he was gone. Each day her fear grew. Each night, she feared something bad was going to happen to Tadmor. Already the unrest was bubbling up in the surface.

In the streets of Mahara, the anger of the people was palpable. It was not open. It was not even evident, according to Marit's eyes and ears across the city.

The stabbings had dwindled as mass arrests were carried out, as the members of the Black Hand were discovered and, one by one, executed in the town square.

But the piety remained: the anger at Javan and, indeed, Marit, continued. One day it would erupt into something worse than before. Civil war was coming. Was Javan up to the task? Had it been a mistake to expel the clerics?

No.

Marit, clutching the railing of her balcony, peered into the city.

The Law of Mazda no longer prevailed. The people were free. That is how Marit saw it.

But others, she knew, in the streets below her, harbored different ideas. They thought the wazir and wazira were blasphemers, enemies of a faith they held dear, condemned to hell and targets for religious killings.

Could she remove such a disease from the people's minds, or was it engrained, too deeply held, too steadfastly believed? Marit did not know. They had won the battle. But could they win the war? She had become more and more doubtful. The zeal was deep. Most did not share it. But enough did. They could not stuff centuries of Mazdahi oppression into a bottle, and expect it to remain inside. Marit could see bloodshed ahead, and endless war. Things would not return to the way they were, centuries ago.

"We will win," she muttered to herself, staring down into the streets below. "We will win?"

Where was Javan? She needed him. Moktata had assumed control of the city, in his absence, and each night parades of warriors marched through the streets, daring anyone to leave their homes. He had made examples of the last members of the Black Hand, torturing out confessions and arresting entire networks of subordinates. No longer did the people fear the clerics; they feared the wazir and wazira.

She recalled, in her youth, that she confessed her belief in Mazda. It had been real to her. If she led a life of exceptional zeal, aiding the clerics in spreading their power, she would achieve paradise.

Only when she reached the palace, and found a paradise in this world, did she question it. Only when she met emissaries from the Continent, who professed faith in not Mazda but Athra lord of fire, or in no god at all, did she begin to wonder.

What lay beyond, at the end of life? She still did not know.

In the darkness there was the sound of a horn. In the distance, set against the mighty walls of Mahara, the front gates were opening. Only one man was important enough to have them opened, just for him.

Relief surged through Marit. She could sleep easy tonight, without worry.

Javan and his warriors were riding through Mahara's streets. She could see them now.

Marit left to done some nice clothes. She would be waiting for him.

~

He entered the bedchamber, still wearing white clothes—now stained brown from sand and mud. The sword was clipped to his side.

He was different.

There was an expression on Marit's face that she had never seen before.

He seemed perturbed. Worried. Afraid.

"What's wrong, Javan?" Marit said.

"Nothing," he answered.

A lie—not normal.

Marit would not sleep easy tonight, like she'd hoped. What would become of the Land of Tadmor?

Where was Yara?

Precious Yara.

Chapter Thirty-Nine: Not Alone

When Yara descended from the mountains, and the green was replaced with red, the fertile soil replaced with barrenness, and the cool replaced with searing heat, she was in as bad a predicament as before. The desert would be harsh and unrelenting. The journey would be long and hard.

But she was in the company of Maryám and a dozen others, and they were well supplied. She was in the company of companions who seemed to care for her, though she was a stranger. She would not have to bear the hatred of Hatzor, not anymore. But she would have to live through the memory of killing her.

When Yara returned to the Temple of the Moon, as a Sister, would they sentence her to die? She would accept whatever punishment that the Goddess required.

The day wore on. They traveled until the sun was a red glow in the sky, sinking beneath the horizon. Canyons and buttes surrounded them. The air was still and silent.

As Maryám and the others bundled together a fire, Yara wandered away from camp, deep in thought.

Tadmor was still around, despite Zathustra's warnings. Perhaps, it was in danger. Perhaps, it was not.

Still, she had to warn her parents, who remained skeptical of the real danger they were in. Yara knew what the Lamia were capable of; she had seen their handiwork.

She could never return to that old life, that pampered existence as the daughter of the wazir and wazira. Moreover, she did not *want* to.She had left it all behind. She had a higher purpose now, one which she relished. Precious Yara was gone; and a warrior was in her place.

She remembered the idol which she had stolen from a Naamer

tomb. She remembered the nightmares she'd had, of the three old women in the desert. Yara rubbed her arms together; it had grown cold.

A screech owl began to cry. She hurried back to camp.

Maryám and the others were huddled around the campfire.

The last bits of the sun were setting into the horizon: a fiery red glow against a pink sky.

They were being watched.

Yara could not see it, but she could sense it in her bones. The same fear that consumed her in the oasis, when the Lamia appeared, had begun to creep up within her now.

Were the Lamia here?

No.

The Lamia, according to her Sisters, resided near water and vegetation. There was none of that here, only dry earth and sun.

As Maryám and the fellow travelers began to talk of their plans when they reached the coast, Yara kept an eye out. The sun was casting long shadows over the buttes and mesas in the distance, and as it sunk further into the horizon, the shadows grew longer.

Yara put a hand on the hilt of her sword, preparing at any moment for an ambush. She had a feeling that one was coming, though she couldn't explain why?

Maryám's eyes were glistening in the light of the flame. She was staring at Yara, examining her. "What is the matter, Yara?" she said.

Yara wondered if this Maryám was a sorceress, if she could read and examine others' minds. It seemed unlikely, but Maryám was perceptive beyond anyone Yara knew. Maryám seemed to know what Yara was thinking and how she was feeling.

It unnerved Yara. It made her wonder if this journey, terrible risk that it was, had been a mistake. Would these strangers rob her and leave her to die in the desert? It was possible. Perhaps, it was even likely.

Yet she would remain here with them. To stray from them was to die. The desert could claim one's life in less than a day. There was no water. There were no markers and no roads. There was no life.

"Don't worry about me," Yara said to Maryám. There was an edge to her voice, one she immediately regretted. But she wanted to be left alone, to her own thoughts and worries.

She wondered if the Temple of the Moon itself had been overcome. Would she reach the sacred Pillars only to find ruins and scorched bodies? Would she even reach the Pillars at all?

"Have some food," Maryám replied.

One of the traveling companions, a man, handed Yara a stick of dried meat. Yara was not hungry. She was too worried to be hungry.

But as the night progressed, and Maryám stopped her inquisitive stares, they began to speak of their great plans to sail across the sea. Yara was soon just background. She nibbled at the dried meat, seeing it was flavored with spices and salt. It was infinitely better than the waybread that Hatzor had bought.

But Yara wondered if she'd been better off with Hatzor, with whom she shared a task and a common purpose. Who knews where this group of commoners would take her?

One of the men in the group took out a lute and began plucking the strings and singing. Others soon joined in.

It was a song in Cathayan style, about a fair maiden and a potion and something about the moon.

Judging by the parts she understood, this was a song she'd heard in traces in the Mountain's Heart Inn. It was a song of the Moon Festival.

In Tadmor, music was mostly squelched. Though not banned outright, the clerics had decreed it immoral.

Maryám had grabbed a tambourine and began striking her leg to the beat. Another woman had taken out a flute; she began to play along. Most had discarded their headscarves, no longer in public, no longer facing judgment from fellow desert folk who might be in Kish. Yara had not worn hers in months; and she never would again.

Song after song progressed. Yara found her attention straying, into the darkness beyond. The darkness was all-encompassing; it was deep. She could not make out much of anything beyond the campfire's light.

But they were not alone. She knew they were not alone.

Chapter Forty: To the Grave

Javan did not know what to think. He did not know what to do. He had not slept in two nights.

He still did not understand what happened to him in the Caves of Karbala. He still did not know who, or what, he had spoken to. He only knew that he feared for Tadmor, and for his own family, more than ever before.

He had mounted a white charger, straining against his own exhaustion. Rebellions had erupted in Magdala and Adwar, and as far away as Ijlib. The Mob—that small but zealous minority—still strained under the yoke of their secular ruler. They did not know, they did not care, that Javan their wazir had their best interests in mind. For centuries, the clerics had set up the law of god side by side with the law of man. They had driven the people of Tadmor to terror. Everyone dreaded the clerics. Their punishments were brutal and inhumane. Their judgments were severe. So why did the rebellions continue? Why, day after day, week after week, did blood continue to be shed?

And now, as he rode out of Mahara, to where his warriors had encamped, he remembered the encounter in the Caves of Karbala. The gravest threat, the most dire danger, did not come from Tadmor, but from without.

Perhaps, he had imagined it. Perhaps, it had just been a dream.

How could it have been real? A ghostly white man in a black hood, demanding fealty before an altar. If it had been a dream, it had been so vivid and lifelike that it caused Javan's insomnia. He had never seen a vision so realistic, so startling. In that moment, he had been convinced of Tadmor's impending doom; now, in the light of day, in the distance of time, he had begun to nurse doubts.

Moktata and Rashad had gathered together two thousand warriors with spears and shields. They were amassed outside Mahara's city walls, just beyond the gate.

Moktata, riding a horse of his own, trotted up to Javan. "Your

Worship," he said.

Javan could not offer a smile or any kind of assurance.

"Magdala is of the greatest urgency," Moktata continued.

Javan frowned and looked at Moktata wearily. "Magdala is almost destroyed… how many times can we put down a rebellion? How many Tammuri can we kill? How many times can this happen?"

Moktata did not start this war. Javan wondered if Moktata's heart was truly in it.

Moktata, the greatest of his emirs, was riding a black horse. A spear was in his hand; a cowhide shield was strapped to his back. As usual, his black hair was tied in a ponytail. In addition to his great skills as a leader, he was the best fighter in the army. He fought with his soldiers, through thick and thin, through good times and bad.

Moreover, his wisdom was unparalleled. He always seemed to know the right choice.

And with Javan's statement, he looked dumbfounded.

It was true, after all. How long could they spill blood? How long could they paper over the root of the problem?

Towns, villages, and cities, had been twice, sometimes thrice, reduced to ruins. The Mob would never accept the rule of the "Blasphemer Wazir."

"In the Land of Sur," Moktata said, "they train elephants. They must be whipped. They must be broken. One day the people will be broken. The Mob will lose their zeal. They will consign themselves to their fate…"

"The Land of Sur is far away," Javan said. It was all he could manage to say.

He had become convinced of his own doom. The grave was just one step away.

Chapter Forty-One: The Old World

Javan was gone again. Marit, alone and unprotected, kept to herself inside her room.

She did not trust any of her servants, anymore, not after Tigra's betrayal. She did not trust her cooks. She did not trust her scullions. She did not trust even the guards who swore to protect her life.

The clerics had, in recent years, banned most non religious texts. Even medical books were viewed with suspicion. The Thul, in one of his sermons in Mahara's city square, had said that "physicians healing the sick are subverting the Will of Mazda; hell awaits them."

Javan had bent to the pressure, over a decade ago. The books had been cleared from the personal library, allowing only space for Mazda's law, ten codices long, and various commentaries on the prophets.

Those commentaries were what Marit now read, sitting inside on her bed. The day was cool. The Feast of the Ten Tables was approaching at the end of the month. As the winds changed across the desert, bringing cold air, Marit elected to stay indoors. She was still not fully healed from her wounds.

In the absence of other entertainments, she had begun reading about the conqueror-prophet Mali.

Born a poor boy in the city of Bezakirah, he had become a zealous convert to Mazda's religion. He had traveled to where the faith was founded, in the faraway city of Kurasan in the Nether Provinces. Mali became zealous beyond anyone in Kurasan; he became consumed with rage at the unbelievers, back home in Bezakirah and especially in "that cesspool and center of filth and vice called Tadmor." The commentaries outrageously claimed that the Tammuri, who worshiped the goddess Isdar, had built temples "of prostitution, where priestesses served as common whores." Centuries later, Marit bristled at Mali's vindicitive commentary on the Beautiful Land. She was hoping for

Mali's failure, but she knew too well how the story ended. She was living it.

As the morning progressed into afternoon, she read of Mali's gathering of armies; of his conquest of Kish and all its surrounding lands; and how he returned to the place of his birth, subjugating the city of Bezakirah and all the Coastal States. He had been defeated twice by the Queen of Tadmor, Issara.

Between bites of her noon meal—lamb shanks roasted in the palace kitchen—she read of how the Queen of Tadmor was slain by her advisor, Rahman, and the Beautiful Land plunged into chaos. Of course, the writers of the commentaries did not call it the Beautiful Land but as "that cesspool of vice and immorality, Tadmor."

A tear formed in Marit's eye as she read of the Fall of Tadmor. The vineyards were slashed and burned. Libraries, which had collected the knowledge of the ancients, went up in smoke. There was a great earthquake across the land, and Mahara's walls crumbled. Mali entered without resistance. Thousands of "pagans" were slaughtered, the commentaries said. A kabakh was built were the Temple of Isdar had been.

At the thought, Marit paused.

The Grand Kabakh was the largest of all in the desert region, from Kish to Bezakirah.

It remained standing, though the cleric—who had denounced Javan—was killed.

Underneath the pitch-black stone, was there a remnant of Tadmor's past? Could it exist underneath the foundations?

She had become consumed with the thought.

She would have to sneak down in the streets, unnoticed.

~

In clothing that covered all of her face, which some of the most religious in Tadmor wore, Marit descended into the city streets unnoticed. She brought no guards. She was completely vulnerable. Only her disguise protected her.

The streets were quiet, but signs of life emerged. Outside the palace, beyond the walls which protected it, a couple was laughing on the street corner. A beggar cried out at Marit, holding his tin.

Though she was rich, she had brought no silver or gold. She had nothing to offer him.

She passed him by, through the network of streets.

There were fewer people, it seemed, than even a year ago. The bloodshed that consumed the streets for a month had taken a toll.

But now, it seemed, it was quiet. The rebellion was not quite as vibrant as before. Peace had returned… peace at the edge of the sword, as warriors patrolled Mahara. This was the best peace they would ever acquire. This was a peace born of fear, a peace of a people who had accepted their fate.

But Marit knew it was for their own good.

~

Through shady avenues and narrow alleys Marit walked, making her way to a place she knew by heart, and a place that, long ago, she had feared.

Now, with open contempt, she looked upon the Grand Kabakh, near the city square.

Its pitch-black stones were carved and fitted perfectly, making it resemble a single piece of rock. Now, no guards stood around it. There were no preachers shouting in its vicinity. There were no fiery sermons, no denunciations of Javan or proclamations of doom to the heathens. It was silent.

A courtyard of cobblestone surrounded it, rectangular in shape like the kabakh itself.

Marit had never seen it this quiet. The clerics were gone. In all their zeal, they had not been able to prevent this. Despite all their fiery declarations of Mazda's favor, despite their proclamations of doom to the impure and unjust, they had not been able to prevent Javan from taking control.

It looked so pristine, the cobblestone, unmarred by the presence of the street preachers.

A warrior stood guard at the entrance. Javan had told them to forbid entry.

Marit approached cautiously. She had not been into the Grand Kabakh in decades, since she was a young girl. She had only glimpsed the kabakh's innards when the Thul brought out the Books of Law on the Feast of Oaths. He had paraded with the hefty tomes in front of the penitent, and fearful, crowd. It was the only time the priceless books, illuminated in gold leaf, were seen by the public. The prophet Mali himself had commissioned them, according to legend.

She approached the warrior, who was bearing a spear in both hands.

He looked at her with scorn, but Marit removed her coverings, bearing her face.

He recognized her instantly. "My lady," he said.

"May I come in?" she said.

"You are asking my permission?" The warrior laughed.

Perhaps, Marit's nerves were strained from entering this place of terror and supposed sanctity. She smiled and laughed along with him.

Out of habit, or perhaps out of fear of Mazda's power, Marit stopped at the entryway. She untied her sandals and entered barefoot.

~

Javan's warriors had kept the candles burning, perhaps out of respect for this still, in many people's minds, sacred place. The roof, the walls, and the floor alike were made of pitch black stone. A long corridor ran its entire length, with rooms shooting out from it at either side. At the very end was a gold door etched in Old Tammuri writing, which Marit could not read. She walked all the way to the end. She laid her hands on the bronze handle and pulled.

The gold door jerked open. A red veil further obscured her view. The candles here had all burnt out. None dared to enter the most holy part of the Grand Kabakh, where the Thul resided.

Dare Marit venture beyond the veil, where the impure could never see? As a girl she had only been as far as the vestibule. Now, she was on the edge of its most sacred space.

This, for certain, was a blasphemy. If the Mob found out, they would riot for days, regardless of pressure.

And in truth, she did not want to disrespect them. She did not want to disrespect anyone.

"But Mali disrespected me," Marit said aloud, to herself. "Mali disrespected my people."

She pushed beyond the veil, which tore at the slightest touch.

~

With a candle grabbed from a sconce in the hallway, Marit shone her light into this secret space. It was mostly empty, with the same black wall as the rest; but in a shelf ahead, there were the Books of Law, three in total, each weighing many pounds. Here were the precepts and customs of the Mazdahi, written by ancient hands, illuminated in gold leaf, preciously preserved and seen only by the people on feast days. Here was the yoke tied around the neck of the Tammuri. Here was the source and symbol of their oppression. Here was the weight on their shoulders.

She grabbed the first volume. She almost fell at its incredible weight, but steadied herself and laid it, flat, on the top shelf.

She opened the book, seeing letters scrawled in Old Tammuri. Marit could barely read the modern language. Education was forbidden to girls.

But translations allowed her to know what was said. These were lists of laws and regulations, of food and drink and Devil's water, thousands of pages long, and after them punishments for various crimes, some so terrible that even the Thul refused to carry them out. If, the clerics said, no crime was committed during life, Mazda may in his mercy allow them heaven.

That was the hope many paupers clung to. And it was rarely, if ever, achieved. What laid beyond? A cruel and capricious god determining their fate? Marit knew where she stood in the eyes of the Mazdahi.

She remembered the Queen of Tadmor, slain by Mali. She remembered the wealth of Ancient Tadmor, the wine flowing like streams from the vineyards.

Here, where she stood, was stolen ground. A temple had once stood here, mighty, of white marble. She would order it deconstruction. Brick by brick, stone by stone, the Grand Kabakh of Mahara would be demolished.

Chapter Forty-Two: The Tower Is Fallen

When Javan and his thousand warriors reached the city of Magdala, its famous tower was no longer standing. The villagers were in outright revolt. Reports had reached him along the road that anyone seen as sympathetic to the wazir had been killed.

Now, he saw a city in ruins, fallen far from its ancient wealth. Amid bodies on the streets, certain homes had been burnt to husks. Magdala had been destroyed.

On the edge of the city, watching on horseback as his warriors poured in, Javan's mind was not at rest. He no longer cared about Magdala or any of the other towns and villages. His mind was in the Caves of Karbala. The imminent doom that awaited.

Could he make a pact with the Devil? His character prevented it. How could he make an agreement with the forces of evil, the Lamia, the Daughters of Shadow? Had he expelled the clerics from the Land of Tadmor, only to let a graver threat in?

In his youth, his grandfather would tell him tales of the Lamia, and of the ghouls, the Sons of Darkness. He had never believed any of them. Now, Javan wasn't sure.

It had to have been a dream, a product of his overworked and beleaguered mind. It did not make sense. A dark emissary of the night, working on behalf of his liege, asking for Javan to swear fealty... an altar for Javan to spill his blood upon. It did not make sense.

"My lord!" Moktata was shouting at him, astride his own horse. A spear was in his hand. A battle had ensued, with all its roaring noise and clashing of sword against sword.

Javan was so disturbed by his encounter in the Caves that even battle could not distract him.

Javan drew his sword and rode in, after Moktata, as his warriors seized control of the city.

By nightfall the rebels had been cleared.

The Tower of Magdala was now in ruins. Would the rest of Tadmor follow?

He peered out into the desert night. He was not alone. They were not alone.

Chapter Forty-Three: Mighty Men

A week after leaving Kish, the mood among Maryám and her fellow travelers had taken a definitive turn for the worse. Yara felt more isolated than ever. Maryám bickered with Maahul, and Maahul with Ali.

Against this backdrop, Yara wondered if fear played a role, if they sensed what she sensed… that they were in danger.

~

Two weeks after leaving Kish, and just miles from the Sacred Pillars, things had settled down somewhat. Maryám had grown cold to Yara. Now, it seemed, Yara was a foreign presence, and one that was not entirely welcome… a presence eating their precious resources. Yet Maahul and Ali had put their differences aside. Maryám no longer argued with Maahul; they had settled matters.

Yara kept quiet, feeling more and more alien, more and more unwelcome.

They were close to the Pillars one night, as the cool settled in and Maahul built a roaring fire.

Yara kept silent as Maryám began to talk. "I wish we had never left Kish. Cathay wasn't safe, but…"

Maahul grunted some curse.

Heading to the Continent had been Maahul's idea.

Yara wanted to withdraw. She could sense a fight coming, after their long peace.

A screech owl was crying in the night. A rocky canyon sheltered them, here. She looked up to the top, and despite the darkness, thought she saw a shadow.

As an argument overtook the camp, Yara slinked away. She laid a hand on her saber, grasping the hilt tightly. She did not want to alarm Maryám and the others. But she did not want any harm coming to them.

Maahul and Maryám had begun to shout, and soon Ali and Warka joined the fray. Despite this, Yara heard the sound of disturbed earth, and a footstep, far above.

"Maryám!" she shouted, rushing to the campfire. "We are not alone!"

Maryám wasn't having any of it. Her cheeks had turned pink as Maahul accused her of cowardice. Her voice was raised.

"Grab your daggers!" Yara screamed as the first of the ghouls came swarming into camp.

As suddenly as a flash of lightning, the arguments among the campfire turned to carnage.

A ghoul had seized Mahul and with its fetid jaws, tore his head from his neck.

Another ghoul had tackled Maryám and gored her chest, sucking out her innards with its worm-like tongue.

Ali bolted away screaming but the ghouls were too fast; he was tackled and ripped to pieces. Yara charged Maryám's attacker and sliced its head off. The other ghouls shrieked and backed away a moment.

Yara seized upon their fear and came out charging, swinging, slashing, screaming. Three ghouls fell dead in the span of a moment. Up above, on the canyon, a wind was blowing. There were drums. Drums.

The rest of the ghouls fled away into the night. The Sons of Darkness were vile, but they were cowards all. Yara braced herself as she looked upon the carnage. Everyone but her was dead or dying. She could not afford to miss a step, or to grieve. She hurriedly scooped up what water and dried meat she could.

The camels had fled, breaking their bonds and running away into the night. Their terror had been so great, they overpowered the binds. Now Yara was left alone.

There was no time to shed a tear for these people, whom she

had gotten to know over the weeks. There was only time for panic.

Drums pounded again. These were martial drums, the drums of war. Yara, with no mount, no way of knowing the way home, grabbed the compass from Maahul's body. With water and enough food to last a few days, she bolted into the night.

Up above the canyon, far in the distance, in the glimmering moonlight, thousands of figures marched in formation. An army was headed west. West toward Tadmor. West toward the Beautiful Land.

~

The sun beat hot upon Yara's neck. Sand covered her body. She had sprinted as long as she could in the night, and half-staggered, half-stumbled into a sleep.

Now the landscape was different. There were no drums. There were no night terrors. There was only the bright and blazing sun, the parched earth, and barrenness more deadly than a thousand ghouls.

She had waterskins, enough to last a day.

As she lay there in the blazing heat, it struck her that she was going to die. How could she escape this? The terrors of the night were one thing; who could stand against the oppression of the sun? In waterless valleys, there was no hope for any living thing.

She stood up and took a sip from her waterskin. She ate some of the dried meat, which had become as sickening to her over these weeks as the waybread. She had to push on. She had to try. If the desert claimed her, the Lily would never know that the Moon Pendant was safe. She would not know that the Temple's most sacred possession was safe, on the neck of the statue in the shrine.

And she would not know the life that it cost. Yara would not receive what was due her, whatever punishment was coming her way.

It could not be. She had to try. Somehow, despite not knowing the way, she had to get back to the Temple of the Moon, to its Pillars, guiding the caravaners like stars in the night sky for centuries.

She hurried along through the desert, going due west, hoping it would amount to something, hoping against hope that the Pillars would emerge, unbidden, from the desert sands. But the likelier outcome, the one she dreaded, was that she would join the legion of the desert's victims. She would succumb to thirst; she would die, and rot, and turn to bone. No one would claim her remains. The Lily and her Sisters would live on in ignorance, not knowing that the Pendant was safe, and that Hatzor had been killed.

~

The sun had grown so hot, blinding in its intensity and brightness, that Yara stumbled. It was midday. She took her waterskin and tried to pour out the last drops. There was none left.

The sands were blowing eastward with the wind.

She was in the middle of the swirling sands. She could go on no further. She stooped down to rest, and collapsed, succumbing to the sun.

A mighty man towered above her, with a bright white beard and lightning in his eyes. He was poking her, urging her to come awake.

It was dusk. The heat had receded.

Yara gasped for air.

"Yara! Yara!" the mighty man said.

He was like a god of old, with the storm within him, the storm in his eyes, the storm all around. A lightning bolt was in his hands; no, it was a staff.

And he did not have a beard of fire; it was a beard of white. He was old, as old as he was mighty.

He was Zathustra.

"Zathustra!" Yara cried out. Despite her thirst and hunger, she jerked up and met him in an embrace. "How did you know I was here? How did you find me?"

Zathustra began to laugh.

"Ah, Yara," he said. "When I left you, I placed a ward on you. I knew where you came and went…"

Yara began to cry, but she feared those last drops of water would kill her. She tried to hold herself together.

"You were just miles from the Pillars. And you were remaining there. I knew you were in danger…"

The horizon was a deep purplish red. The sun was aglow to the west. The heat of the day was sinking away fast. Yara was as cold as she was thirsty.

"I was traveling with some Kish folk," Yara began. "Actually, they were Tammuri…"

"The Lily of the Valley told me you were traveling with a fellow Sister."

Yara frowned. Punishment was nigh. "She is dead," she said.

"Dead," Zathustra said with no small amount of incredulity. "What killed her?"

"I did."

Speechless, Zathustra stood by as Yara grabbed his hand and hoisted herself up onto her feet.

He offered her a waterskin and she guzzled it down without hesitating.

When she had drunk it dry, she still felt famished and dizzy.

But she had confessed. A great weight had been lifted from her shoulders. Whatever came next, she would face with bravery and resolve.

~

The stars were spread across the night's blue canvas, and the moon was bright white, a waning crescent, when Yara and Zathustra passed through the Pillars.

Yara had privately doubted whether Zathustra would ever return from Indjar. But returned, he had… and he had saved her life.

She was still weak, stumbling and staggering at times, but remained focused on coming home. Her mind swam from the lack of food and water, but she was committed to return to the Temple and proclaim the mission was accomplished… and accept her punishment.

At times, on the long walk from the Pillars to the Temple, she recalled the lives just lost… of Maryám, sweet Maryám, of Maahul, of brave Mali. She had known them only a little while on this earth; and now they were gone.

The trauma still remained; in the darkness, her memories raced in a swirl of terror and grief. She heard no drums, but she knew the army was marching: the Lamia, the ghouls, and the restless dead, marshalling in the name of the King of the Dark.

The Temple emerged in sight and Yara's fear and panic melted away. There were candles in the windows. Up on the observatory tower, torches were burning, casting light onto the roof below. To the side of the Temple, the pomegranate trees were in bloom. In the dim light Yara caught sight of a Sister attending to the camels in the stable. Here, all was well with the world. Here, Yara was safe.

At the door, Yara removed her sandals, perhaps out of habit, perhaps out of fear of further punishment.

~

In the courtyard, at the edge of the pool, Ruby was curled up like an orange and black ball.

There were cubs near her, male and female. One came bounding toward Yara, crossing the distance between them in the blink of an eye. He batted her with his paws, not drawing any blood.

Yara laughed.

She bent down and gave the warlike cub a scratch; he bit her but his teeth were soft and drew no blood.

Yara laughed again.

"I wonder," she said, half to herself, half to Zathustra, "who is Ruby's sire."

"Ruby was a lonely tigress." The Lily's voice stunned Yara and seized her with fear. She had emerged from the darkness of the colonnade and was standing before Yara, now, with a wry smile. "But sometime, not long after you left, a tiger came by. He gave Ruby, and us, a few daughters and sons."

Yara rose up onto her feet; the cub skittered away, back toward his mother and playmates.

The Lily seemed ready for battle. Her saber was clipped to her side on her belt. She was smiling, but that smile quickly faded. "You have returned. With Zathustra.

"Where is Hatzor?"

"She is dead," Yara answered. "I killed her."

~

In a closed-off room, down a series of hallways, was what appeared to be a functional tribunal.

The Lily took her seat on a wooden chair, raised high above Yara.

"What is the status of your mission, Sister?" she said.

There was no anger on the Lily's face, only grief.

"The Moon Pendant was taken to the mountain shrine. It remains there."

Zathustra had let them alone, but as the Lily spoke, other Sisters were filtering in, and lining up behind her.

The Lily nodded. "And what happened to Hatzor?"

Everything was still a mystery to Yara. "Hatzor… she was

jealous that you gave me the Moon Pendant to keep. She attacked me, and I defended myself."

"Do you have witnesses?" The Lily's voice had taken a somber tone.

"If I do," Yara said, "they are dead now… killed along the desert road, by ghouls and their companions…"

"Surely, there are witnesses." The Lily was insistent. Her eyes were welling with tears.

"Not even a sparrow saw it," Yara answered.

"Then, according to the law of the Goddess, I sentence you to die," the Lily said. "But run… run, Precious Yara, before I carry it out!"

~

Even in her darkest moments, Yara did not expect such a harsh sentence. Nor, after facing death, did she expect to struggle so much against what justice required.

She fled, crying, from the temple gates, with Zathustra a step behind her.

She had lost her parents; she had lost her Sisterhood. Now her purpose was taken from her.

She supposed she was lucky to be alive.

~

At the Pillars, an exhausted Yara slumped on the marble base.

Zathustra could not comfort her, but he was trying. She had blocked out his voice. She had blocked out everything but her own grief.

Zathustra had followed her out here, out into the darkness of the night, where the terrors could grab him. He looked so pitiful: an old man grasping a great green book, thin and wrinkled, with a staff to keep him steady. How could he comfort her? How could he tell her everything was going to be all right?

"I came back from Indjar for you… Don't run away from things."

No longer did he sound like a powerful sorcerer, but instead a doddering old man. Yara had closed her ears to him. "Don't speak to me," she said.

In the distance, the shadows stirred: the dark shape of a ghoul scurried off, away from the ruins.

"The ghouls are afraid of you," Zathustra said. Apparently, he had seen it too. "When they go to sleep in the daytime, they check their tombs for *you.*"

Yara laughed, despite herself.

"I would tell you to return with me to Indjar," Zathustra said, "but I will not return. Not with you. It is dangerous, too. I will take you to the coasts… I will put you on a ship."

Yara knew nothing of the Continent. She knew less of it than she did of Cathay. Would the farmers and goatherds of the inland empire accept refugees? Would the king take them in?

"I will not take your advice," Yara said. "After all, you are the one who said Tadmor is lost…"

"The King of the Dark was encamped around it months ago. It is lost, Yara, I am sorry… I know it is hard."

Yara laughed again, coldly. "But you are wrong." She remembered Maryáms words. Tadmor was thriving months ago, despite Zathustra's follies. "My friend, Maryám…" She stopped right there, thinking of her, dying, at the hands of a ghoul. "She was there when you said Tadmor was gone. The Beautiful Land remains."

Zathustra didn't seem convinced. In the light of the moon, his shoulders swelled. He was as prideful as ever. "If you go to Tadmor, you go to your doom. I assure you."

"Then to my doom, I will go," Yara said. Zathustra knew nothing. "And you are going with me."

Chapter Forty-Four: Ruins

The sting of guilt hit Marit as she watched her workmen, armed with pickaxes and sledgehammers, complete their work. The Grand Kabakh had been reduced to rubble, and that rubble was being carted away.

What have I done, she thought on occasion.

Her parents, now long dead, would have disowned her over this. They would have joined the Mob in calling for her death. But she had changed; the world had changed.

Workmen were carting off the black rubble. Soon it would all be gone. The Books of Law had been carted into the palace. Perhaps, tonight, Marit would throw them into the fire. Perhaps, she would keep them. But it did not matter; they were a relic of the past.

In place of the Grand Kabakh, she would build a temple, in the manner of the Queen of Tadmor. Mali had humbled Tadmor; but Tadmor would have the last laugh.

The old world would return.

The new is fading... the world the ancients bequeathed shall return to us.

Chapter Forty-Five: Prince of the Air

A cold wind was blowing, and the sun's heat seemed faint.

It was the thirtieth day since the man in black approached Javan.

Or, at least, it was the thirtieth day since he had dreamed it.

Javan stood in the city square of Mahara, surrounded by a coterie of warriors. For the first time in years, pipes were playing.

The scent of baking pastries was thick.

The Feast of Ten Tables was underway across Mahara, and bakers throughout the city made cookies in the shapes of the prophet's famed tablets, with writing in date honey.

But Javan did not feel jubilant, not at all. Though there were children playing, and adults laughing with hot drinks in hand, Javan's stomach was unsettled. After the defeat in Mahara, the spirit of the rebels seemed to have broken. An uneasy peace, at the end of a sword, had spread over Mahara; and bit by bit, it seemed life was returning to normal.

Better than normal, Javan ventured to say.

He did not normally leave the palace during the Ten Tables festivities. But he wanted to take a look at what the city had become, what the people thought, and how they were behaving.

It seemed everyone was in good spirits. Far better than he.

Javan feared the night. He feared the future. But he would go to the Caves of Karbala. He would offer his blood to save the Land of Tadmor, so that the laughter and revelries would continue, from this day until the days of their grandchildren.

~

He departed with Moktata, who alone knew the way.

Astride a camel he led Javan through the desert, up and down the steep and ever-changing dunes. The desert had relinquished some of its heat, but the sun was still intense, and Javan quickly became parched.

His hands were trembling on the reins.

Moktata did not know why Javan wanted to return to the caves. He did not know what dark purpose drew him here. But he would find out soon enough.

The sun was bright and blazing, reflecting against the sand.

As Javan grew thirstier and hungrier, and dizzy on camel-back, the sun began to sink.

When the caves appeared, a dark blot against the horizon, it was sundown and the sky was painted in hues of red and gold. Javan's shaking had reached its apogee, but it seemed when he saw that the caves were near, whatever dark spirit haunted him left. He had become calm and serene.

By the time they reached the caves, the day had turned to night. Only the moon lit the way, but ahead, there were torches… dozens of them, lined up in a procession.

Their bearers were wearing hoods.

The panic returned. Javan had not imagined it. He had imagined nothing.

"What is this?" Moktata cried.

He still did not know. He only knew that he was afraid; afraid for his own life, and for Moktata's.

"Go back home!" Javan shouted.

"What?" Moktata said.

They were at the edge of the caves, and the sound of the bubbling springs was evident.

"Go back to Tadmor!" Javan insisted. "Go back to Mahara. Watch over my wife. Go now! I am the wazir, the leader of the army. It is my command!"

Moktata could not argue with that. "My lord… I will not abandon you!"

"Go!" Javan shouted. His scream, his anger, was motivated

above all by fear… fear for Yara… fear for Marit. Fear for Tadmor.

His harsh tone spurred Moktata to turn around and flee quickly, away from the caves, into the chill of the desert night.

He dismounted from his camel. The trembling had returned. His breath was turning to fog. He buckled, collapsing to his knees. He retched. He looked up, seeing a column of men in black hoods, carrying torches, leading the way to the altar.

Against the sound of the wind, a drum rose up, deep and hollow in its timbre. The beat was slow and steady. He heard voices, some talking, some laughing. A cold presence washed over him. Goosebumps formed on his hands and forearms. He felt lifted up, not by his own accord; in an instant, he was standing upright. He had been given wings like the servant of an ancient god.

He walked forward, feeling light. It felt like his feet did not touch the ground.

Music began as he walked down the way; a choir was singing, like the sound of wailing women.

He could scarcely see. He had begun to float; when he took too great a step, it took a while for him to descend to the ground.

He had grown dizzy, but the panic had faded. He focused on walking ahead, and walking softly so that he would remain on firm footing. He was disoriented. The sound of the ghostly choir filled his head.

As he made his way forward unsteadily, walking gingerly and haphazardly ahead, the sound of the choir pulsed and faded in succession. The stars seemed to have lost their luster; instead of bright light they glowed dully. The earth itself seemed unsteady and Javan strove not to fall. Slowly but surely, he walked ahead, across the rocky ground. He zigged and zagged his way through the parade of torches.

The altar came into view.

Behind it was a giant of stone, a marble statue carved of black rock: with seven arms and ten heads and flaring tongues.

Then the statue moved, and Javan screamed. He fell face-first onto the ground. The torch bearers began to laugh.

Javan scrambled to get up, but in his light, almost weightless state he quickly fell again, then bounced through the air.

What is happening? Surely, this is a dream…

When he landed, he was much closer to the black altar. He carefully made his way ahead, putting one foot ahead of the other.

A figure in a black hood stood behind it, in the shadow of the ten-headed giant. Others were with him, in black hoods. Behind them were scores of slavering ghouls.

But the priest, standing before the altar, was a mere servant. His master was elsewhere… and Javan did not ever want to meet him.

The panic returned as he reached the altar. He tripped on the pebbles surrounding it, almost falling face first.

An icy hand grabbed him and all the heat left his body.

When he stood up, he was shaken and numb.

The priest had removed his hood. There was an iron mask on his face, and twin red glows pierced the eye-slits. A sword of dark metal was clipped to his side.

"Pledge you, Javan, to the King of the Dark?" he said. His voice was caustic. "Pledge you your kingdom, your life?"

"I pledge!" Javan cried. "I pledge!"

"Then show me…"

Javan swept his sword from its sheath. He slashed his palm, crying out in the pain. He smeared the blood all over the altar.

He knelt before the priest.

"I pledge my life and my kingdom to the King of the Dark… there is no other king in the desert but him."

The hooded torch bearers began to laugh.

The choir began to laugh.

Javan had begun to rise up in the air; the earth no longer had a hold on him.

He began to cackle.

The laughter consumed him, and soon he lost control. He

thought of the Fall of Tadmor, and he cackled. He could not believe his luck. His subjects would fall; the people would fall. But Javan would live.

He was rising up into the air, as if by a wind. But when he looked down he saw his body still there, frozen in a pose, with his palm bleeding.

Javan ignored it as he drifted upwards. The laughter consumed him; it had overtaken his soul.

Chapter Forty-Six: A New Temple

The day after Ten Tables, with Javan gone again, Marit could have retreated into her bedchamber. Instead she had left the quiet comforts of the palace and, with a retinue of warriors protecting her, made her way to the ruins of the Grand Kabakh, what would one day be the Temple of Isdar.

There were no angry mobs. There had not been a murder in weeks. The people of Mahara had settled their grievances. Her husband, Javan, the Reformer, was on the cusp of absolute victory.

When she reached the ruins, she saw the cobblestone was destroyed and the stone had largely been removed. Great blocks of marble had been set out. They would be carved into pillars, in the manner of the ancients.

And Marit would dedicate this sacred space in the name of her daughter Yara.

It was a grand ambition. There were no blueprints for such a building. The architects did not know much of how to make of it.

Marit had not consulted her husband. She had consulted only herself, and a handful of Mahara's best architects. There were coins from that ancient age, which emerged occasionally in the desert sand. But there was not much to go on.

Only the Pillars of the Moon, and the ruins of a temple which had been gone a thousand years, offered any type of clue.

She watched the masons, questioning what she would do, questioning how the people would react.

The clerics no longer had a say. The Thul could no longer raise his Mob.

She looked to the sky, and for the first time in a long time, saw a cloud emerging. It was dark and purple in color, unlike any she'd seen before.

Rain, she thought. She would relish each moment.

Chapter Forty-Seven: Dreams

In the morning, Yara and Zathustra set out. Yara had lost track of time, but a brisk wind was blowing. She guessed it was around Ten Tables. It was the rare holiday that Yara liked, with its pastries and date honey. But that was gone, now. It was all gone. Could she return, now? Would her parents forgive her?

She didn't think so. She had been expelled by the Sisterhood; but she was still a servant of the Goddess. She could not tarry long in Tadmor, wherever her journeys took her.

~

The first night, and the second night, they heard only the sound of screech owls and night birds. The remainder of the journey was peaceful; there were no ghouls, no night terrors, only quiet and peace.

~

In Magdala, the tower had crumbled. It lay in bits and pieces, strewn amid the debris.

A cloud covered the sky, deep and purple, and occasional flashes of light lit up the firmament.

The road to Mahara, the road Yara knew, was lined with skulls; they had been nailed to posts.

"There are no people," Yara said.

Zathustra waved ahead. "Go on, Yara. It is you who wanted to visit Tadmor."

~

Roads Yara had known from childhood were empty, without

man, camel, or horse. Villages she had seen before were empty, and in the eerie light of the clouds, the shadows of the homes and huts were long and dark.

She had begun to grow afraid.

When they reached Mahara, Yara stopped.

The city walls were forbidding, but the gate was open. Up in the center of the city, a bright white eminence had taken the place of the sun, glowing and pulsing.

"Zathustra… I am afraid."

Zathustra touched her hand. "Precious Yara… I had warned you."

"There are no ghouls… there are no Lamia…" Yara was speaking mostly to herself. "Where are they? Where are they?"

Even the sight of a ghoul with its slavering jaw and foaming mouth would be a welcome sight to her. She wanted to see life, not just emptiness, not just death.

"Mother and Father…" Her eyes welled with tears.

"They are dead," Zathustra said. "As all are in Tadmor…"

At Zathustra's words she sank to her knees. She began to weep.

Mother, Father… she had come all this way, and Zathustra was right. They were gone… Gone forever.

Zathustra helped her up.

She tried to swallow her sadness, but it was a great pit, an emptiness inside, which she could never recover from.

Feebly she entered the gates, seeing abandoned houses, abandoned buildings. No one was here. No one was alive. The only sound was the wind. The only light was the eminence, hovering above.

She looked up at the white glow. She thought she saw a face.

Zathustra grabbed her hand and pulled her forward. "Come on," he snapped.

She stumbled ahead. She looked behind her, into the fields beyond the gates. Dark shadows were emerging; humanoid shadows, bent over and lurching. Ghouls.

Suddenly, she did not want their company.

She walked ahead, on the streets, toward the palace, her home. She hoped beyond hope that Mother and Father were alive. It still could be. It still could happen. She could see them again. Things could return to the way they were…

Tears streaked her cheek as they entered the city square. Its cobblestone spaces, once filled with merchants and stalls of all kinds, were completely gone. There was no one in sight. Zathustra, one step ahead, was casting a long shadow which stretched entirely across the square.

"Come," said Zathustra, and Yara followed.

~

In the corridors and hallways Yara knew, in the rooms where she'd played hide and seek with the servants, in the feasting hall where they served pastries and sweets on her birthday, it was all different. Instead of people, there were long shadows cast across objects. Instead of servants scurrying in and out there was a draft blowing, a cold air which caused Yara to seize up and cover her body in goosebumps.

At the throne room she stopped and screamed.

A skeleton was sitting there; it was dressed in Father's clothes.

Beside him, on a smaller throne where her mother sat, was another skeleton, dressed in Mother's finest.

Beneath her Father's body, a placard read: "Javan, Wazir in Life, King in Death."

Ghouls poured in from another room. Yara screamed.

Zathustra turned.

It was too late. They were going to die.

Yara jerked awake. She and Zathustra were in the desert, encamped in twilight. Zathustra was standing over her with his great green book.

She recalled the events of the day; the petty arguments she'd had about the camels. "I saw…"

"You saw a vision," Zathustra answered. "A vision of what will be."

Yara's eyes were streaked with tears, like in the dream. She did not want to see those images. She did not want to witness her Mother and Father, dead…

"You are a liar!" Yara said.

Zathustra glared. "I have never told a lie. I am a holy man… I am upright…"

He seemed upset even at the insinuation.

"We are a day from Tadmor… you can still turn back, Yara."

She looked to the horizon, to the dunes of the desert she had known and feared all her life. Where could she go? What could she do? The Sisterhood had betrayed her. All she had was Zathustra… Zathustra, and Tadmor.

Zathustra, Tadmor, and a glimmer of hope…

"I will go," Yara said. "With or without you… I don't care what you say."

Zathustra looked upon her with pity. "As you wish, young girl. As you wish, Precious Yara…"

~

In the middle of the day, Tadmor appeared in the horizon.

Yara had decided not to wear conservative dress. The ghouls would not care about anything but her flesh. She had seen no clerics in the vision.

The Tower of Magdala was in ruins. She halted her camel.

It was as the vision stated. Dare she risk death? Dare she risk an attack? She would join the dead…

But what did she have? What else did she have, except a glimmer of hope?

Zathustra, perhaps seeing her hesitance, said, "We can still turn back."

"No," she answered.

They pressed on, toward the ruins of the tower, toward Tadmor.

The sunlight shone down upon a vibrant market square.

There were merchants shouting; there were stalls and tables featuring all manner of goods, dates, flour, meat, and more.

"You lied…"

"No," Zathustra said.

They had stopped before the market square.

"No, no," Zathustra was murmuring. "This is impossible!"

Yara gazed upon her old friend. He seemed frazzled, genuinely confused. "Perhaps," she said, "your visions are worth nothing."

"They've never been wrong before…"

In the square, there were women with heads uncovered, baring their hair for all to see. There was a cask of wine being sold.

"What…" Yara mumbled. "What is this…"

She did not understand. How could things have changed in just months? How could Tadmor have become so different?

"Onward," Zathustra said. His voice was jubilant, despite his error. "Onward, to Mahara…"

~

The streets of Mahara were packed with people, more people than Yara ever remembered. The air pulsed with the sound of music, with the flute and trumpet and pipe and tambourine.

"What is this?" Yara cried. She could not hide her shock.

Everything had changed… everything was different. And it had happened so quickly.

In the city square, a merchant was selling monkeys. A woman was selling purple dyes. There were wine-sellers, openly hawking their produce on the street. There were smiles on the faces of the people of Mahara; they were bathed in sunlight.

A joy was rising up in Yara, a joy she'd never known before. She hurried as quickly as possible toward the palace. Mother and Father could yet be alive… they could yet live on this earth…

The guards recognized Yara. They let her by.

She turned to Zathustra. "Come on," she said.

But he only smiled and shook his head. "Our paths were crossed; now they diverge. Fare well, Yara. Fare well. Enjoy this… enjoy Tadmor's salvation."

But Zathustra seemed disturbed, somehow. He was thinking deeply, and his expression had turned sorrowful.

"Fare well, friend," she said. "If your journeys ever take you to Tadmor, come stop by."

Zathustra waved her away. "Goodbye, my dear." He turned and left.

Yara would never see him again.

With her camels in the stables, Yara entered the palace. The corridors were warm and swarming with servants. Many recognized her and hugged her as she walked along. Everyone, it seemed, thought she was dead.

When Yara entered the throne room, Mother screamed and came running. "Yara, Yara, precious Yara…" She grabbed her and wrapped her arms around her in a tight embrace.

Father was more reticent. He had left his throne, but his eyes were filled with a warm and radiant glow.

"You look," he said, "like a servant of the Goddess."

How did Mother and Father know? How did they speak of the Goddess that way, not fearing the clerics?

Father's hand was scarred; it had been sliced, so deep the wound would never heal.

"What happened to your hand?" Yara said. Mother had not relented of her embrace.

"I cut it," he said. "I was preparing chicken…"

Father never cooked, but Yara supposed there was a first time for everything. "Mother, there are women with their hair uncovered… there is wine in the market… what has gone on? How has the Thul not stormed Mahara?"

"Ah, ah, Precious Yara," Mother said. "The old world is returning… the new order of things is passing away…"

Yara did not know how to respond. She did not know what Mother meant. But here she would remain, at least for now. She would remain in the palace, in her parents' care, until the Goddess called upon her once more.

Epilogue

The Thul was enraged. He had called upon the true believers in the Coastal States, and the desert villages. He had amassed an army of ten thousand.

Ten days after the Feast of Ten Tables, he entered Mahara, and the Blasphemer Wazir met him with all his warriors.

The Thul's armies were destroyed, killed to a man. They scattered throughout Tadmor, leaving him to be captured.

The next night, he was hanged in the city square.

Glossary

Bezakirah: A large town on the desert's edge, near the sea, several hundred miles from Tadmor.

Beautiful Land, the: An ancient term for Tadmor, describing its natural beauty and blessed resources.

Cathay: A nation far to Tadmor's east, the main center of silk production. It is known for its wealth and bountiful food. The Dragon Emperor, who rules Cathay, is said to outstrip the King of Kings in wealth. It is among the most populous nations in the known world, with large cities and ports.

Continent, the: A generic term for the vast central imperial heartland.

Date honey: An extremely sweet condiment made from dates.

Devil's water: A term for alcoholic beverages, usually referring to wine but also to beer.

Desert languages: Languages spoken across the desert, all of which are mutually intelligible. Tammuri is among them.

Dwemer: A region far northeast of Tadmor, considered remote and exotic. The region is mountainous and known for its iron ores and high quality weaponry.

Dragon Emperor: The ruler of Cathay. He is considered by his subjects as a divine figure, worthy of worship and religion. Many believe he is the most powerful man in the world.

Dragon's tar: A black substance, easily ignitable, found in certain places throughout the desert.

Feast of Ascension: A day celebrating the conqueror-prophet Mali's storming of Mahara and his subsequent entry into heaven, riding up into the sky on a winged horse. Celebrants don black turbans, in the style of Mazda.

Feast of Ten Tables: A day celebrating the prophet Aadzor's revelation of the law, which he wrote on ten stone tablets. According to legend, these were the original precepts of the Law of Mazda. The day falls in the winter season.

The One God: An epithet for the god Mazda, whose worship was introduced centuries ago to Tadmor.

Ghoul: Creatures of filth and decay who live near tombs. They live in the desert and feast on decaying flesh, preferring the taste of human above all. In human settlements near the desert, they are reviled for their habit of eating hanged men who are left to rot.

Houri: According to legend, beautiful, supernatural women who can be found in certain oases in the desert.

Jinn: Creatures of air and fire known to haunt the desert and certain isolated places. They are known to be found near places of exceptional beauty. They can control lightning and wind.

Kabakh: A temple of Mazda, constructed of black stone, rectangular in shape. Worshippers are forbidden to enter. All such temples are built wherever the religion of Mazda holds sway.

Kish: A city in the foothills of the Heavenly Mountains. It guards a passageway through those mountains which leads to Cathay.

Nether Provinces: An impoverished region, north-west of Kish, which is mountainous and cold. It is home to the village of Muammar, birthplace of the prophet Aadzor, who founded the faith of Mazda. In recent times, it has become a site of poverty as the faith of Mazda and the wealth of the clerics spread westwards.

Mahara: The largest city and capital of Tadmor. The wazir rules from the palace here. The city also serves as the center of the priesthood of Mazda in Tadmor.

Mazda: The principal god worshiped in Tadmor. All other religions are banned from the region, on penalty of death.

Mazdahi: A term for the followers of Mazda, but especially his most zealous and devoted followers.

Pagans: According to the worshipers of Mazda in Tadmor, the ancient inhabitants who did not adhere to the religion.

King: The King of Kings rules over many kingdoms throughout the

Southern World. Tadmor is one of many regions under his domain. The nation he leads is called Fharas and is considered to have hegemony over the lesser states.

Stridge: A bloodsucking bird known to haunt the desert. It is strictly nocturnal and is a feature of scary tales.

Spice Cities: A distant confederation of cities, known for their fabulous wealth and corrupt politics. Each city is led by a leader called a Mercantor.

Sur: The Land of Sur or Kingdom of Sur is a distant jungle kingdom, known as the Kingdom of Elephants. Its people have much in common with Cathay.

Tadmor: Known as the Land of Wells, Tadmor is a region in the middle of the desert, surrounded by the swirling sands. It is blessed with arable farmland and numerous deep wells which provide an endless source of water. Thanks to its positioning in the middle of the desert, it is often a stop for caravans traveling to Cathay and beyond.

Tamurri: The language of Tadmor. It is mutually intelligible with that of the coastland region and Bezakirah.

Thul: The faith leader of a mokaa, or episcopal province, among the followers of Mazda. He is the religious and supposedly military leader of that mokaa. Many mokaa encompass across the desert, the greatest of which is the Mokaa of Tadmor. Mokaa are found wherever the followers of Mazda have any number.

Wazir: A governor of a province, subservient to the king. Wazirs rule with great autonomy over their lands, and must collect taxes from their subjects.

Wazira: The wife of a wazir.

Ziggurat: A stepped pyramid which was the center of religious life in ancient Tadmor and the surrounding regions, before the desert encroached on them. They now are spread throughout the desert, mostly forgotten, but many contain buried treasure because they doubled as tombs for kings.

About the Author

Cursed at birth with a wild imagination, Andrew Cooper spent his youth dreaming of worlds more exciting than Earth.

He is a graduate of the Odyssey Writing Workshop. His stories have appeared in Morpheus Tales, Fear and Trembling, Residential Aliens and Mindflights, among others.

Contact the Author

Visit **www.aj-cooper.com** to sign up for the newsletter and stay up-to-date on new releases.

Find him on Facebook at:

www.facebook.com/AJCooperauthor

www.ingramcontent.com/pod-product-compliance
Lightning Source LLC
Chambersburg PA
CBHW051301210726
48287CB00002B/610